Masquerade

By Melissa de la Cruz

Blue Bloods
Masquerade

Look out for:

Revelations
The Van Alen Legacy

Masquerade

A

Blue Bloods

NOVEL

Melissa de la Cruz

www.atombooks.co.uk

ATOM

Published in the United States in 2007 by Hyperion
First published in Great Britain in 2010 by Atom
Reprinted 2010 (four times), 2011

Copyright © 2007 by Melissa de la Cruz

Extract from *Revelations* by Melissa de la Cruz
Copyright © 2008 by Melissa de la Cruz

A CIP catalogue record for this book
is available from the British Library.

ISBN 978-1-905654-77-2

Printed and bound in Great Britain by
Clays Ltd, St Ives plc

Atom
An imprint of
Little, Brown Book Group
100 Victoria Embankment
London EC4Y 0DY

An Hachette UK Company
www.hachette.co.uk

www.atombooks.net

For my brother, Francis de la Cruz,
stalwart ally and kindred spirit

And for my husband, Mike Johnston,
without whom the Silver Bloods would not exist

We become so accustomed to disguise ourselves to others,
that at last we are disguised to ourselves.

—François Duc de la Rochefoucauld

. . . the thing I am becomes something else. . . .
The shadow is cast.

—Bauhaus, "Mask"

ONE

*T*he pigeons had taken over St. Mark's Square. Hundreds of them: fat, gray, squat, and silent, pecking at the pieces of *sfogliatelle* and *pane uva* bread crumbs that careless tourists had left behind. It was noon, but the sun was hidden behind clouds, and a gloomy pall had fallen over the city. The gondolas were lined up on the docks, empty, their striped-shirted gondoliers leaning on their oars, waiting for customers who had not arrived. The waters were in low tide, the dark stain of the higher levels visible on the building facades.

Schuyler Van Alen rested her elbows on the rickety café table and put her head in her hands, so that the bottom of her chin was hidden underneath her oversize turtleneck. She was a Blue Blood vampire, the last of the Van Alens— a formerly prominent New York family whose influence and largesse had been instrumental in the founding of modern-day Manhattan. Once upon a time, the Van Alen name had been synonymous with power, privilege, and patronage. But that was a long time ago, and the family fortune had been dwindling for many years: Schuyler was more familiar with penny-pinching than shopping sprees. Her clothes—the black turtleneck that hung past her hips, cutoff leggings, an army flak jacket, and beaten-up motorcycle boots—were thrift-store castoffs.

On any other girl, the ragged ensemble might look as though it had been thrown together by a homeless vagrant, but on Schuyler it became raiment equal to royalty, and made her delicate, heart-shaped features even more striking. With her pale, ivory complexion, deep-set blue eyes, and mass of dark, blue-black hair, she was a stunning, impossibly lovely creature. Her beauty was made even more benevolent when she smiled, although there was little chance of that this morning.

"Cheer up," Oliver Hazard-Perry said, lifting a small cup of espresso to his lips. "Whatever happens, or doesn't happen, at least we had a bit of a break. And doesn't the city look gorgeous? C'mon, you've got to admit being in Venice is so much better than being stuck in Chem lab."

Oliver had been Schuyler's best friend since childhood—a gangly, floppy-haired, handsome youth, with a quick grin and kind, hazel, eyes. He was her confidant and partner in crime and, as she had learned not too long ago, her human Conduit—traditionally a vampire's assistant and left-hand man, a position of exalted servitude. Oliver had been instrumental in getting them from New York to Venice in a short period of time. He had been able to convince his father to let them accompany him on a business trip to Europe.

Despite Oliver's cheerful words, Schuyler was glum. It was their last day in Venice and they had found nothing. Tomorrow they would fly back to New York empty-handed, their trip a complete failure.

She began ripping apart the label on her Pellegrino bottle, tearing it carefully so it unwound into a long thin strip of green paper. She just didn't want to give up so soon.

Almost two months before, Schuyler's grandmother, Cordelia Van Alen, had been attacked by a Silver Blood, the mortal enemies of the Blue Blood vampires. Schuyler had learned from Cordelia that, like the Blue Bloods, Silver Bloods were fallen angels, doomed to live their eternal lives on earth. However, unlike the Blue Bloods, Silver Blood vampires had sworn allegiance to the exiled Prince of Heaven, Lucifer himself, and had refused to comply with the Code of the Vampires, a stringent rule of ethics that the Blue Bloods hoped would help bring about their eventual return to Paradise.

Cordelia had been Schuyler's legal guardian. Schuyler had never known her parents: her father died before she was born, and her mother had fallen into a coma soon after giving birth to her. For most of Schuyler's childhood, Cordelia had been aloof and distant, but she was the only family

Schuyler had had in the world, and for better or worse, she had loved her grandmother.

"She was sure he would be here," Schuyler said, disconsolately tossing bread crumbs at the pigeons that had gathered underneath their table. It was something she had been saying ever since they'd arrived in Venice. The Silver Blood attack had left Cordelia weakened, but before her grandmother had succumbed to the passive state (Blue Blood vampires are continually reincarnated immortal beings), she had pressed on Schuyler the need to find her missing grandfather, Lawrence Van Alen, whom she believed held the key to defeating the Silver Bloods. With her last breath, Schuyler's grandmother had instructed her to travel to Venice, to comb the city's crooked streets and winding canals for any sign of him.

"But we've looked everywhere. No one has ever even heard of a Lawrence Van Alen, or a Dr. John Carver," Oliver sighed, pointing out that they had made dozens of inquiries at the university, at Harry's Bar at the Cipriani, and at every hotel, villa, and pensione in between. John Carver had been a name Lawrence had taken during the Plymouth settlement.

"I know. I'm beginning to think he never even existed," Schuyler replied.

"Maybe she was wrong—too weak and disoriented and confused about where to send you," Oliver suggested. "This could end up being just a wild-goose chase."

Schuyler mulled the possibility. Perhaps Cordelia had been wrong, and maybe Charles Force, the leader of the Blue Bloods, was right after all. But the loss of her grandmother had affected her terribly, and Schuyler was nursing a fevered determination to carry out the old woman's final wish.

"I can't think like that, Ollie. If I do, then I've given up. I have to find him. I have to find my grandfather. It hurts too much to think about what Charles Force said. . . ."

"What did he say?" Oliver asked. Schuyler had mentioned a conversation she'd had with Charles before they had left, but had kept the details vague.

"He said . . ." Schuyler closed her eyes and remembered the tension-filled encounter.

She had gone to visit her mother in the hospital. Allegra Van Alen was as beautiful and remote as ever, a woman who lingered between life and death. She had slipped into a catatonic state shortly after Schuyler was born. Schuyler had not been surprised to find a fellow visitor at her mother's bedside.

Charles Force was kneeling by the bed, but he stood up quickly and wiped his eyes when he saw Schuyler.

Schuyler felt a stab of pity for the man. Just a month ago, she had believed him to be the personification of evil, had even accused him of being a Silver Blood. How off the mark she had been.

Charles Force was Michael, Pure of Heart, one of the archangels who had voluntarily chosen exile from Heaven to help his brethren who had been cast out during Lucifer's revolt and cursed to live their lives on earth as the Blue Bloods. He was a vampire only by choice, not sin. Her mother, Allegra Van Alen, was the only other vampire who shared this distinction. Allegra was Gabrielle, the Uncorrupted, the Virtuous. Michael and Gabrielle had a long and entangled history. They were vampire twins, blood-bound to each other, and had been born brother and sister in this cycle.

The bond was an immortal vow between Blue Bloods, but Gabrielle had forsaken the vow when she had taken Schuyler's Red Blood father, her human familiar, as husband instead.

"Do you know why your mother is in a coma? Or chooses to be in a coma?" Charles had asked.

Schuyler nodded. "She swore never to take another human familiar after my father died. Cordelia said it was because she wanted to die herself."

"But she cannot. She is a vampire. So she lives," Charles said bitterly. "If this is what you call living."

"It is her choice," Schuyler said, her voice even. She did not like the judgment inherent in Charles's words.

"Choice," Charles cursed. "A romantic notion, but nothing more." He turned to Schuyler. "I hear you are going to Venice."

Schuyler nodded. "We leave tomorrow. To find my grandfather," she declared. *It is said that the daughter of Gabrielle*

6

will bring us to the salvation we seek, her grandmother had told her. *Only your grandfather knows how to defeat the Silver Bloods. He will help you.*

Cordelia had explained that throughout the history of the world, Silver Bloods had preyed on Blue Bloods, consuming their blood and their memories. The last known attacks had happened in Plymouth, when the vampires had crossed to the new world. Four hundred years later, in New York City, when Schuyler had started her sophomore year at the elite Duchesne School, the attacks had started again. The first victim was a fellow student—Aggie Carondolet. Soon after Aggie's death, the body count had increased. Most disturbing to Schuyler, all of the slain had been Blue Blood teens, taken during their most vulnerable period—between the years of fifteen and twenty-one, before they were fully in control of their powers.

"Lawrence Van Alen is an outcast, an exile," Charles Force said. "You will find nothing but confusion and sorrow if you travel to Venice," the steely-eyed magnate declared.

"I don't care," Schuyler muttered, her eyes downcast. She gripped the hem of her sweater tightly, twisting it into knots. "You still refuse to acknowledge that the Silver Bloods have returned. And already there have been too many of us who have been taken."

The last killing had happened shortly after her grandmother's funeral. Summer Amory, last year's Deb of the Year, had been found drained in her penthouse apartment in

Trump Tower. The worst part about the Silver Bloods was that they didn't bring death—no—they brought a fate worse than death. The Code of the Vampires expressly forbade them from performing the *Caerimonia Osculor*, the Sacred Kiss, the feeding on blood—on their own kind. The *Caerimonia* was a regulated ritual, with stringent rules. No humans were ever to be abused, or fully drained.

But Lucifer and his legions discovered that if they performed the Kiss on other vampires instead of humans, it made them more powerful. Red Blood held the life force of only one being, while Blue Blood was more potent, holding in it an immortal bastion of knowledge. The Silver Bloods consumed a vampire's blood and memories, sucking them to complete dissipation, making the Blue Blood a slave to an insane consciousness. Silver Bloods were many beings trapped in one shell, forever. Abomination.

Charles Force's frown deepened. "The Silver Bloods have been banished. It is impossible. There is another explanation for what has happened. The Committee is investigating—"

"The Committee has done nothing! The Committee will continue to do nothing!" Schuyler argued. She knew the history that Charles Force clung to—that the Blue Bloods had won the final battle in ancient Rome, when he had defeated Lucifer himself, then known as the maniacal Silver Blood emperor Caligula, and sent him deep into the fires of Hell by the point of his golden sword.

"As you wish," Charles sighed. "I cannot stop you from going to Venice, but I must warn you that Lawrence is not half the man Cordelia wished him to be."

He lifted up Schuyler's chin, as she stared at him with defiance. "You should take care, Allegra's daughter," he said in a kinder tone.

Schuyler shuddered at the memory of his touch. The past two weeks had done nothing but prove that Charles Force might have known what he was talking about. Maybe Schuyler should just stop asking questions, go back to New York, and be a good girl, a good Blue Blood. One who didn't question the motives or actions of The Committee. One whose only problem was what to wear to the Four Hundred Ball at the St. Regis.

She blew out her bangs and looked beseechingly across the table at her best friend. Oliver had been a faithful supporter. He had been right by her side throughout the whole ordeal, and during the chaotic days right after her grandmother's funeral.

"I know he's here, I can *feel* it," Schuyler said. "I wish we didn't have to leave so soon." She put the bottle, completely stripped of its label, back on the table.

The waiter arrived with the check, and Oliver quickly slipped his credit card in the leather tablet before Schuyler could protest.

They decided to hitch a ride on a gondola for one last

tour of the ancient city. Oliver helped Schuyler into the boat, and the two of them leaned back on the plush cushion at the same time, so that their forearms pressed against each other. Schuyler inched away just a tiny little bit, feeling slightly embarrassed at their physical proximity. This was new. She had always felt comfortable with Oliver in the past. They had grown up together—skinny-dipping in the pond behind her grandmother's house on Nantucket, spending sleepovers curled up next to each other in the same double-wide sleeping bag. They were as close as siblings, but lately she had found that she was reacting to his presence with a newfound self-consciousness she couldn't explain. It was as if she had woken up one day and discovered her best friend was also a boy—and a very good-looking one at that.

The gondolier pushed off from the dock, and they began their slow voyage. Oliver took pictures, and Schuyler tried to enjoy the view. But as beautiful as the city was, she couldn't help but feel a wave of distress and helplessness. If she didn't find her grandfather, what would she do then? Aside from Oliver, she was alone in the world. Defenseless. What would happen to her? The Silver Blood—if it had been a Silver Blood—had almost taken her twice already. She pressed a hand to her neck as if to shield herself from the past attack. Who knew if or when it would come back? And would the slaughter stop, as The Committee hoped— or would it continue, as she suspected, until all of them were taken?

Schuyler shivered, even though there was no chill in the air, looked across the canal, and saw a woman walking out of a building.

A woman who looked eerily familiar.

It can't be, Schuyler thought. It's impossible. Her mother was in a coma, in a hospital room in New York City. There was no way she could be in Italy. Or could she? Was there something about Allegra that Schuyler did not know?

Almost as if she had heard her, the woman looked straight into Schuyler's eyes.

It was her mother. She was sure of it. The woman had Allegra's fine blond hair, thin aristocratic nose, the same knife-blade cheekbones, the same lissome figure, the same bright green eyes.

"Oliver—it's—oh my God!" Schuyler exclaimed, pulling on her friend's coat. She pointed frantically across the canal.

Oliver turned. "Huh?"

"That woman . . . I think it's my . . . my mother! There!" Schuyler said, pointing toward a figure running swiftly, disappearing into a crowd of people leaving the Ducal Palace.

"What the hell are you talking about?" Oliver asked, scanning the sidewalk where Schuyler was pointing. "That woman? Are you serious? Sky, are you out of your mind? Your mother's in a hospital in New York. And she's catatonic," Oliver said angrily.

"I know, I know, but . . ." Schuyler said. "Look, there she is again—it's her, I swear to God, it's her."

"Where do you think you're going?" Oliver demanded, as Schuyler scrambled to her feet. "What's gotten into you? Hold on! Sky, sit down!" Underneath his breath he muttered, "This is a huge waste of time."

She turned around and glared at him. "You didn't have to come with me, you know."

Oliver sighed. "Right. As if you would have gone all the way to Venice on your own? You've never even been to Brooklyn."

She exhaled loudly, keeping her eyes focused on the blond woman, itching to be out of the slow-moving boat. He was right: she owed him big-time for accompanying her to Venice, and it annoyed her that she was so dependent on him. She told him so.

"You're *supposed* to be dependent on me," Oliver explained patiently. "I'm your human Conduit. I'm supposed to help you navigate the human world. I didn't realize that would mean being your travel agent, but hey."

"Then *help* me," Schuyler snapped. "I need to go. . . ." she said frantically. She made up her mind and jumped from the gondola to the sidewalk in one graceful leap—a leap no human would have been able to execute, since they were a good thirty feet away from the nearest *marciapiede*.

"Wait! Schuyler!" Oliver yelled, scrambling to keep up. *"Andiamo! Segua quella ragazza!"* he said, urging the gondolier to follow Schuyler, but not quite sure that the man-powered boat would be the best way to chase a fast-moving vampire.

Schuyler felt her vision focus and her senses heighten. She knew she was moving fast—so quickly that it felt as though everyone else around her were standing still. Yet the woman was moving just as fast, if not faster, soaring across the narrow channels that wormed through the city, dodging speedboats and flying toward the other side of the river. But Schuyler was right at her heels, the two of them a blur of motion across the cityscape. Schuyler found herself unexpectedly exhilarated by the pursuit, as if she were stretching muscles she didn't know she had.

"Mother!" She finally felt desperate enough to call out as she watched the woman leap gracefully from a balcony to a hidden entryway.

But the woman didn't turn back, and quickly disappeared inside the door of a nearby palazzo.

Schuyler jumped to the same landing, caught her breath, and followed the woman inside, more intent than ever to discover the mysterious stranger's true identity.

imi Force surveyed the industrious scene inside the Jefferson Room at the Duchesne School and sighed happily. It was late on a Monday afternoon, the school day was over, and the weekly Committee meeting was well underway. Diligent Blue Bloods were gathered in small groups at the round table, discussing last-minute details for the party of the year: the annual Four Hundred Ball.

Blond, green-eyed Mimi and her twin brother, Jack, were among the young vampires who were going to be presented at the ball this year. It was a tradition that reached back centuries. Induction into The Committee, a secret and vastly powerful group of vampires that ran New York, had been only the first step. The public presentation of young Committee members to the entire Blue Blood society was a bigger one. It was an acknowledgment of one's past history and future responsibilities. Because Blue Bloods returned in

different physical shells, under new names in every cycle—
what vampires called the length of a human lifetime—their
presentation or "coming-out" was highly important in the
recognition process.

Mimi Force didn't need a herald with a trumpet to tell
her who she was, or whom she had been. She was Mimi
Force—the most beautiful girl in the history of New York
City and the only daughter of Charles Force, the Regis,
a.k.a. head of the coven and superior badass, known to the
world as a merciless media magnate whose Force News
Network spanned the globe from Singapore to Addis Ababa.
Mimi Force—the girl with hair the color of woven flax, skin
like fresh buttercream, full pouty lips that rivaled Angelina
Jolie's. She was the underage sexpot with a reputation for
cutting a reckless swath through the city's most eligible young
heirs: hot red-blooded boyfriends otherwise known as her
human familiars.

But her heart had always been, and always would be,
much, much closer to home, Mimi thought as she looked
across the room at her brother, Jack.

So far, Mimi was satisfied. Everything was shaping up to
be picture-perfect for the night at the St. Regis Hotel. This
was the biggest party of the year. Unlike that tacky little cir-
cus they called the Oscars, with its sniveling actresses and
corporate shilling, the Four Hundred Ball was a strictly old-
fashioned affair—about class, status, beauty, power, money,
and blood. Bloodlines, that is, and more specifically, Blue

Bloodlines. It was a vampire-only ball: the most exclusive event in New York, if not the world.

Absolutely no Red Bloods allowed.

All the flowers had been ordered. White American Beauty roses. Twenty thousand of them, specially flown in from South America for the occasion. There would be ten thousand roses in the garland entrance alone, the rest scattered among the centerpieces. The most expensive event planner in the city, who had turned The Metropolitan Museum into a Russian wonderland straight out of *Dr. Zhivago* for the Costume Institute's Russian exhibit, was also planning to hand-make ten thousand silk roses for the napkin rings. And to top it all off, the entire ballroom would be scented by gallons of rosewater perfume pumped into the air vents.

Around Mimi, The Committee conferred on last-minute issues. While the junior members, high school kids like herself, were occupied with busywork—filing RSVP cards, checking off guest lists, confirming logistics for the two fifty-piece orchestras' stage requirements and lighting—the senior coven, led by Priscilla Dupont, a well-known Manhattan socialite whose regal visage graced the weekly social columns, was involved with more delicate matters. Mrs. Dupont was surrounded by a group of similarly thin, polished, and well-coifed women, whose tireless work on behalf of The Committee had led to the preservation of some of New York's most important landmarks and funded the existence of the city's most prestigious cultural institutions.

Mimi's extra-sensitive hearing picked up on the conversation.

"Now we come to the question of Sloane and Cushing Carondolet," Priscilla said gravely, picking up one of the ivory linen place cards scattered in front of her. The cards were embossed with the name of each guest, and would be placed at the front reception with a designated table number.

There was a murmur of disapproval among the well-heeled crowd. The Carondolets' growing insubordination was hard to ignore. After they had lost their daughter Aggie a few months ago, the family had shown signs of being distinctly anti-Committee. Rumor had it they were even threatening to call for an impeachment of Mimi's father.

"Sloane can't be with us today," Priscilla continued, "but she has sent in their yearly donation. It's not as big as it has been in the past, but it is still substantial—unlike some other families I won't mention."

Donations to the Four Hundred Ball benefited the New York Blood Bank Committee, The Committee's public name, which was organized ostensibly to raise money for blood research. The money it brought in was also used in part to fight AIDS and hemophilia.

Every family was expected to make a magnanimous donation to its coffers. The combined offerings fueled The Committee's multimillion-dollar budget for the entire year. Some, like the Forces, gave above and beyond the call of duty, while others, like the Van Alens, a pitiful branch of a once-powerful clan, had struggled for years to come up with the requisite amount for their tithe. Now that Cordelia was gone, Mimi wasn't even sure if Schuyler knew what was expected of her.

"The question is," Trinity Burden Force, Mimi's mother, said in her lilting voice, "is it *appropriate* for them to sit at the head table as they usually do, knowing what they have said about Charles?" Trinity posed the question in a way that let the rest of The Committee know that she and Charles would rather dine on ashes than dine with the Carondolets.

"I say shaft them at the back table with all the other fringe families!" BobiAnne Llewellyn declared with her forceful Texan bray. She made a joking slash across her neck, if only to display the thirty-carat diamond on her ring finger. BobiAnne Llewellyn was the second and much younger wife of Forsyth Llewellyn, who currently served as junior senator for New York.

Several ladies seated around Priscilla Dupont shuddered ever so slightly at the suggestion, even if they privately agreed with it. BobiAnne's crass way of putting it was distinctly not the Blue Blood way of doing things.

Mimi noticed her friend Bliss Llewellyn look up at the sound of her stepmother's grating voice. Bliss was one of The Committee's newest members, and her face had turned as red as her curls when she'd heard BobiAnne's guttural laugh boom across the room.

"Perhaps we can reach a compromise," Priscilla noted in her gracious manner. "We will explain to Sloane that they shall not sit at the head table this year, seeing as they are still in mourning and we respect their grief. We will place the Van Alen girl at their table as well. They cannot argue with that, seeing as they were great friends of Cordelia's, and, as her granddaughter, she too has suffered a loss."

Speaking of Schuyler—where was that little wretch? Not that it was Mimi's problem, but it annoyed her that Schuyler hadn't even bothered to show up for today's Committee meeting. She'd heard someone say that Schuyler and her human sidekick, Oliver, had gone to Venice, of all places. Venice? What the hell were they doing in Venice? Mimi wrinkled her nose. If one had to abscond to Italy, wasn't the shopping in Rome and Milan better? Venice was just wet and stinky, in Mimi's opinion. And how were they able to get permission from the school to do so?

Duschene did not look kindly upon self-scheduled school vacations—even the Forces had been reprimanded when they had taken the twins out of school last February for a ski vacation. The school had already allocated an official "ski week" in March on the calendar that all families were supposed to follow. But tell that to the Forces, who maintained that the powder on Aspen Mountain in March was deeply inferior to February's snowfall.

Mimi threw a silk rose across the table at her brother, Jack, who was involved in a lively discussion with his subcommittee over security issues, blueprints of the St. Regis ballroom spread out in front of them.

The rose fell into his lap, and he looked up, startled.

Mimi grinned.

Jack colored a bit, but returned her smile with a dazzling one of his own. The sun shone through the stained-glass windows, framing his handsome face with a golden glow.

Mimi thought she would never get tired of looking at him: it was almost as gratifying as looking at her own reflection. She was glad that after the truth of Schuyler's heritage—a half blood! Practically Abomination!—had been revealed, things between the two of them had gone back to normal. What passed for normal around the Force twins, anyway.

Hey handsome, Mimi sent.

What's up? Jack replied, without speaking.

Just thinking of you.

Jack's smile deepened, and he threw the rose back at his sister so that it landed in her lap. Mimi tucked it behind her ear and fluttered her eyelashes appreciatively.

She checked over the RSVP cards once again. Since the ball was a community affair, it would be a party dominated by the Elders and the Wardens—an older crowd. Mimi pressed her lips tightly together. Sure, it would be a fun party—the most glamorous event ever—but suddenly she had an idea.

What about an after-party?

For Blue Blood teens only? Where they could really let loose without worrying about what their parents, Wardens, and Committee leaders thought?

Something more edgy and adventurous . . . something only the crème de la crème could attend. A cold, glittering smile played on her lips as she imagined all her silly little peers at Duchesne begging for an invitation to the party. All in vain, Mimi thought. Because there would be no invitations. Only a text-message sent to the right people on the night of the Four Hundred Ball would reveal the location of the after-party. The Alterna-vampire Ball.

Mimi glanced over at Jack, who was holding a sheet of paper in front of his face, covering his handsome visage. And she suddenly remembered a scene from a past life of theirs: the two of them, bowing to the Court at Versailles, their faces concealed behind ornately beaded and feathered masks.

Of course!

A masquerade ball.

The after-party would require elaborate masks.

No one would be sure who was who—who had been invited and who had not—creating the most *exquisite* social anxiety.

She liked this idea very much. Any time she could exclude other people from having fun, Mimi was always ready.

THREE

*I*t's not like she hasn't had this dream before. Of being cold and wet, and of not being able to breathe. All the other dreams had been like this, except this one felt real. She was freezing, shivering, and as she opened her eyes to the murky darkness, she sensed another presence in the shadow. A hand, grasping her arm, lifting her up, up, up toward the light, and breaking the surface.

Splash!

Bliss took a ragged, coughing breath, and looked around wildly. It was no dream. This was real. She was submerged in the middle of a lake.

"Hold still, you're too weak. I'll swim us to shore." The low voice in her ear was soothing and calm. She tried to turn around to look at his face, but the voice interrupted. "Don't move, don't look back, just concentrate on the shore."

She nodded, rivulets of water dripping from her hair into

her eyes. She was still coughing, and felt an enormous need to retch. Her arms and legs were weak, although there was no current. The lake was placid and still. It was hardly even a lake. When Bliss's eyes adjusted to the dark, she saw that she was in Central Park, in the middle of the man-made lake where, last summer, before she'd enrolled at Duchesne, her parents had taken her and her sister to the boathouse restaurant for dinner.

The boats were nowhere to be found this time. It was almost the end of November, and the lake was deserted. There was frost on the ground, and for the first time that evening, Bliss felt a cold seeping into her veins. She started to shake.

"It'll pass. Your blood will heat up, don't worry. Vampires don't get frostbite." That voice again.

Bliss Llewellyn was from Texas. That was the first thing Bliss said to new acquaintances. "I'm from Texas," as if identifying her home state went a long way to explaining everything about herself: the accent, the big curly hair, the five-carat diamond rocks on each ear. It was also a way for Bliss to hold on to her beloved hometown, and a life that seemed more and more remote from her current reality as just another pretty girl in New York.

In Texas, Bliss had stood out. She was five foot ten (with the hair height, she was easily six feet tall), fierce, and fearless—the only cheerleader who could execute a tumbling leap off the top of a fifty-person pyramid and safely land feet first on the soft grass of the football field. Before she discovered she was a vampire and capable of such physical dexterity, Bliss had chalked up her coordination to luck and practice.

She had lived with her family in a sprawling, gated mansion in an exclusive Houston suburb, and had driven to school in her grandfather's vintage Cadillac convertible—the one with real buffalo horns on the hood. But her father had grown up in Manhattan, and after a fruitful run as Houston's leading politician, had abruptly uprooted the family when he ran—and won—New York's empty senate seat.

Adjusting to the frenzy of the Big Apple after life in Houston was difficult for Bliss. She felt uneasy in all the glamorous nightclubs and exclusive parties Mimi Force, her self-appointed new best friend, dragged her to. Give Bliss a jug of Boone's, a few girlfriends, and a DVD of *The Notebook*, and she was happy. She didn't like hanging out at clubs, feeling like a wallflower while watching Mimi have all the fun.

But her life had suddenly picked up when she'd met Dylan Ward, the sad-faced, black-eyed boy with the sexy smolder who had walked, cigarette-first, into Bliss's life in a back alley on the Lower East Side just a few months ago. Dylan had been a misfit at Duchesne, too—a sullen, alienated rebel with a bunch of loser friends, including Oliver Hazard-Perry and Schuyler Van Alen, the two most unpopular kids in their year. Dylan had been more than a friend; he was an ally, not to mention a possible boyfriend. She blushed to remember his deep, penetrating kisses—oh, if only they had not been interrupted the night of the party. If only . . .

If only Dylan were still alive. But he had been taken by a Silver Blood, turned into one of them and then killed when he had come back to visit her—to *warn* her. . . . Bliss blinked back tears, remembering how she had found his jacket crumpled on her bathroom floor and covered in blood.

Bliss had thought that that was the last time she would ever see Dylan again, and yet . . . this boy who had rescued her . . . his low voice in her ear—it had been so familiar. She didn't dare to hope; she didn't want to believe in something that couldn't be true, that couldn't possibly be real. She had clung to him as he pulled her steadily to the shore.

This wasn't the first time Bliss had woken up in an unexpected place, only to find herself inches from danger. Just last week she had opened her eyes to find herself perched on the topmost ledge of the Cloisters Museum, high up in Fort Tryon Park. Her left foot had been dangling off the edge, and she had caught herself just in time to pull back and save herself from a dangerous fall. Bliss realized she probably would have survived the fall anyway, with only a few scratches, and wondered idly that if she did want to commit suicide, what options would be available to an immortal anyway?

And then today she had found herself in the middle of the lake.

The blackouts—the nightmares of someone stalking her, and of being here but not here—were getting worse. They had begun the year before: excruciating, head-pounding migraines accompanied by terrifying visions of crimson eyes with silver pupils, and sharp, glittering teeth . . . and of running down endless corridors while the beast chased her, its foul breath sickening in its intensity . . . catching up to her, bringing her down to the ground, where it would devour her soul.

Stop it, she told herself. Why think of that now? The nightmare vision was gone. The beast—whatever it was— resided in her imagination only. Wasn't that what her father had said? That the nightmares were simply part of the transformation? Bliss was fifteen, the age at which the vampire memories resurfaced, the age in which the Blue Bloods began to realize their true identities as immortal beings.

Bliss tried to recall everything that had happened earlier that day, if there was any clue as to how she could come to find herself half drowned in the Central Park lake. She had gone to school as usual, and afterward had attended another tedious Committee meeting. The Committee was supposed to teach her and all the new inductees how to control and use their vampire senses, but for the last two months the organization had been more invested in planning a fancy party than anything else. Her stepmother, BobiAnne, had attended the meeting, embarrassing Bliss with her screechy voice and her tacky outfit, a head-to-toe-logo'd Vuitton tracksuit. Bliss hadn't realized they made casual wear out of the same brown canvas as the luggage. She thought her stepmother looked like one big gold-and-brown train case.

Afterward, because her father was home for a change, the family had dined at the new Le Cirque that had recently relocated to sumptuous quarters at One Beacon Court. The famed New York dining hall catered to the powerful and wealthy, and Senator Llewellyn had spent the evening shaking hands with the other well-heeled patrons—the mayor, the broadcaster, the actress, the other senator from New York. Bliss had ordered her foie gras rare, and had enjoyed slathering gooseberry jam on the thick, rich, creamy goose liver on her plate.

When dinner was over, they had attended an opera, in the family's private box. A new Met production of *Orfeo ed Euridice*. Bliss had always loved the tragic story of how Orpheus descended into Hell to rescue Eurydice, only to lose her at the very end. But the stentorian rumbling and mournful singing had rocked Bliss to sleep, leading her to dream of the watery abyss of Hades.

That was where her memory ended. Was her family still in the theater? Her father seated like a stern, grave idol, his hands placed under his chin, watching the show intently while her stepmother grimaced and yawned, and her half sister, Jordan, silently mouthed all the words. Jordan was eleven years old and an opera freak—freak being the definitive word, in Bliss's estimation.

They were near the dock now, and the steady hand hoisted her up the ladder next to the pier. Bliss slid on the slippery ledge, but found she could walk. Whoever he was, he was right: her vampire blood was warming her up, and in a few minutes she wouldn't even notice that it was forty degrees outside. If she had been human, she would have been dead, drowned for certain.

She looked down at her damp clothing. She was still wearing the same clothes she had worn to dinner and the opera. An intricately embroidered black satin Temperley dress—ruined now. So much for dry-clean only. Only one of her five-inch patent leather Balenciaga platforms remained. The other one was probably at the bottom of the lake. She looked askance at the opera program she was still holding tightly in her hand, and released it, letting it flutter to the ground.

"Thank you . . ." she said, looking behind her to finally see the face of her savior.

But there was nothing behind her but the calm blue waters of the man-made lake. The boy was gone.

OCTOBER 1, 1870
THE MYSTERIOUS DISAPPEARANCE OF MAGGIE STANFORD

———

Oil man's daughter disappears on night of society ball.
Was she drugged?

THE NEW YORK POLICE ARE puzzled over the mysterious disappearance of sixteen-year-old Maggie Stanford, who walked out of the home of Admiral and Mrs. Thomas Vanderbilt three weeks ago during the annual Patrician Ball held in their home at 800 Fifth Avenue and has not been seen since by her family or relatives. Maggie Stanford is the daughter of Mr. and Mrs. Tiberius Stanford of Newport. The detectives have worked industriously on the strange case but have been unable to to find any clews.

The disappearance of Miss Stanford was reported at the Tenth Precinct police station as having occurred on Friday, August 22. On that evening, according to her mother, Dorothea Stanford, who is known in society, Maggie was presented at the Patrician Ball and led the quadrille. Maggie is of a quiet and retiring disposition. She weighs ninety-five pounds, is fragile, pretty, and delicate, and her home relations are of a pleasant character. She has dark red hair, green eyes, and winning ways. Her engagement was announced to Alfred, Lord Burlington, Earl of Devonshire, on the evening of the ball.

Mrs. Stanford told the police she thought her daughter had been decoyed or abducted by some person of evil influence. The Stanford family has offered a substantial reward for any information leading to her return. Tiberius Stanford founded Stanford Oil, the most profitable organization in the United States.

———

But she was right here. Schuyler was certain. The woman she was chasing had disappeared through the door of the very same palazzo that Schuyler was now standing in, and yet the woman was nowhere to be found.

Schuyler looked around. She was inside the lobby of a small, local inn. Many of the magnificent floating palaces of ancient Venice had been turned into tourist-friendly pensiones, shabby little hotels, where guests didn't mind the crumbling balustrades and peeling paint because their glossy brochures had promised them they were experiencing a slice of the "authentic" Italy.

An old woman with a black scarf around her head looked up curiously from the registration table. *"Posso li aiuto?"* Can I help you?

Schuyler was confused. There was no sign of the blond woman anywhere in the room. How could she have hidden herself so quickly? Schuyler had been right at her heels. The room was empty of closets or doors.

"Ci era una donna qui, si?" Schuyler said. A woman just came in here, yes? She was grateful that the Duchesne School made their students take not one but two foreign languages, and that Oliver had urged her to take Italian, "so we can order better at Mario Batali's restaurants."

The old lady frowned. *"Una donna?"* She shook her head. The conversation continued in rapid Italian. "There is no one here but me. No one came in but you."

"Are you certain?" Schuyler demanded.

She was still questioning the landlady when Oliver arrived. He pulled up to the side of the building in a sleek speedboat. He'd found that a water taxi was more suitable to his needs than the man-powered gondola.

"Did you find her?" he asked.

"She was just here. I swear. But this lady says no one came in."

"No woman," the old lady said, shaking her head. "Only the Professore lives here."

"The Professore?" Schuyler asked, her ears keen. Her grandfather had been a professor of linguistics, according to the Repository of History, the Blue Blood archive that held all the knowledge and secrets of their race. "Where is he?"

"He has been gone many months now."

"When will he return?"

"Two days, two months, two years—it could be anytime.

Tomorrow or never," the landlady sighed. "No one knows with the Professore. But I am lucky, he always pays his bills on time."

"Can we—can we see his room?" Schuyler asked.

The landlady shrugged and pointed to the stairs.

Her heart beating in her chest, Schuyler ascended the stairway, Oliver close behind.

"Wait," Oliver said as they reached a small wooden door at the front of the landing. He jiggled the knob. "It's locked." He tried again. "No dice."

"Damn," Schuyler said. "Are you sure?" She reached around him to try. She turned the knob and it clicked open.

"How do you do that?" Oliver marveled.

"I didn't do anything."

"It was totally locked," he said.

Schuyler shrugged and pushed on the door gently. It led to a neat, spare room with a single bed, a worn wooden desk, and shelves of books stacked up to the ceiling.

Schuyler pulled a book from the lower shelves. "*Death and Life in the Plymouth Colonies* by Lawrence Winslow Van Alen." She opened to the first page. It was inscribed in elegant handwriting: "To my dear Cordelia."

"This is it," Schuyler whispered. "He's here." She peered at several more books on the shelves and found that many of them bore spines that declared L. W. Van Alen as their author.

"Not right now, he is not," the landlady said from the

doorway, making Schuyler and Oliver jump. "But the Biennale ends today, and the Professore has not missed one yet."

The Biennale, the biannual art exhibit in Venice, was one of the most definitive, influential, and exhaustive presentations of art and architecture in the world. For several months every other year, the entire city was taken over by an international collection of artists, art dealers, tourists, and students eager to partake of the historic art festival. It was an event Schuyler and Oliver had missed during the weekend, due to their fruitless search for her grandfather.

"If it's closing today," Schuyler said, "we've got to hurry."

The landlady nodded and left the room.

Schuyler wondered again about the woman who had looked so eerily like her mother. Had her mother led her to her grandfather? Was she helping Schuyler in some way? Was it just her spirit that Schuyler had seen?

They hurried down the stairs and found the landlady shuffling papers at the reception desk.

"Thank you for all your help," Schuyler said, bowing to the old woman.

"Eh? Excuse me. *Posso li aiuto?*" the old woman snapped.

"The Professore, the Biennale, we are going to try and find him now."

"Professore? No, no. No Professore . . ." The old woman made the sign of the cross and began shaking her head.

Schuyler frowned. "No Professore? What do you think she means by that?" she asked Oliver.

"He leave . . . two year ago," the landlady said in halting English. "He no live here no more."

"But you just said . . ." Schuyler argued. "We were just talking, upstairs. We saw his room."

"I never see you in my life, his room is lock," the landlady said, looking shocked and sticking determinedly to her stilted English even though it was obvious Schuyler was fluent in Italian.

"Eravamo giusti qui," Schuyler argued. But we were just here.

The landlady balefully shook her head and muttered to herself.

"There's something different about her," Schuyler whispered to Oliver as they walked out of the inn.

"Yeah, she's even more cranky now," Oliver cracked.

Schuyler turned back to look at the cross old woman again, and noticed that she had a mole underneath her chin from which a few stray hairs had sprouted. And yet the old woman who had spoken to them earlier had not been afflicted with such a mole, Schuyler was sure of it.

imi looked at her vibrating cell phone as she exited her AP French class.

Am I on the list?

Another text message. It was the seventh one today. Could everyone *please* calm down?

Somehow, in less than twenty-four hours, the news that the fabulous Mimi Force was planning an after-party to the Four Hundred Ball had gone out to the entire New York City teen vampire elite. Of course, Mimi herself had told Piper Crandall, the biggest gossip in the school, and Piper had made sure everyone knew exactly what was going down. There was a secret location. The Force twins were hosting. But no one would know if they were invited until the night of the event. Sheer social torture!

Just say Y or N!!!!

She deleted the text without replying.

Mimi walked down the back staircase at Duchesne that led to the cafeteria in the basement. As she passed by, several Blue Blood teens tried to capture her attention.

"Mims . . . heard about the after-party . . . Great idea, do you need any help? My dad can get Kanye to DJ," offered Blair McMillan, whose father headed the largest record label in the world.

"Hey, Mimi, I'm invited, right? Can I bring my boyfriend? He's an RB . . . Is that cool?" Soos Kemble wheedled.

"Hey, sweetie, just making sure you got my RSVP. . . ." Lucy Forbes called out, blowing Mimi an exaggerated air kiss.

Mimi smiled graciously at all of them and put a finger to her lips. "I can't say anything about anything. But you'll all find out soon enough."

Downstairs in the cafeteria, underneath the gold baroque mirror that hung across from the fireplace, Bliss Llewellyn picked listlessly at her sushi roll, as if it were a particularly distasteful specimen. Mimi was supposed to meet her for lunch, and she was late as usual. Bliss was glad of the reprieve, since it gave her a chance to lose herself in the events of the night before.

Dylan. It had to be him. The stranger in the park who had saved her from drowning. Bliss had to believe he had survived the Silver Blood attack. Perhaps he was now in hiding, and maybe he would be in danger if he revealed his identity. Like a superhero, she thought dreamily. Who else would have sensed her distress? Who else could have swum through the cold waters of the lake to reach her? Who else could have been so strong? Who else could have made her feel so safe?

Bliss hugged this information to herself like a warm blanket. Dylan was *alive*. He had to be.

"Not hungry?" Mimi asked, sliding in next to her.

In answer, Bliss pushed away her tray and made a face. She shoved all thoughts of Dylan out of her mind.

"What's all this about an after-party everyone's been harassing me about? No one believes me when I tell them I have no idea what's going on. You and Jack are throwing some kind of bash after the ball?"

Mimi looked around to make sure no one could overhear, and only when she was certain they were beyond earshot did she speak. "Yeah, I was going to tell you about it today."

She filled Bliss in on the details. She had secured the perfect spot—an abandoned synagogue downtown. There was nothing Mimi enjoyed more than advocating a night of debauchery in a once-sacred space. The Angel Orensanz Center was a neo-Gothic building in the middle of the Lower East Side. It had been designed as a synagogue in 1849 by a Berlin architect who modeled it after the cathedral of Cologne. Mimi wasn't the only New Yorker who liked to throw over-the-top extravaganzas in the space: the center had already played host to several fashion shows during Fashion Week, which was how she got the idea in the first place. Mimi didn't care about points for originality, she only cared about being where the action was, and right now, desecrated synagogues were hot.

"The inside is a mess," Mimi said gleefully. "There are like, rotting columns and exposed beams . . . It's like a beautiful ruin," she whispered. "We're going to light the whole place with tea light candles—no electric lights at all! And that's it, no other decor. The place has enough atmosphere. It doesn't need anything."

Mimi ripped out a sheet of notebook paper from her binder and passed it to Bliss. "This is who I'm thinking for the party. I wrote it down during my French quiz." Mimi was enrolled in AP French, but the class was a joke. Once her vampire memories resurfaced, she had discovered she was already fluent in the language.

Bliss looked down at all the names. Froggy Kernochan. Jaime Kip. Blair McMillan. Soos Kemble. Rufus King. Booze Langdon.

"These are all Committee members. But not even *all* of the Committee members," Bliss noted.

"Exactly."

"You're not inviting Lucy Forbes?" Bliss asked, aghast. Lucy Forbes was a Blue Blood senior, and Head Girl of the school.

Mimi wrinkled her nose. "Lucy Forbes is a drip. A goody-goody." Mimi had had a vendetta against the girl ever since Lucy had reported that Mimi had abused her human familiars by feeding on them without adhering to the forty-eight hour rest period mandate.

They went down the list, Bliss proposing a name and Mimi rejecting it.

"How about Stella Van Rensslaer?"

"Freshman! No frosh at this shindig."

"But she's going to be inducted next spring. I mean, she *is* a Blue Blood," Bliss argued. All the names of potential Blue Blood vampires were available to Committee members so they could watch out for their younger brethren, the way Mimi had taken Bliss under her wing earlier that year.

"Ugh. No," Mimi said.

"Carter Tuckerman?" Bliss proposed, thinking of the friendly, skinny boy who spent Committee meetings taking copious notes as secretary.

"That geek? No way."

Bliss sighed. She hadn't seen Schuyler's name on the list either, which bothered her.

"And what about . . . you know . . . 'significant others,' the familiars?" Bliss asked. Blue Bloods used the term "human familiar" to describe the reliant relationship between the mortal and immortal races. Human familiars were lovers, friends, vessels from which the vampires drew their greatest strength.

"No Red Bloods at this party. This is like the Four

Hundred Ball, but even more exclusive. Vampires only."

"People are going to be really upset about this," Bliss warned.

Mimi smiled her cat-that-ate-the-canary smile. "Exactly."

*T*he Venice Biennale was located in several overlapping pavilions, so that visitors wandered through a long series of darkened rooms, searching as video installations crackled to life in unexpected corners. Faces projected on vinyl balls expanded and contracted, shrieking and giggling. Flowers blossomed and withered on the screens. A rush of Tokyo traffic sped by, claustrophobic and threatening.

When Schuyler and Oliver had first arrived in Venice, Schuyler had been fired up with a wild, almost feverish, energy. She was relentless in her search, dogged and determined. But her enthusiasm had flagged when it became clear that finding her grandfather in Venice would not be as easy as she had assumed. She had come with nothing but a name—she didn't even know what he would look like. Old? Young? Her grandmother had told her Lawrence was an exile, an outcast from the Blue Blood community. What if all those years of isolation had led to madness and insanity? Or worse, what if he was no longer alive? What if he had been taken by a Silver Blood? But now, after seeing the Professore's room, she was filled with the same fierce hope as when she had first arrived. *He is here. He is alive. I can feel it.*

Schuyler drifted from one room to the next, scanning the dark places for a sign, a clue that would lead her to her grandfather. She thought most of the art was intriguing, if somewhat overwrought, with just a hint of pretension. What did it mean that a woman kept watering the same plant over and over again? Did it even matter? As she looked at the video, she realized she was the same as the woman, trapped in a Sisyphean task.

Oliver had already skipped ahead several installations. He took the same amount of time to study each piece— approximately ten seconds. Oliver claimed that that was all he needed to understand art. They were supposed to call each other if they found anything, although Oliver had pointed out that neither of them knew what Lawrence Van Alen actually looked like. Oliver was not as convinced as Schuyler that a visit to the Biennale would be fruitful, but he had held his tongue.

She stopped at the entrance to a room bathed in a crimson haze. A single light cut through the entire space, projecting a glowing orange equator through the expanse of red light. Schuyler walked inside and paused for a moment, admiring it.

"It's an Olaf Eliasson," a young man standing next to her explained. "It's beautiful, isn't it? You can see the influence of Flavin."

Schuyler nodded. They had studied Dan Flavin in Art Humanities, so she was familiar with the work. "But then again, doesn't all fluorescent art come under the influence of Flavin?" she asked saucily.

There was an awkward silence, and Schuyler started to move away, but her companion spoke again. "Tell me. Why have you come to Italy?" the handsome Italian boy asked in perfectly accented English. "You are obviously not an art tourist, one of those with the big cameras and their cultural guidebooks in tow. I would bet you have not even seen the new Matthew Barney."

"I am looking for someone," Schuyler replied.

"At the Biennale?" he asked. "Do you know which venue?"

"There are others?" Schuyler asked.

"Of course, this is only the *giardini*; there is also the *Arsenale* and the *corderie*. The whole city of Venice transforms for the Biennale. You are going to have a hard time finding just one person. Almost a million people visit the Biennale— the garden itself has thirty pavilions."

Schuyler's heart sank. She had no idea the Biennale was such a vast and confusing collection of places. She had walked along the promenade, past other buildings before entering the Italian pavilion, but she had no idea what stretched beyond. The gardens were a vast landscape filled with buildings from every era, each one built by its host country. Each building had its own style and housed its own country's art.

If what the boy was saying was true, going to the Biennale to look for the Professore was akin to searching for a needle in the middle of a haystack.

Useless.

Impossible.

A million people every year! Which meant there must be thousands upon thousands of people at the exhibit right now. With those odds, she might as well give up immediately.

Schuyler despaired. She would never find her grandfather now. Whoever he was, wherever he was, he did not want to be found. She wondered why she was even being so forthright with the boy, but she felt she had nothing to lose. There was something in his eyes that made her feel comfortable, safe.

"I am looking for someone they call the Professore. Lawrence Winslow Van Alen."

The boy studied Schuyler coolly as she looked around at the glowing red room. He was tall and slim, with a hawkish nose, jutting cheekbones, and a dash of thick, caramel-blond hair. He wore a white silk scarf around his neck, a finely tailored wool jacket, and gold-rimmed aviator frames pushed back on his handsome forehead.

"One should not seek those who do not wish to be found," he said abruptly.

"Excuse me?" Schuyler asked, turning to face him,

startled by his unexpected reply. But by then the boy had ducked behind a thick black felted curtain and disappeared.

Schuyler exited the Italian pavilion onto the rough stones of the main promenade, punching Oliver's number into her cell phone as she ran after the boy.

"You rang?" Oliver asked with comic obsequiousness.

"There's a boy—tall, blond—looks like a race-car driver. Aviator shades, driving gloves, tweed coat, silk scarf," Schuyler described, panting as she ran.

"Are you chasing a model? I thought we were looking for your grandfather." Oliver laughed.

"I was talking to him. I told him the name of my grandfather, then he disappeared. I may be on to something— Hello? Ollie? You there? Hello?" Schuyler shook her cell phone, and noticed she had no bars. Damn. No signal.

Moving through the garden exhibitions was like being in a time machine. There were Greco-Roman atriums interspersed with bold, clean modernist structures. Buildings were hidden behind long paths and camouflaged in forestry. Schuyler sighed, helpless for a moment.

But she was not helpless. She could sense him. She saw his silhouette pass behind a reproduction of a Greek theater. He darted through the columns, disappearing in and out of her vision. Schuyler lunged forward, careful to keep her speed in check this time, in case any of the scattering of tourists noticed something odd.

She spotted the boy dashing through a grove of trees, but was confounded when she arrived at the spot. Before her stood only a building. She moved quickly up the steps and into the structure. Once inside, she understood why she had been confused.

The interior of the building had been constructed to resemble an exterior patio; trees sprang up through the open roof, making the room appear as if it were outside. Sculptures were dotted throughout the white stone covered courtyard. All around her, she heard voices speaking in Italian, the tour guides' proud declarations the loudest of all.

Concentrate, she told herself. Listen for him. For his footsteps. She closed her eyes, trying to sense him, trying to zero in on his particular scent, remembering the combination of leather and cologne from his silk scarf, and looking as if he had just exited a fast, shiny new sports car. *There!* She spotted the boy standing at the far end of the space.

This time, she was unafraid to use her speed, her strength. She ran so fast she felt as if she were flying, and as before, she was exhilarated by the chase. She was even stronger than when she had chased after the woman who looked like her mother earlier that afternoon, she could feel it. She was going to catch him.

He was moving farther back into the garden. The buildings gradually became more modern, their shapes almost frightening. She passed through a building made only of glass, its walls etched with words and names. Another was composed of plastic tubes colored brightly and glowing like candy. She saw his shape moving within.

Inside, the pavilion was dark. A glass floor separated the viewer from the art below. Or at least she assumed it was art. All she could see was a writhing mass of toy robots grinding and climbing over each other endlessly as colored lights flashed in red, blue, and green in the darkness. She sensed movement, and from the corner of her eye, saw the boy's head moving quickly out of the room on the other side.

"STOP!" She called.

He looked at her, smiled, and then disappeared again.

Schuyler walked back out to the garden path, once again scanning for him among the crowd. Nothing.

Oh, what was the use?

She thought for a moment. She tried to imagine Lawrence and where he might be; why he might be drawn to this place. The Biennale.

Then she remembered the map in her back pocket. She pulled it out and studied the serpentine pathways that connected the pavilions. She felt silly for a second, having not thought of it sooner. She folded up the map and walked swiftly to her new destination.

Her cell phone rang. Oliver.

"Sky, where are you? I was worried."

"I'm fine," she said, annoyed to be interrupted. "Listen, I'll call you back. I think I know where he is."

"Where who is? Schuyler, where are you going?"

"I'll be fine," Schuyler said impatiently. "Ollie, please don't worry about me. I'm a vampire."

She hung up the phone. Minutes later she was standing in front of a small, red brick building. A modest construction compared to the mostly outlandish structures in the exhibit. Its facade was Georgian, Early American, with white painted trim and neatly detailed wrought iron handrails. It was a relic from another time, and the kind of place—reminiscent of the early colonial settlements.

No sooner had she stuffed the map back into her pocket then she saw the boy again. He looked as if he had aged during the chase: his breath was shallow, and his hair was askew.

He looked startled to find her there. "You again," he said.

Now was her chance. Cordelia had instructed her, before she had expired in this cycle, that if she ever found Lawrence, or anyone whom she thought would be able to lead her to him, that Schuyler must say the following words.

She said them now, clearly, and in the most confident voice she could muster.

"Adiuvo Amicus Specialis. Nihilum cello. Meus victus est tui manus." I come to you for aid as a secret, special friend. I have nothing to hide. My life is in your hands.

He looked into her eyes with an icy stare that could only belong to Schuyler's kind, and her words faded into silence.

"Dormio," he ordered, and with a wave of his hand, she felt the darkness come upon her as she fainted.

MARCH 15, 1871
ENGAGEMENT BROKEN

———

Lord Burlington and Maggie Stanford
Will Not Marry.
Maggie Stanford Still Missing.

THE ENGAGEMENT OF MAGGIE Stanford, the daughter of Mr. and Mrs. Tiberius and Dorothea Stanford of Newport, and Alfred, Lord Burlington of London and Devonshire, has been broken. The wedding was to have taken place to-day.

Maggie Stanford mysteriously disappeared on the night of the Patrician Ball six months prior. Superintendent Campbell has continued to investigate. The Stanford family suspects foul play, although no ransom note or sign of kidnapping has yet been discovered. A substantial reward has been offered for any information concerning Maggie Stanford's whereabouts.

———

*I*t was a jewel box of a room, high up on the highest floor of one of the tallest skyscrapers in midtown Manhattan, a building made of glass and chrome, and as Mimi looked out over the magnificent New York skyline, she caught her reflection in the plate glass window and smiled.

She was wearing a dress. But not just any dress. This was a couture confection of thousands of chiffon rosettes hand-stitched together to create an ethereal, cloudlike elegance. The strapless bodice hugged her tiny twenty-two–inch waist, and her lustrous gold locks spilled over her creamy shoulders and toned lower back. It was a six-figure dress, a one-of-a-kind showstopper that only John Galliano could create. And it was hers, at least for one night.

She was in the celebrity dressing department at Christian Dior. An exclusive showroom that was by invitation only. All around the racks that surrounded Mimi were dresses flown straight from the Paris runways—samples that only models and model-thin socialites could ever dream of wearing.

Here was the Dior that Nicole Kidman wore to the Oscars, there was the gown Charlize Theron wore to the Golden Globes.

"Stunning," the Dior publicist pronounced with a quick nod of her head. "Absolutely, this is the one."

Mimi took a flute of champagne from the silver tray proffered by a white-gloved servant. "Perhaps," she acknowledged, knowing that with the dress's fifty foot–long train, she would cause a commotion when she entered the party.

Then Bliss appeared in the doorway.

Mimi had invited her friend to join her, thinking it would be fun to have an audience watch her try on dresses. Mimi liked nothing more than to have a fawning friend envy her good looks and social privileges. She hadn't expected the publicist at Christian Dior to fall over herself and encourage Bliss to borrow a dress as well. But ever since Bliss had been signed by the Farnsworth Modeling Agency, and her face and figure had been emblazoned all over town in the "Stitched for Civilization" jeans advertising campaign that she had starred in with Schuyler Van Alen, the little Texas rose had become a bona fide New York celebrity—a fact Mimi had yet to forgive. Bliss had even been chosen as *Vogue*'s "Girl of the Moment," and there were Web sites devoted to her every move. Mimi had to face the awful truth: her friend was famous.

"You guys—what do you think of this?" Bliss asked.

Mimi and the publicist turned. Mimi's smile faded. The publicist ran over to Bliss Lwelleyn's side.

"Gorgeous!" she declared. "I only wish John were here to see you in it."

Bliss was wearing a plush velvet dress of the darkest green—almost black—that dramatically offset her cascading reddish-gold curls. Her pale, ivory complexion looked almost translucent against the deep rich, dark jeweled color of the gown. It had a plunging, outrageously low neckline, cut from collarbone to belly button, revealing a generous amount of cleavage but stopping short of anything obscene. The bodice was embroidered with a thousand Swarovski crystals that twinkled against the fabric like stars in the night sky. It was a fantastic, entrance-making dress, the kind of dress that propelled unknown actresses into A-list movie stars, a contender against Elizabeth Hurley's famed Versace safety pins.

"I like it." Bliss nodded. She towered over Mimi in her jeweled stilettos, and the two of them looked at themselves in the mirror.

Against Bliss's severe yet sexy gown, Mimi in her pale-pink rosettes suddenly looked inconsequential, and Mimi's smile withered underneath the lights as Bliss twirled and danced around the room.

"It only looks heavy," Bliss said, lifting the hem. "But it's so light."

"It's made from Venetian silk—some of the best in the

world," the Dior rep explained. "Ten Belgian nuns went blind making it," she joked. "So girls, I suppose we're all set?"

Mimi shook her head. There was no way in hell she would allow Bliss to steal the spotlight—her night—away from her. She had her heart set on being the single most beautiful girl in the room, and there was no way she would be able to do that if Bliss upstaged her in that insanely opulent gown.

Visiting the celebrity dressing department had been her idea, but now Mimi had to opt for Plan B. She wouldn't be content with a gown from the runway—she had to have a gown custom-made and designed for herself only, by the master. Balenciaga.

They left the showroom and crossed the street to grab a quick lunch at Fred's, the restaurant on the top floor of Barneys. The hostess seated them immediately in a comfy, four-person booth near the window, where they could be seen by the tony crowd. Mimi noted Brannon Frost, the Blue Blood editor in chief of *Chic*, seated across from them with her fourteen-year-old daughter, Willow, a freshman at Duchesne.

Bliss's color was high and her face glowed happily. She was still talking about the dress.

"Yeah, totally, it looked great on you," Mimi said in a flat voice.

Her friend's smile wavered, and Bliss swallowed a gulp of

water to camouflage her disappointment. Mimi's disinterest was a cue that all discussion about Bliss's ball gown was now over. Bliss quickly regrouped. "But *yours* was ah-ma-zing. Pink is so your color."

Mimi shrugged. "I don't know. I think I'm going to look somewhere else. Dior is so outré, don't you think? De trop, as they say. A little over the top. But of course, if that's what you're looking for, it's fabulous." She said condescendingly as she paged through the leather-bound menu.

"So where do you think you'll go?" Bliss asked, trying not to feel the sting of Mimi's little barbs. She knew she had looked great in that dress, and that Mimi was just jealous— Mimi was always that way. The last time they went shopping, they had both found a gorgeous baby-lamb fur coat at Intermix, a trendy downtown boutique. Mimi had allowed Bliss to buy it, but only after she'd disparaged wearing fur. "But you go ahead, dear. I know some people don't care about the suffering of tiny little animals." In the end, Bliss had purchased the coat, but she had yet to wear it. Score one for Mimi Force.

The bitch was just green-eyed with envy. I rocked that dress, Bliss thought, then immediately felt ashamed to be thinking of her friend that way. Was Mimi really jealous? What did the beautiful Mimi Force have to be jealous about, *ever*? Her life was like, perfect. Maybe Bliss was reading too much into her reaction. Maybe Mimi was right—maybe the dress was too much. Maybe she shouldn't wear it after all. If only someone else had been with her at the showroom, some-one like Schuyler, whom Bliss knew would be able to offer an honest opinion. Schuyler didn't even realize how pretty she was; she was always hiding in those bag-lady layers of hers.

"I don't know where I'm going to find a ball dress," Mimi said airily. "But I'm sure I'll find something." She wasn't about to share the ace up her sleeve this time. God help her if Bliss got the same idea to ask the Balenciaga designer to make her a ball dress as well.

The waiter arrived and took their orders, two steak au poivres. Rare.

"Bloody." Mimi smiled, showing just a hint of her fangs so that the waiter did a double take.

"Raw," Bliss joked, handing back the menu, although she wasn't really kidding.

"Anyway," Mimi said, taking a sip of water and looking around the lively restaurant to see if anyone was looking at her. Yes. Several women—tourists, by the looks of their pastel cardigans and eighties-era scrunchies—seated in Siberia, were whispering and talking about her. "That's Mimi Force. You know, Force News? Her dad's that gazillionaire? There was a story about her in last week's Styles. She's like, the new Paris Hilton."

"As I was saying, it's not really about the dress. It's about a date," Mimi said.

"A date?" Bliss gagged. "I didn't know we had to find dates for this thing."

Mimi laughed. "Of course you need a date, silly. It's a ball."

"So who are you taking?"

"Jack, of course," Mimi replied promptly, as if it were the most natural thing in the world.

"Your brother?" Bliss asked, shocked. "Um, like, ew?"

"It's a family thing," Mimi huffed. "Twins always go as each other's dates. And besides, it's not like . . ."

"It's not like?" Bliss prodded.

Mimi had been meaning to say, It's not like he's really my brother, but this was neither the time nor place to explain their complicated and immortal romantic history and the bond between them. Bliss wouldn't understand. She didn't have full control of her memories yet and would not be coming out at the ball until next year.

"Nothing," Mimi said, as their entrées were set before them. "Ooh. I think this one is still breathing." She smiled as she cut into her steak, releasing a river of red blood on the immaculate white plate.

A date, Bliss thought. A date for the Four Hundred Ball. Bliss knew there was only one guy in the world she wanted as an escort.

"So what about you? Maybe you can take Jaime Kip," Mimi suggested. "He's totally hot and so available." Actually, Jaime Kip had a girlfriend, but since she was a Red Blood, in Mimi's mind she didn't count.

"Listen, Mimi, I need to tell you something," Bliss

whispered. She hadn't meant to confide in Mimi, but she couldn't keep her thoughts and hopes to herself any longer. Especially since they were talking about boys.

Mimi raised an eyebrow. "Go on."

"I think Dylan is alive," Bliss said, explaining in an almost incoherent rush how she had found herself half drowned in the Central Park lake, only to be rescued by a boy—a boy whose face she never saw, but whose voice had been only too familiar.

Mimi looked pityingly on her friend. Through her father, Mimi had heard what had happened. Dylan had been attacked and killed by a Silver Blood. There had been no hope for his survival. They had never found his body, but Bliss's testimony to The Committee about the tragic evening had spelled out his fate loud and clear.

"Bliss, darling, I think that's really sweet how you think this guy, your so-called 'savior,' was Dylan. But there's no way. You know as well as I do that . . ."

"That what?" Bliss asked defensively.

"That Dylan's dead."

The words hung in the air between them.

"And he's never coming back, Bliss. Ever." Mimi sighed and put down her knife and fork. "So let's get serious. Do you want me to set you up? I think Jaime Kip is such a hottie."

hen Schuyler woke up, she was lying in an enormous king-size bed in the middle of a vast room furnished in what can only be described as Early Medieval Royalty. An immense and foreboding tapestry depicting the death of a unicorn decorated the far wall, a gargantuan gold chandelier lit with a hundred dripping candles hung from the ceiling, and the bed itself was piled with all manner of thick and woolly animal pelts. The whole place conveyed a brutal, primitive elegance.

She blinked her eyes and her hands went flying up to her neck. But there were no bite marks. She was safe from that, at least.

"Ah, you are awake."

Schuyler turned to the sound of the voice. A uniformed maidservant in a black dress with a white apron curtsied. "If you please, follow me, Miss Van Alen," she said. "I am supposed to take you downstairs."

How did she know my name?

"Where am I?" Schuyler asked, kicking off the covers and stuffing her feet back into her motorcycle boots that she found on the floor.

"The Ducal Palace," the maid answered, leading Schuyler out of the room and toward a winding stairway lit by hanging torches.

The *Palazzo Ducale*, or the Doge's Palace, was the seat of the Venetian government for centuries and housed its administrative and legislative arms, as well as council rooms and the doge's private residence. Tourists were welcome to visit the grand halls and galleries. Schuyler herself had already seen the palace on the officially sanctioned tour.

She realized she was in one of the private residences, the roped-off section of the palace that was not open to the public.

The maid motioned for her to follow, and Schuyler walked down the stairway to a long hall. At the end of it was an immense oak portal, carved with assorted hieroglyphics and pagan symbols.

"You will find him here," the maid said as she opened the door.

Schuyler walked inside and found a roomy library of baronial splendor. Red velvet curtains were draped over the double-height windows. Walnut shelves were lined with leather-bound books. Animal rugs and trophies abounded.

A stooped, gray-haired gentleman in Harris tweeds sat in a massive leather chair in front of a roaring fire.

"Come forward," he ordered.

Next to him was the handsome young Italian boy from the Biennale. He nodded at Schuyler and motioned to the chair in front of them.

"You put a spell on me," Schuyler accused.

The boy acknowledged this was so. "It was the only way to make sure of your identity and your true intentions. Do not worry, you were not harmed."

"And? So are you satisfied?"

"Yes," the boy said gravely. "You are Schuyler Van Alen. You are staying at the Hotel Danieli with Oliver Hazard-Perry Senior and his son, Oliver. You are on a quest of some kind. Allow me to bring you some excellent news. Your quest is over."

"How so?" Schuyler asked warily.

"This is the Professore," the boy said.

"You have been looking for me, I hear," the Professor said jovially. "I am not so popular these days with American students. A long time ago, I had many little pilgrims come to see me lecture. But not anymore. Tell me, why have you come?"

"Cordelia Van Alen sent me," Schuyler said.

At the mention of her name, the Professor and the boy exchanged a meaningful glance. The warmth of the hearth brought heat to Schuyler's cheeks, but it wasn't just the blaze that brought a red blush to her pale skin. Saying Cordelia's name so boldly made her feel vulnerable. Who were these strange men? Why had they taken her here? Had she been right in invoking Cordelia's call for help?

"Tell me more," the Professor encouraged, leaning forward and assessing Schuyler keenly.

"Cordelia was my grandmother . . ." Schuyler said. Even if these were enemies, there was no backing out of it now. She scanned the room for exit points: she noticed a hidden door built into one of the library walls. Maybe she could escape through there, or else she could stun both the old man and the boy with a spell of her own and fly out through the window.

"Was?" the boy asked.

"She has expired in this cycle. She was attacked," Schuyler inhaled sharply. "By a Silver Blood. Croatan."

"How can you be sure?" the boy demanded. "The Silver Bloods have not been heard of since the seventeenth century. Their existence has been legislated out of Blue Blood history."

"She told me herself."

"But she was not—taken?" the boy asked in a hoarse voice.

"No. Thankfully. The attack did not drain her of all her blood and memory. She will live to return in the next cycle."

The boy leaned back in his chair. Schuyler noticed he was fiddling with the car keys in his left hand, and his right knee was moving up and down in impatience to hear the rest of her story.

"Continue," the Professor urged.

"Cordelia said that the key to defeating the Silver Bloods lay in finding her husband, Lawrence Van Alen, who has been in hiding. She thought if she sent me—if she sent me to Venice I might find him. Have I?"

The old man's eyes twinkled. "Perhaps you have."

"Grandfather, I come to you for help. Cordelia said it was imperative that . . ."

There was a throat-clearing noise from the boy. Schuyler turned to him.

"I am Lawrence Van Alen," the boy said, leaning forward. The boy's features shifted—not so much melted, but phased out—changed, so that he appeared to be an older gentleman. But this was not the stoop-shouldered, white-haired grandfather of Schuyler's imagination. This was a tall, thin man with the same leonine hair as the boy's, except it was flecked with silver, and still there was the aristocratic, hawkish nose and the arrogant chin.

It was as if the room shrank in his presence. He was a commanding figure, and the sharpness of his gaze was intimidating. Here was a man who would be a worthy rival to Charles Force, Schuyler thought.

"You are a shapeshifter," Schuyler said admiringly. "Is this your real form?"

"As much as any form can be real," Lawrence replied. "Anderson, you may excuse us."

The elderly gentleman winked at Schuyler and exited

the room, closing the creaky wooden door with a hush.

Schuyler settled in her chair, noticing the faded Aubusson rugs on the hard stone floor. They were similar to the ones in Cordelia's library on 101st Street.

"Your Conduit?"

Lawrence nodded. He stood up and walked over to the recessed bar across from the fireplace, opened a lower cabinet, and removed a bottle of port wine. He poured two glasses of the scarlet liquid and handed Schuyler a glass.

"I had a feeling," she said, accepting the drink. She sipped it slowly. It was sweet without being cloying, full-bodied and delicious. Alcohol had no effect on vampires, but most of them still enjoyed the taste.

"I thought you might. You almost turned to address me, but caught yourself. How did you know?"

"The lord of the manor typically seats on the left, where you were, while he was seated on your right," Schuyler said. It was a law of medieval etiquette she had learned from Cordelia's endless lessons on Blue Blood history. The king was always seated on the left, while his queen, or any lesser personage was seated on the right.

"Ah, very observant. I forgot. I am getting old."

"I'm sorry Cordelia couldn't be here," Schuyler said softly.

Lawrence sighed. "It is all right. We have been separated now for more than a century. One gets used to solitude. Perhaps one day it will be safe for us to be together again."

He leaned back on his chair and removed a cigar from his front pocket. "So, you are Allegra's daughter." He said, breaking off the corner of the cigar with a silver cigar cutter. "I have been watching you. I knew you were looking for me the minute you arrived in Venice. I sensed something in the air—I thought it was your mother—but it was a different energy. You saw me."

"You were the woman on the street that I saw today. You had taken Allegra's form," Schuyler realized aloud. It all made sense now.

Lawrence nodded. "I do sometimes. If only because I have missed her for a very long time."

He took a quick puff from the cigar and exhaled. "I was wary of coming out to you until I was certain of your identity. I have many enemies, Schuyler. They have been hunting me for centuries. You could have been one of them."

Schuyler sat up suddenly, almost spilling her drink. "The lady at the pensione? That was you as well. At least at first."

Lawrence chuckled. "Yes. Of course."

"So that was why she said she had never seen us before when we came down the stairs. She was telling the truth." Schuyler set her empty glass on the small side table across from her chair, taking care to place it on one of the gold-plated coasters.

"Marie is an honest landlady, I'll give her that." Lawrence smiled.

"Why did you show us your room?"

"I didn't mean to, but you were chasing me and I had to seek shelter in one of my secret hiding places around the city. I have many addresses, you know. One needs them if one is going to hide successfully. Marie was telling you the truth; the room was locked. But it opened for you. I took that as a good sign. I thought I would give you a clue—see if you would be able to find me in the Biennale. You did well. You were drawn to the Olafur Eliasson as was I."

"But why did you run away from me again? I was chasing you."

"And you almost got me. My God, the speed of you— you are unbelievably strong. It took all of my energy just to stay ahead of you. I was still unsure of your intentions or your identity. You surprised me by finding me in front of the Colonial building. I'm sorry I had to use that sleep spell on you."

"Why do you choose to trust me now?" Schuyler asked.

"Because only Allegra's daughter would know the correct *Advoco Adiuvo*, the invocation you used. Cordelia and I had agreed that if we ever went looking for each other, our emissaries would use those words from the Sacred Language. Without the *Advoco*, you would never have found me in a thousand years, regardless of your powers. But I had to put you to sleep to stall for time while I made sure you had not been corrupted. I had to take you somewhere safe, where we would not be observed."

Schuyler nodded. She had guessed as much.

"So now you have found me, what do you want?" Lawrence asked, looking at Schuyler through a haze of smoke.

"I want to know about the Silver Bloods. I want to know everything."

he next day was the beginning of finals week at Duchesne. Unlike at other schools, students at the exclusive institution actively looked forward to examinations since it meant a flexible schedule and marked the advent of the coming school holidays. Bliss consulted her chart as she hurried through the school's double-height, gold-brass and glass doors. That day she had English and AP American History. The next day, German and Biology. She had a Social Justice test on Wednesday, no exams on Thursday, and only a French recitation on Friday.

As she ran up the grand staircase to the third floor, she noticed that all around her, girls were dressed down in yoga pants, T-shirts, and worn Ugg boots, while the boys wore faded sweatshirts, holey jeans, and sneakers.

What was going on? She herself was wearing her usual attire: pressed stovepipe jeans tucked into knee-high buckled pirate boots, and a Stella McCartney sweater over a ruffled Derek Lam blouse. Why did everyone else look as if they had stumbled out of bed and had gotten dressed in the dark?

"Hey, Bliss!" Mimi yelled as she sped out of the second-floor library.

Bliss was surprised to find Mimi in an outfit she would never be caught dead in otherwise. Mimi had pulled back her long blond hair into a garish red-and-blue bandanna and was wearing hardly any makeup (in fact, Bliss noted a small pimple on Mimi's chin). An oversize Duchesne lacrosse T-shirt borrowed from her brother, Jack, hung on her skinny frame, and she completed the look with low-slung flannel pajamas and comfortable shearling slippers.

"Hey!" Bliss called.

"Can't talk—late for my Chem final," Mimi explained, hurrying downstairs, her slippers flip-flopping on the marble.

"Did you just get here?" Soos Kemble asked, following Mimi. She was wearing an oversize Oxford sweatshirt and saggy jersey leggings, her thin blond hair a frizz. This was the girl who arrived in school every day with her hair perfectly blow-dried, wearing designer outfits that cost in the five-figure range.

"Yeah." Bliss shrugged. "Why?"

"Everyone else has been here since dawn." Soos yawned. "It's the only way to get the best cubicles in the lib during finals."

Interesting, Bliss thought. She would never quite

understand the unspoken rules at Duchesne, but apparently looking like a "grind" or a "nerd" was the height of fashion during exams. You had to appear like you were slaving away and totally serious about tests. Even the Blue Bloods, with their hyperintelligence, still needed to cram.

Tomorrow, Bliss promised herself, she would arrive at school in her oldest pajamas. She hated sticking out like a sore thumb. It was just another way to broadcast the fact that, unlike her classmates, she hadn't been a student at Duchense since pre-pre-kindergarten. Would she always be an ignorant outsider? Bliss wondered if she should be annoyed that Mimi hadn't told her about the casual dress code, but then realized Mimi probably had better things to worry about than advising Bliss on what to wear to finals.

When Bliss arrived at the History room, almost everyone in class was sitting down quietly and waiting for their professor to hand out the tests. Bliss took a seat in the back of the room, looking around to see if Schuyler or Oliver were there. She wanted to tell them her news of Dylan's return. Surely they would believe her, even if Mimi did not.

No such luck.

Then she remembered the two of them had been given permission to take their exams early so they could travel to Venice for two weeks. Lucky bastards.

Bliss looked down at her blue composition notebook. The first question had concerned the *Mayflower* journey, Pilgrims, and the founding of the thirteen colonies. Since she had lived through it, all she'd had to do was close her eyes and she could see their desolate settlement. She was sure to pull top marks.

Bliss felt confident she had aced the exam as she stood up and handed in her paper. Jack Force was in her class, and he gave her a friendly smile as he turned in his paper after she did. He held the door open for her so they could walk out together.

"How are you?" he asked once they were in the hallway next to the grand staircase.

"Great," she said. "I feel like a cheat, I mean . . . you know."

He nodded. "I know what you mean. All we have to do is close our eyes, right?"

"It's like we have an open textbook or something," Bliss said.

"Well, it's not as if we *have* to use it," Jack mumbled.

"Excuse me?" Bliss asked.

"Nothing." Jack shrugged. He had a faraway look in his eyes, and Bliss wondered what was going on with him. She didn't know him very well, although she hung out with him often enough since Mimi always liked to have him around.

"Good luck this week," Jack said, slapping her on the back in a brotherly fashion.

"You too," Bliss called. She looked at her watch. She had several hours before her next exam. Maybe she could grab a quick bite from a corner deli and then try to score one of those cubicles in the library—if there were any left.

As she walked down the stairs, a girl fell into step with her. Bliss raised an eyebrow. "Yes?"

It was Ava Breton, a fellow sophomore—a Red Blood—and yet very popular. Almost all of Ava's friends were Blue Bloods, although she didn't know it. Bliss noticed there were telltale marks on her neck, which meant that Jaime Kip, her Blue Blood boyfriend, had made her a familiar. Interesting.

"Bliss, can I ask you something?" Ava asked, tucking a hair behind her ear. Ava was wearing a thin, long-sleeved American Apparel T-shirt over her boyfriend's basketball shorts, and gray thermal underwear.

"Sure."

"Do you know anything about this party that Mimi and Jack Force are throwing next week?"

Bliss shifted uncomfortably. "I . . ."

"It's okay. I mean, Jaime is being really weird about it. I know he's going to that ball at the St. Regis with his parents—seriously, how lame is that? But I thought it was weird he didn't even invite me to the after-party."

"I'm sorry." Bliss said, feeling uncomfortable. She hated when people were left out of the fun. She remembered what her life had been like before Mimi had taken her under her wing. She didn't have it in her heart to exclude people. It was so shallow and snobby, and so Mimi. It certainly wasn't Bliss. Anyway, what was the harm? Maybe the Four Hundred Ball was exclusively for Blue Bloods, but the after-party was for teenagers. In Bliss's opinion, the more the merrier. If someone wanted to join, what was the harm, really?

"I just—it's just—I mean, I know everyone else will get an invite," Ava said, biting her lip. "And what if I don't . . ."

"It's downtown at the Angel Orensanz Center at midnight," Bliss blurted out. "And it's a masquerade party. You'll need a mask, some sort of disguise, to get in."

A rapturous smile appeared on Ava's face. "Thank you, Bliss. Thank you SO MUCH."

Damn.

Now she'd gone and done it.

She'd invited a Red Blood to the party. Mimi was going to be seriously pissed.

opeless. Everything was hopeless now. Her grandfather had turned out to be useless: a scared old man
with nothing to live for but his books, his cigars, and his port
wine. What had she expected? A tutor, a guide, a patron . . .
a father. Someone who would take the burden off her shoulders for a while.

As she packed her bags in her hotel room the next morning, Schuyler remembered Lawrence's parting words.

"I am sorry, Schuyler. Cordelia was wrong in sending you to
me."

He then began to pace in front of the fire. "The truth is, I
no longer have any interest in Blue Blood affairs. I have washed
my hands of their plight, ever since Roanoke. They chose to
follow Michael then, as they have always done," he said, meaning the coven leadership had reinstalled Michael as Regis

when the crisis at Roanoke had been discovered and it looked as if the Silver Bloods had returned. "And if I'm not mistaken, they still choose to follow him today as Charles Force." Lawrence shook his head. "When he turned his back on the family and renounced the Van Alen name, I vowed that I would never return to the coven.

"Alas, you have traveled to Venice in vain. I am an old man. I would prefer to live out my immortal life in peace. I have nothing to offer you."

"But Cordelia said . . ."

"Cordelia placed too much faith in me, as always. The key to defeating the Silver Bloods lies with Charles and Allegra, not with me. Only the Uncorrupted can save Blue Bloods from the Silver Blood Abominations.

"I am sorry I cannot be of much help. I swore off the Blue Bloods forever when I went into exile."

"Then Charles Force was right about you," Schuyler said, her voice shaking.

"How do you mean?" Lawrence asked darkly.

"He said you weren't half the man Cordelia wished you to be. That I would only find sorrow and confusion if I traveled to Venice."

Lawrence stepped back as if he had received a physical blow. His face registered a myriad of emotions—shame, anger, pride—but he remained silent. In the end, he abruptly turned his back on her and left the room, slamming the door behind him.

* * *

Well. That was that. Schuyler zipped up her carryall, lugged it over her shoulder, and walked out to the elevator, where Oliver was waiting. He didn't say hello or good morning.

She knew that if she wanted to, she could catch a glimpse of his mind—his thoughts broadcast as if on satellite radio. But she always switched the signal. She didn't feel it was right to pry. Besides, she didn't need any of her special powers to figure out he was still annoyed with her for not calling him the night before.

Lawrence's chauffeur had brought her back to the hotel late the previous evening, and Schuyler had found several frantic messages from her friend on her cell phone and hotel voice mail. She would have called him back, but it was so late she hadn't wanted to wake him.

"I thought you were dead," Oliver accused.

"If I was, you could have my iPod."

"Ha. Yours sucks. It doesn't even have video."

Schuyler repressed a smile. She knew Oliver couldn't stay mad at her for long.

"Anyway, you missed a hilarious European music awards show on TV. David Hasselhoff swept all the categories."

"Sucks to be me."

He grunted. "Dad's gone, he took an earlier flight. Had to get back for some shareholders' meeting."

Schuyler glanced sideways at her friend. Oliver's chestnut shag covered his forehead, and his warm hazel eyes, flecked with green and topaz, were filled with hurt and concern. Schuyler restrained herself from touching his neck, which looked so vulnerable and inviting. Lately she had been sensing a new desire in her blood to *feed*. The thirst was a low hum, like music in the back of your head that you didn't even notice, but once in a while it would raise its voice, and there was no mistaking it. She found herself drawn to Oliver in a new way, and she blushed when she looked at him.

It occurred to Schuyler that her human father had been her vampire mother's familiar, and Allegra had taken him as her husband—against vampire law. For the first time in the history of the Blue Bloods, the lines between the races had blurred, and the result had been Schuyler. Half human, half vampire. *Dimidium Cognatus.*

Schuyler had been made aware of her ancestry only a few months ago, but now she understood that her blood was her destiny, formed in an intricate pattern of veins underneath her skin. Blood calling for blood. Oliver's blood . . .

She'd never noticed how handsome her best friend was. How soft his skin looked. How much she wanted to reach out with her fingers and touch that spot below his Adam's apple, and kiss him there, and then, maybe, to prick the skin with her teeth, to sink in her fangs . . . and *feed*. . . .

"Where were you, anyway?" Oliver asked, breaking her train of thought.

"It's a long story," Schuyler said. The elevator doors opened and they both stepped inside.

* * *

As they made their way in a rickety cab through the cobble-stone streets to the tiny regional airport, Schuyler filled Oliver in on everything that had happened, and her friend listened attentively.

"It's a goddamn shame," Oliver said. "But maybe he'll change his mind one day."

Schuyler shrugged. She had pleaded her case, she had done as her grandmother had asked, but she had still been spurned. She really didn't think there was anything she could do about it anymore.

"Maybe, maybe not. Let's stop talking about it," she sighed.

Their flight to Rome was delayed, so Schuyler and Oliver killed time by browsing the duty-free and souvenir shops. Oliver grinned as he showed Schuyler a racy Italian magazine.

Schuyler grabbed several magazines, a bottle of water, and gum to ease the air pressure in her ears during take-off and landing. She was waiting on line for the cashier to ring her up when she noticed a stack of Venetian masks. The city was full of sidewalk vendors hawking them, even though Carnevale was still a few months away. She had hardly paid any attention to the cheap trifles, but one mask in particular in the airport display caught her eye.

It was a full-face mask with only holes for eyes, and was made of the finest porcelain, with gold-and-silver beading.

"Look," she said, holding it up to show Oliver.

"What do you want that tacky thing for?" he asked.

"I don't know. I don't have anything to remind me of Venice. I'm getting it."

Their flight to Rome was bumpy, and the flight to New York was even worse—so much turbulence that Schuyler thought she would go crazy from her teeth chattering against each other every time the plane bounced. But once she looked out the window and saw the New York skyline, she felt a rush of love for the city, tinged with sadness to know that there was no one waiting for her at home except two loyal servants who were now her legal guardians, as per Cordelia's will. At least there was Beauty, her bloodhound, a true friend and protector. Beauty was another part of the transformation, a part of Cordelia's soul that had transferred to the physical world to protect Schuyler until she was in full control of her powers. She had missed her dog.

They made their way to the concourse to retrieve their bags from the carousel, weary from their journey. After traveling for almost fifteen hours straight, both of them looked peaked, and it was dusk when they arrived in New York. They walked out to find a light dusting of snow. It was the first week of December, and winter had finally arrived.

Oliver found his family's car and driver idling by the curb, and led Schuyler toward the black Mercedes Maybach. They settled inside the cozy leather interior, Schuyler thanking the gods for giving her Oliver. His family fortune (intact) definitely came in handy during times like these.

The two of them were quietly absorbed in their own thoughts as they rode back to the city. Traffic was light on the freeway for a change, and they made it to Manhattan in half an hour. The car drove over the George Washington Bridge and exited on 125th Street, making its way down Riverside to the Van Alen mansion on the corner of 101st and Riverside.

"Well, this is me," Schuyler said. "Thanks again for every-thing, Ollie. I wish it had worked out with my grandfather."

"Yeah, no worries. 'Protect and serve,' that's my motto."

Oliver leaned over to kiss her on the cheek like he always did, but at the last minute Schuyler turned her head so that their noses bumped into each other.

"Oops," she said.

Oliver looked embarrassed, and they embraced awk-wardly instead.

What was wrong with her? He was her best friend. Why was she acting so lame? She was about to open the car door when he cleared his throat. She turned to him. "Did you say something?"

"So, uh, I guess you're going to that thing tonight, huh?" he asked, scratching his chin.

Schuyler blinked. "Thing?"

"That, uh, Four Hundred Ball," Oliver said, rolling his eyes and making exaggerated scare quotes with his fingers. "The big bloodsuckers shindig."

"Oh, right." She had almost forgotten about that. Her presence would be required as part of The Committee. She was too young to be officially presented at the ball, unlike Mimi and Jack Force. Jack Force—for weeks now she had suppressed her feelings for him, but the thought of the Four Hundred Ball brought his image to the forefront of her mind. Tall, painfully handsome, the sun shining on his golden hair and skin, laughing with his piercing green eyes, showing his even, dazzlingly white teeth.

Jack had been the first to suspect there was more to the story of Aggie's death than anyone on The Committee would have liked to believe. He was the one who had been determined to find out the truth. She had sought him out after she had been attacked, and after he had comforted her, they had kissed. The memory of his kiss was still pressed like an imprint on her lips. If she closed her eyes she could still smell him, clean and fresh like newly laundered linen, with a hint of woodsy aftershave.

Jack Force . . .

Who had turned his back on her when she had mistakenly accused his father of being a Silver Blood.

She wondered if Jack had a date for the ball, and if he did, who it was. She felt a bright flare of jealousy at the thought of another girl in his arms.

"Do you want to go with me?" She hadn't even given any thought to a dress or a date until Oliver mentioned it.

Oliver blushed and looked pained. "It's, um . . . vampires

only. Kind of a rule. No human familiars or Conduits allowed."

"Oh, I'm sorry, I didn't know." Schuyler said. "Maybe I won't go."

Oliver looked out the window, where snow had covered the rooftops and sidewalks with a glaze of white crystal.

"You should," Oliver said quietly. "Cordelia would have wanted you to."

Schuyler knew he was right. She was the remaining Van Alen in New York. She would have to represent the family. "All right, I'll go. But I'll leave early and maybe we can meet up later on?"

Oliver smiled wistfully. "Sure."

The Forces had booked the four-bedroom presidential suite at the St. Regis. Almost all the rooms in the hotel were taken over by Blue Blood families. It was a tradition, since it meant a simple ride in the elevator to the ballroom and guaranteed less crinkling of the ladies' gowns.

Charles Force fastened his remaining cuff link. He was a tall, proud man with a handsome head of silver hair. He was wearing white tie and tails, as well as white gloves. The tailcoat was beautifully cut in the traditional fashion, with a two-button closure and a velvet stripe down the side of the trousers. He stood in the living room with his hands clasped behind him, waiting for the women in his family to finish dressing.

His son, Jack, was dressed similarly, and looked dashing in his tailcoat. Jack had chosen a pointed collar that lay flat on his dress shirt rather than the traditional butterfly collar that turned up against the chin.

Jack had been quiet all day, and suddenly he swung his legs off the couch and stood up. He looked his father in the eye. "What did you say to Schuyler before she left?"

"Still concerned about the Van Alen girl?" Charles asked. "I would think that after she wrongly accused me of being Abomination, you would have lost interest in her."

Jack shrugged. "I'm not concerned, father. Just curious," he said. During the ruckus that had surrounded Dylan's disappearance and Cordelia's passing, his father had taken Jack into his confidence, telling him the truth of Schuyler's ancestry. That night, Jack had also discovered the truth about his relationship with his sister. Mimi was his other half, for better or worse, his best friend and worst enemy, his twin in more ways than one.

But although Jack had reconciled himself to the truth of his family, questions remained: what was The Committee hiding? Had a Silver Blood truly returned? His father acted as if the entire situation were completely resolved, since the killings had abruptly stopped several months ago.

Charles sighed. "I simply told her that her journey to Venice would be useless. She has gotten it into her head that her grandfather is somehow going to provide the necessary answers to all of her silly questions. But he shall not. I know Lawrence very well; he will stay out of it as he always has. She has embarked on a fruitless journey."

Jack had guessed as much. He was aware of his father's dislike of Lawrence Van Alen, and his newly surfacing memories confirmed it.

"Any more questions for me?" Charles asked.

Jack looked down at his patent-leather shoes, shined especially for the occasion. He could see his brooding reflection on their shiny surface.

"No, Father." He shook his head. How could he doubt his father? Charles Force was Michael, Pure of Heart, the Regis. A vampire by choice rather than sin, and infallible.

"Good," Charles said, brushing the lint off Jack's black tailcoat and admonishing his son to stand up straight. "This is the Four Hundred Ball. Your formal presentation to our people. I'm proud of you."

"Trinity, my dear? Are you ready?" Charles called from the living room.

Jack saw his mother, Trinity Burden Force, walk out of her dressing room and smile affectionately at her husband. She was dressed in a deep-red silk charmeuse ball gown with a sweetheart neckline and a plunging back. The two of them would open the ball with their entrance. But Jack knew from his father that Trinity had not been honored in this fashion in the past. In fact, this would be only the sixteenth year that Allegra Van Alen did not take her place by her brother's side. The sixteenth year that Gabrielle would not lead the coven.

* * *

In an adjoining suite, Mimi Force was draped in a plush Turkish bathrobe, sitting on a gilt-back chair while a bevy of stylists and manicurists surrounded her, tending to every inch of her. Her hair was being brushed back into a graceful chignon, while another assistant held an industrial-strength hair dryer. Two of the most well-known makeup artists in the city were working on their final touches: one was brushing on lipstick, the other dotting her face with bronzer.

All the while, Mimi held a cell phone to her ear while she blew on her nails, painted a pearly "Socialite."

"Oh my God, it's a madhouse in here, sorry—I can't hear you that well. What time did you say you guys were getting there?

"We're at the hotel. Yeah, the penthouse. Sorry, do you mind? Excuse me, hello, you there," she said sharply to the goateed stylist with the hair dryer. "You almost singed my ear off," she said, giving him a dirty look. "Sorry, Bliss, I gotta go."

Mimi flipped her cell phone closed, and the activity around her came to a standstill.

"Are we done?" she asked.

"Look." The stylist handed her a mirror.

"Polaroids!" Mimi demanded.

One of the black-shirted assistants took a quick snap.

Mimi checked her reflection as well as the photograph. She studied herself critically, searching for any detectable flaw, no matter how minute. Her hair was brushed and styled to a burnished sheen, and framed her face like a golden crown. Her skin glowed; a dark smoky shadow brought out the green in her eyes, and her lips looked stained with freshly picked roses.

"Yes, I think that will be all," she said regally, dismissing her entourage with a wave of the hand and without a trace of gratitude. Mimi considered it a privilege for them to work on her, not the other way around.

Soon after, her maid entered the room bearing a white cardboard box the size of a small child's coffin. It had been messengered over to the hotel at the last minute, and Mimi clapped her hands when she saw it.

"It's here!" her maid said happily, having been the unlucky recipient of Mimi's tantrums at the fact that the ball was starting in a few hours and her dress had still not arrived.

"I see that. I'm not an idiot," Mimi snapped.

She ran over to the box, laid it on the bedspread, and ripped open the brown parcel paper like a whirling dervish.

After leaving the Dior showroom, Mimi had complained to her mother about the lack of proper ball gowns, and Trinity had secured her an appointment at the Balenciaga atelier to meet with the head designer himself.

Over the course of the five-hour meeting, Mimi had rejected and dismissed countless designs, causing the designer to rip up more than several dozen sketches.

"What is it you're looking for?" he had asked, completely exasperated. "You're pickier than a bride."

Mimi inhaled sharply. "Exactly." She closed her eyes and saw herself and Jack together—during their first bonding. The dress she'd worn then was simple, white, merely a sheet, like a toga, and they had walked barefoot down the streets of Venice together, hand in hand, for the ceremony.

"White, the dress has to be white," she murmured. "White like snow. Transparent like tears."

Now, there it was, nestled in deepest tissues. The dress of her dreams.

It was made of the thinnest white silk satin, and when she picked it up, it felt like a whisper between her fingers, it was so fragile. Just as she had ordered, it was severe in its simplicity. It looked like nothing on the hanger—like a plain white piece of cloth. It was corded with a heavy silver chain at the hips, and had a sexy, unexpected keyhole cut out at the hip bone—the one concession to modern fashion she had allowed.

Mimi shrugged off her bathrobe, tossing it to the floor. She stood in the middle of the room, completely nude as her maid held the dress aloft. Mimi stepped into it, feeling the light, gossamer fabric fluttering about her like mist, settling against her slim form.

"Go," she said curtly to her maid. The frightened servant almost tripped on the bathrobe in her haste to leave.

She tied the cord around her waist and assessed the tanned skin that peeked through the cutout. When she stood in front of the light, her form would be shown in complete blackened silhouette; every curve of her body, every line from neck to breast, from waist to hips to her endless legs, she would be at once covered and yet exposed, clothed and unclothed, garbed and yet nude.

No underwear necessary.

It was spectacular.

"Wow."

She smiled. That didn't take long.

She turned around to face her brother.

Jack was standing in the doorway to her room, leaning a hand on the doorknob. Charles had sent him to collect his sister. His fine, platinum hair was brushed back from his forehead, and there was a tender look on his face.

You look . . . He sent.

I know. . . .

They had gone back to their old habits of talking without speaking—Jack letting his sister into his every thought, his every memory.

His eyes glazed over. She could see what he saw through his eyes, and she knew he was remembering that first night as well. She could see the cloudless Venetian sky, their footsteps light and quick over the bridge. She could see herself through his eyes, an eternity younger—how young they had been then—at the dawn of the world, before the wars, before the dark.

How did you find . . . *is it the same one?*

No, sadly that dress is gone to the Tiber river. . . . Silk does not keep a thousand years, my darling. This is a new one, for a new bonding.

"But not yet," Jack blurted.

Their shared vision disappeared, and Mimi was annoyed to find herself wrenched out of a very pleasant memory.

"No, not yet," Mimi allowed. They would not be bonded officially until their twenty-first birthday. According to vampire law, the bond—the holy matrimony between vampires—was an immortal vow, but the ceremony could not be performed until they were of age. The two of them were obligated to renew their bond in every cycle, although this was the first time that they had been born as twins to the same family, confusing matters due to pesky human laws. But no matter. They were vampire twins, which had a different meaning among their kind. It meant their souls had twinned in heaven, where they had pledged their love.

The bond could not be performed until they had both come into their full memories and mastered their powers. Vampire twins sometimes spent cycles looking for each other, and bonded couples had to be old enough to be able to recognize the latest reincarnation of their spouse in a new physical shell.

She knew that in the entire history of the vampires, there was only one couple that had forsaken their bond. Gabrielle as Allegra Van Alen had forsaken Michael, Charles Van Alen Force, in this cycle. She had married—*married*—in a church, a holy sanctuary, had said the words, had pledged her troth to a human! To her human familiar! And look what happened . . . Gabrielle trapped in a coma forever, caught between life and non-death. Condemned to eternal silence.

"But why wait?" Mimi asked. "I've known who you were ever since I could see. And you know who I am now."

Mimi was referring to the night in her father's study when Jack's memories had finally rushed back, allowing him to finally see what was right in front of him all along. They were two who were one. She was his. For eternity.

"I love you, you know," Mimi said. "You make me crazy, but God help me, Jack, I do."

Jack bent his head so that his nose was buried in Mimi's hair. It smelled of honeysuckle and jasmine, and he inhaled deeply.

"I love you too," he replied.

"My God." Trinity said, with a sharp intake of breath.

Mimi and Jack slowly parted from their embrace and looked to see their mother standing at the open doorway.

"Mimi, you are only sixteen. And that is certainly not a dress for a sixteen-year-old," Trinity accused, her voice shaking.

"Should I remind you I am centuries older than you, 'Mother'?" Mimi sniffed. She was coming of age now, the memories flooding back, and Mimi did not want to have to play at being Red Bloods anymore, with typical nuclear family dynamics.

"Charles," Trinity said. "Control your children."

"Mimi, you look beautiful," Charles said, kissing his daughter on the forehead. "Let's go."

Trinity scowled.

"Come, darling, it is time to dance," Charles said soothingly, taking his wife's hand and leading her out of the room.

"Shall we?" Jack asked, holding out his hand.

"We shall." Mimi smiled.

And together the Force twins walked out, arm in arm, to the party of the year.

few blocks away, in an altogether different penthouse—the Llewellyns' outlandish triplex, nicknamed "Penthouse des Rêves" due to its awesome, if surreal, extravagance—Forsyth Llewellyn was standing in front of a secret compartment behind the shoe closet. He quickly turned the knob on the vault two clicks to the right, then three clicks to the left, and stepped back as the five-inch stainless steel door swung open.

"Daaaad, what's this all about?" Bliss asked, standing beside him. "I'm supposed to meet Jaime in the lobby at eight." She was holding Miss Ellie, her Chihuahua, in her arms. Miss Ellie was her canine familiar, named after her favorite character, on *Dallas*, of course.

Just as promised, Mimi had set Bliss up with Jaime Kip. It was a total friend-date. Jaime had absolutely no interest in Bliss, and vice versa. In fact, it was Jaime who had suggested they meet in the St. Regis lobby since they were both attending with their families. Bliss got the distinct impression Jaime had asked to be her escort for the sole purpose of getting Mimi off his back. Mimi could be quite pushy when she wanted to be.

Bliss crossed her arms and looked around at her stepmother's enormous dressing room. It never failed to impress guests during the ritual house tour. The "closet" was easily two thousand square feet. It had a step-down Roman bath lined with travertine marble and was equipped with dancing showerheads along the side, so that you bathed in the midst of a fountain. There was an endless hallway of mirrors that masked a series of compartments that housed five thousand items of designer clothing, which had been catalogued and archived by BobiAnne's personal assistant. Too bad so much of what was inside was, in Bliss's opinion, vulgar and tasteless. BobiAnne had never met a marabou-trimmed leopard-print poncho that she didn't like.

BobiAnne was absorbed in her own toilette, and Bliss could hear her stepmother's gravelly laugh echo around the dressing chamber as she gossiped with her two stylists.

Bliss looked at herself in the infinity of mirrors. She had decided to wear the green Dior after all. Her father and stepmother had simply gasped when they saw her.

"My dear, you are so beautiful," BobiAnne had whispered, clasping her stepdaughter in her bony arms made stringy by too much Pilates. It was like being hugged by a skeleton.

BobiAnne was forever praising Bliss's good looks to the heavens, and disparaging her own daughter's rather plain appearance. Jordan, who at eleven was too young for the ball, had peeked in while Bliss was getting dressed and rendered her own judgment. "You look like a slut."

Bliss had thrown a pillow at her sister's retreating back.

After showing her parents the dress, her father had taken her aside and led her to the safe. He pulled open several of the suede-lined drawers custom-made to BobiAnne's exact specifications. Bliss could see the sparkle of her stepmother's many diamond tiaras, necklaces, rings, and bracelets. It was like the inside of Harry Winston. In fact, rumor had it that when the Texans had moved to Manhattan, the senator's wife had cleaned out the vaults at all the major diamond merchants in order to celebrate their ascendance in the city's social realm.

He pulled out a long black velvet box from a bottom drawer.

"This was your mother's," he said, showing her a massive cushion-cut emerald set in a platinum necklace. The emerald was as large as a fist. "Your real mother's, I mean. Not BobiAnne."

Bliss was struck silent.

"I want you to wear it for this evening. This is an important time for us, for our family. You will honor your mother's memory with this jewel," Forsyth said, clasping the necklace around his daughter's neck.

Bliss knew little of her mother, only that she had cycled out early for an unknown reason. Her father never talked about her, and Bliss had grown up understanding that her mother was a painful subject. There was little to remember her by, and what few photographs remained were washed-out and faded, so that her mother's features were almost indistinct. When Bliss asked about her, her father only said to "channel her memories," and that she would meet her mother again if time allowed it.

The dog in Bliss's arms went berserk, snapping and growling at the stone.

"Miss Ellie! Stop!"

"Silence!" Forsyth ordered, and the dog jumped from Bliss's arms and high-tailed it out the door.

"You scared her, Daddy."

Bliss looked at the emerald, which had nestled itself inside her cleavage. It was heavy against her skin. She didn't know if she liked it or not. It was so big. Had her mother really worn this?

"The stone is called the Rose of Lucifer, or Lucifer's Bane," the senator explained with a smile. "Have you heard the story?"

Bliss shook her head.

"It is said that when Lucifer fell from heaven, an emerald fell from his crown. The emerald was called the Rose of Lucifer, the morning star. Some other stories even call it the Holy Grail."

Bliss absorbed the information quietly, not knowing what to think. Her mother owned a jewel linked to the Silver Bloods?

"Of course," Forsyth said, shaking his head, "it's only a story."

At that moment, BobiAnne entered the room wearing a frightful Versace dress that looked like metallic vinyl siding spray painted on her body.

"How do I look?" she asked her husband sweetly.

Bliss and her father exchanged a glance.

"Very pretty, darling," her father said with a frozen smile. "Shall we? The car's waiting."

In front of the hotel a phalanx of photographers had gathered, and a swelling crowd of curious onlookers were being held back by security gates and a legion of New York's Finest. As each black town car pulled up to the entrance, flashbulbs exploded in a cacophony of staccato bursts.

"Here we go," BobiAnne exclaimed joyfully as she stepped out of the car and leaned on her husband's arm.

But the paparazzi were only interested in Bliss.

"Bliss! Over here! Bliss! One for me! Bliss—this way!"

"What are you wearing?"

"Who made that dress?"

A few of the photographers and reporters were polite enough to ask the senator and his wife what they thought of the party, but it was obvious Bliss was the main attraction.

There were only ten steps from the curb to the hotel

entrance, but it took Bliss a good half hour to get there.

"It's madness," Bliss remarked, looking pleased when she finally arrived in the pink and gold lobby and found her date waiting impatiently by the front reception table.

The St. Regis Ballroom had been transformed into a twinkling winter wonderland: the crystal chandeliers were hung with softly beaded strings of rhinestones, and glorious American Beauty roses bloomed everywhere, from the soaring, six-foot-tall centerpieces (so heavy that the tables had to be reinforced) to the massive garlands on every archway. A snow-white carpet on the marble floor led the way from the front reception room into the ballroom proper.

"Senator and Mrs. Forsyth Llewellyn," the herald announced as the politician and his wife appeared at the top of the stairs. A spotlight shone on them, and the percussionist played a dramatic drumroll.

"Mr. James Andrews Kip. Miss Bliss Llewellyn."

The four of them walked slowly into the party.

The two fifty-piece orchestras faced each other across the expanse of the ballroom, playing a serene waltz as the Blue Bloods displayed their finery—the men dashing and suave in their tails, the women preternaturally thin and impossibly stylish in their couture ball gowns. It was a magical sight. The Committee had really outdone themselves this time. The whole ballroom was filled with a dazzling, white brilliance: the antique crystal chandeliers shone, and the terrazzo floors gleamed.

Jaime deposited Bliss at her table, saluted her, and promptly disappeared for the rest of the evening. So much for that. Bliss found Mimi standing with her parents at the front of the reception line.

"Wow, look at that!" Mimi said, zeroing in on the necklace immediately. "What a rock!"

"It was my mother's," Bliss explained. She told Mimi the legend of Lucifer's Bane.

Mimi took the emerald in her hands, stroking its glacial coldness. Once she touched it, she was transported back to that final battle, flashes of the black day, trumpets sounding in the distance, Michael with his flaming sword, the banishment, and then the cold. The cold . . . waking up immortal on earth and dying to *feed*.

"Oh." Mimi's eyes glazed, her hand still cupping the stone. And then she dropped it as if it had burned her.

Bliss was startled. She knew something had happened to Mimi, the flash of insight, the memory spike when she had touched it. And yet when Bliss touched the stone herself, nothing happened. It was just a dead piece of jewelry. Lucifer's Bane. It gave her shivers.

"It's the Heart of the Ocean," Mimi cracked. "Just promise me you won't throw it off the deck of the *Titanic*."

Bliss tried to laugh. But the stone, fifty-five carats, weighed heavily on her skin.

Rose of Lucifer. Lucifer's Bane. The Prince of the Silver Bloods, his most precious possession, hung around her neck like a noose. She shuddered. Part of her wanted to rip it off her throat and throw it as far away as she could.

*T*he Van Alen mansion on the corner of 101st and Riverside had once been one of the largest and most majestic homes in all of New York. Countless generations of the family had entertained presidents, heads of state, foreign dignitaries, Nobel prize–winning laureates, as well as Hollywood royalty and the occasional flavor-of-the-month bohemian—artists, writers, and their ilk. Yet now it was a mere shadow of its former self: the cornices were chipped, there was grafitti on the side of the building, the roof leaked, and the walls were riddled with cracks, as the family had been unable to maintain its upkeep over the years.

Schuyler dragged her suitcase up the steps and rang the bell.

Hattie, her grandmother's loyal maid, answered and let her inside.

The living room was as dark and shrouded as when

Schuyler had left. For years Schuyler and Cordelia had lived in only a quarter of the rooms in the vast house—kitchen, dining, and their two bedrooms. Everything else was locked and unused, which Schuyler had always attributed to Cordelia's penury. Her grandmother kept almost all the furniture in the house under canvas sheets, windows were curtained, and entire wings of the house were off-limits.

Hence the mansion was akin to a musty old museum, filled with antique artifacts and expensive art objects that were hidden and kept under lock and key.

Schuyler made her way to her room, where Beauty greeted her with a cheerful and resonant bark, and only then did Schuyler feel like she was truly at home.

Now the only problem was what to wear. The invitation had stated White Tie, which Schuyler understood to mean long, formal gowns for the women. She dimly remembered Cordelia getting ready for the yearly Four Hundred Ball, donning a succession of stiff, Oscar de la Renta ball gowns with elbow-length opera gloves. Perhaps she would be able to find something in Cordelia's closet.

She made her way to her grandmother's bedroom. She hadn't been inside since the fateful evening of the attack. She dreaded being in there, remembering how she had found her grandmother lying in a pool of blood. But she comforted herself with the knowledge that Cordelia had managed to survive the attack, and she had been able to bring enough of Cordelia's blood to the medical center. They would keep it resting until the next cycle. Cordelia would return one day. She was not dead. She had not been taken by the Silver Blood.

"Looking for something, Miss Schuyler?" Hattie asked, popping her head in and finding Schuyler standing with her hands on her hips in front of her grandmother's closet.

"I need a dress, Hattie. For the ball tonight."

"Mrs. Cordelia had a lot of dresses."

"Yes." Schuyler frowned, removing several hangers and assessing the dresses that hung on them. They were very old-fashioned, with huge mutton sleeves or peplums. Several were very Reagan-eighties: shoulder pads that rivaled those on Alexis Carrington's Nolan Miller originals on *Dynasty*. "I just don't think these are going to cut it."

"Miss Allegra had dresses too," Hattie said.

"My mother? My mom's dresses are still here?"

"In her room, on the third landing."

Her mother had grown up in the same house, and Schuyler wished, not for the first time, that her mother was around to help her with her current dilemma. Hattie led her upstairs to the next floor, down the hallway, to a corner room in the back.

Schuyler's heart beat in nervous excitement.

"It's a shame about Miss Allegra," Hattie said as she opened the door. "The room's just like it was when she was eighteen. Before she eloped and married your father."

The room was pristine. Schuyler was shocked to see that there were no cobwebs in the corners, or a layer of dust everywhere. She had expected a crypt, a mausoleum, but it was a bright and cheerful room, with crisp Italian linens on the bed and billowing white curtains on the windows.

"Mrs. Cordelia always insisted we keep it up. For whenever your mother wakes up."

Schuyler walked toward the armoire in the middle of the room and opened one of its doors.

She reached inside and pulled out a shirt on a hanger. Valentino, circa 1989.

"Are you sure she had ball gowns?"

"She had a cotillion. She was presented at the Four Hundred Ball on her sixteenth birthday," Hattie explained. "Chanel made the dress. It should be in there."

Schuyler patiently went through each hanger. At last, in the farthest reaches of the closet, she found a black garment bag embroidered with the double-C logo.

She laid the bag out on her mother's bed and unzipped it slowly.

"Wow," Schuyler breathed, removing a carefully preserved dress. She held it up to the light. It was a gold dress with a tight, strapless corset bodice and a princess skirt with folds and folds of voluminous fabric.

She held it up against herself. It would fit, she knew it would fit.

When Schuyler entered the St. Regis Ballroom, the whole room stood still. The guests stared at her as she stood by the entrance, illuminated under the spotlight, uncertain about where to go next. A few gasps could be heard from the crowd.

Jack Force, for one, couldn't take his eyes off her.

Like almost everybody in the room, for one brief moment, he had believed that Gabrielle, Allegra Van Alen, had returned to them.

*T*he Four Hundred Ball, also known as the Patrician Ball, never wavered from the tradition set by its original organizers in the late nineteenth century, when the Blue Bloods first came into prominent position in society. The ten-course meal, with breaks in between for dancing, was set on $75,000-a-piece gold service—solid gold plates, gold flatware, and gold-crusted crystal goblets.

Along the length of the four rectangular tables, with a hundred seats at each, was a pile of sand, and each place setting was set with a golden trowel. Guests were encouraged to "dig" for treasure—their parting gifts. The Committee had been able to convince sponsors to provide expensive, eye-popping jewelry set with rubies, sapphires, and diamonds as party favors. The Junior Committee, led by Mimi, had added a modern touch: "alphabet" necklaces from Me & Ro, intricate Peruvian peacock earrings by Zani, and the most coveted piece of the season, Kaviar and Kind's diamond-encrusted shark-tooth pendant.

The menu was just the same as it had been on the night of the first Patrician Ball: a first course of Consommé Olga, then Filet Mignons Lili, Vegetable Marrow Farcie, followed by a roast duckling and sirloin of beef, accompanied by creamed carrots and parmentier potatoes.

Several towering ice sculptures depicting New York's greatest momuments and institutions, including the new MOMA building, renovations funded by Blue Blood money, and the proposed Frank Gehry port, championed by none other than Senator Llewellyn himself, were arranged next to the bars that lined the room, and champagne flowed from hidden spigots in the ice.

Mimi barely touched her food, getting up from her seat to circulate among the glittering crowd. Every prestigious family in New York, all the old names were represented: the Van Horns, the Schlumbergers, the Wagners, the Stewarts, the Howells and the Howlands, the Goulds and the Goelets, the Bancrofts and the Barlows. Members of the clan who had remained in England were represented, as well as several more exotic branches. A vastly rich Blue Blood family who had splintered from the main group centuries ago and settled in what was now modern China had just arrived from Shanghai, a city that they had recently helped rebuild. Their sixteen-year-old twin daughters, two gorgeous long-limbed Chinese socialites, would be among those presented at the ball that evening.

But there was no family more respected or revered than the Forces. Mimi was a princess among her people, and she walked through them, accepting their admiration, their deference.

She looked for her brother. He had been by her side all evening but had disappeared between the fish and meat course. By all rights they should be doing this together. Tonight was the night the coven would recognize that they had found each other, and that when the time came, they would be renewing their immortal vows.

Where was he?

She cast her mind across the room, looking for his signal. Ah, there he was, by the head table, talking to a friend on the lacrosse team, Bryce Cutting. She saw him stop and look in her direction with a sudden, joyous smile on his face.

She smiled back and waved at him, but he didn't return the wave.

Annoyed, she turned around—maybe he wasn't looking at her after all?

And that's when she noticed who was standing right behind her, at the top of the staircase, commanding the attention of the entire ballroom.

Schuyler Van Alen.

In a dress that even Mimi herself would die to wear.

Schuyler found her seat next to the dour parents of Aggie Carondolet. It was apparent that the Carondolets had felt slighted by their seating, and they hardly spoke a word to Schuyler except to inform her that they were truly sad about Cordelia. She found Bliss sitting by herself at the front table, and waved to her. Bliss waved back. "Come over," Bliss mouthed.

She gathered up her gold skirts and walked over to Bliss's side. The two girls hugged warmly.

"Sky, I have to tell you something—about Dylan," Bliss said.

"Oh?" Schuyler raised an eyebrow.

"I think he's . . ." but before Bliss could finish, a boy walked over and asked her to dance. "Sure." Bliss shrugged. "I'll tell you later," she said to Schuyler.

Schuyler nodded. As she dejectedly walked back to her seat, she wondered what Bliss was about to tell her. Bliss was her only friend at the ball. What was Schuyler doing here, anyway? Why had she come? For Cordelia? For the Van Alen name? No. She had to be honest. And this was where the truth hurt. She had wanted to see Jack Force again. But it was agony.

There he was, attentively at his sister's side, the two of them gliding through the ballroom, entwined at the hip. Jack keeping a hand on Mimi's tiny waist. Schuyler had heard whispers from the Elders and the Wardens at the adjoining table . . . something about a bond . . . something about the two of them and an immortal vow.

The next course was served, roast squab and a cold

asparagus vinaigrette. It looked delicious, but the food tasted dry and mealy on her tongue.

"Jack," Mimi whispered softly in his ear as they made their way around the room. "It's time." Ever practical, she decided to ignore what she had seen earlier. Mimi was a master of self-deception. If something bothered her, she refused to even acknowledge its existence. In her mind, Schuyler Van Alen was a temporary, if annoying, infatuation.

But for Jack, the sight of Schuyler Van Alen had only served to ignite a feeling he had been repressing for months. A disquieting thought nagged at his conscience. Why did Schuyler affect him in such a powerful way? Was it the resemblance to Allegra? Was that all? Or was it something new . . . something he wasn't prepared for and didn't expect? He shook his head, disgusted and ashamed of himself. His rightful place was by his sister's side. He would just have to act as if Schuyler did not exist.

"They are waiting for us to lead the quadrille," Mimi said, and Jack dutifully escorted his sister to the dance floor, where three other young couples were waiting. It was part of Four Hundred tradition that the young who were going to be presented would lead in this dance, and the teens in the foremost quadrille were chosen because of their family's hierarchy in The Committee. Aggie Carondolet would have been one of the dancers had she lived.

Mimi thought the quadrille was just a fancy name for

square dancing, but she enjoyed it even so, as Jack led her through the cross-over, the balance, and then the circle eight, ending with the four ladies' grand chain, which placed her in the front of the group, as it should be.

After the dance, the Blue Blood teens remained frozen in their position in the middle of the dance floor, waiting to be formally presented to the assembly, called out by their current and true names by the Regis.

"Dehua Chen," was called, and one of the imperial Chinese beauties stepped forward.

"Known to our people by her true name, Xi Wangmu."

The Angel of Immortality.

"Deming Chen." Her sister was called next. The two of them were identical in their serene, otherworldly beauty, with skin the color of toasted milk; silky-straight, ebony-black hair; sexily slanted almond eyes; and an incongruous splattering of freckles across their button noses.

"Known to our people by her true name, Kuan Yin."

The Angel of Mercy.

Several other Blue Blood teens were called, rounding out the former heavenly pantheon.

At last, a lone spotlight was shone on the Force twins. Mimi gripped her brother's hand tightly.

"Madeleine Force." Mimi stepped forward, her chin held high.

"Known to our people by her true name, Azrael."

The Angel of Death.

"Benjamin Force." Jack bowed his head.

"Known to our people by his true name, Abbadon."

The Angel of Destruction.

The twin Angels of the Apocalypse. This was their immortal destiny. This was their place. The clan's most powerful vampires after the Uncorrupted. Lucifer's former lieutenants, who had turned their backs on the Prince of Heaven after the Fall. In Rome, they had hunted and slain the Silver Blood spawn. Only by their strength had the Blue Bloods survived the millennia.

Jack smiled at Mimi, and they both bowed low to the coven.

They had their work cut out for them.

*T*he coffee had been served in its golden carafes, and dessert—the traditional Waldorf pudding along with peaches in chartreuse jelly, as well as chocolate and vanilla éclairs and a light-as-air meringue cake topped with Amaretto whipped cream—had been served and (lightly) consumed. Powdered cheeks were pressed against powdered cheeks in good-bye. A wonderful time had been had, it was agreed, and a ridiculous amount of money had been raised, breaking records from last year, even.

All around the St. Regis Ballroom, Mimi's text messages were being delivered. For select vampire teens, the evening had just begun.

After-party. Angel Orensanz. Midnight. Masks A Must. No Text. No Entry.

There was a buzzing through the crowd by the cloakroom and the elevators among the invitees, as well as cries of confusion and disappointment among those who had not received the text.

"Are you going to change?" Bliss asked Mimi, following her out the door.

"Are you crazy? I'm going to wear this dress until they pry it off my cold dead body," Mimi joked. "Come upstairs. We have the best selection of masks."

Mimi was in high spirits. The ball had been a blast and all, but now it was time to par-tay.

Schuyler walked out to the sidewalk, hugging her black fur coat, an old one of Cordelia's, around her shoulders. She found Julius, her grandmother's driver, waiting patiently for her by the curb in the old Crown Victoria.

"Where to?"

She was about to say "home" when her phone buzzed. Oliver, for sure. Nope. It was a text message from a blocked number.

Directing her to Angel Orensanz, the abandoned synagogue on the Lower East Side. Masks a must? What was this all about?

"Did you get the message?" Cicely Appelgate called excitedly from the next car over. Cicely was part of Mimi's crew, and Schuyler wondered why she was bothering to talk to her.

"Uh, yeah."

"See you there!" Cicely said gaily. "Great dress, by the way!" she added admiringly. "My mom said it's definitely vintage Chanel."

So that was it. Sometimes it seemed to Schuyler that high school was so silly. If you dressed a certain way, or looked a certain way, or had the "right" things—like a designer handbag, or the newest cell phone, or an expensive watch—your life was much easier. Schuyler never had any of those things. Cordelia had been strict with her allowance, and she had always been the kid in secondhand sweaters and items from last year's clearance bin.

But the dress, and the fact that it was from a respected and expensive design house, had changed Cicely's perception of her. For the evening, at least.

"Home, Miss Schuyler?"

She had promised to call Oliver the minute she left the party. She had told him that she was only going to stay for a few minutes and depart soon after dinner, but it was already eleven thirty. He would be jet-lagged, Schuyler thought. He's probably passed out in front of the television by now.

The text message must be for the party downtown that other kids at the ball were talking about—the buzz about Mimi Force hosting some kind of bacchanal that evening. Should she go? What could it hurt? Besides, if Mimi was there, that meant Jack would be there too. She thought of how handsome he'd looked in his coattails, and the way he'd stared at her when she'd entered the party, his green eyes boring into hers. Not too long ago, he had been the one who was hell-bent to find out the truth about the Silver Bloods, but he had backed off all of a sudden. But maybe there was still a chance she could convince him to join her in her fight. Since her grandfather had refused to help, she was now adrift. But with Jack at her side . . . She made up her mind.

"Let's go home, Julius, but just for a minute," Schuyler decided. "I just need to pick up something. A souvenir from Venice. Then we're going downtown."

November 24, 1871
Engagement Announcement Follows
Disappearance of Former Fiancée

English Lord to Marry Vanderbilt Heiress

The formal announcement of the engagement of Caroline Vanderbilt, the daughter of Admiral and Elizabeth Vanderbilt of 800 Fifth Avenue, to Alfred, Lord Burlington, of London and Devonshire, is the sequel to the mysterious disappearance of Lord Burlington's former fiancée, Maggie Stanford, the daughter of Tiberius and Dorothea Stanford of Newport.

Maggie Stanford mysteriously disappeared on the night of the Patrician Ball held at Admiral and Elizabeth Vanderbilt's home over a year ago upon the announcement of her engagement to Lord Burlington. The engagement was broken eight months ago while Maggie Stanford was still missing.

As yet, the wedding day of the couple has not been set.

*L*ike many of the guests, when Bliss arrived at the after-party, she gasped in delight. The abandoned synagogue was lit by a thousand tea light candles, casting long and gloomy shadows on the walls. Mimi was right, it looked like a beautiful ruin, and there was something spooky and romantic about dancing only in firelight.

The masks lent the evening an eerie glamour, since all the guests were still in their ball finery. The boys were so handsome in their tailcoats, and the girls gorgeous in their couture ball gowns, and everyone looked a little bit wicked with all those masks.

Bliss fixed the feathered and jeweled mask on her face. It was a little hard to see everyone from behind it. She noticed Schuyler arrive. Good. Bliss had forwarded the message to Schuyler without Mimi knowing.

The DJ was spinning Bauhaus, a dark, violent tune, "Burning from the inside . . ."

A boy in white tie and tails walked up to Bliss, his face hidden underneath a sad Pierrot mask.

He motioned toward the dance floor.

Bliss nodded and followed him. He held out his hands and she stepped into his embrace.

"So you have survived," he whispered, his mouth close to her ear, so that she could feel his breath blow softly.

"Excuse me?"

"I would have hated to let you drown." He chuckled.

"You . . ."

He put a finger to his lips, or rather to the lips of the Pierrot mask.

"I missed you . . ." Bliss said. Dylan. It had to be him. He had found her again. How clever to show up at a masquerade party, where he could appear without causing a fuss.

"I haven't been gone for long," he said earnestly.

"I know, but I was worried. . . ."

"Don't be. Everything will be all right."

"Are you sure?"

"Yes."

Bliss danced joyfully. He had returned! He had returned to be with her. She was elated.

The song ended. The boy in the mask bowed low. "A pleasure."

"Wait—" Bliss called, but already he had disappeared into the throng, and when she looked around, she saw a dozen boys dressed similarly in their black tails, but none were wearing a mask with a sad clown face, one tear glinting below the eye.

Schuyler walked despondently from room to room. She should have called Oliver after all, if only to have some company. This party didn't seem to be as exclusive as the Four Hundred Ball. She noticed a few of her human classmates were there looking a bit nervous, as if they weren't sure they were welcome. She could tell human from vampire: the vampires glowed in the dark—the gift of *Illuminata* made them recognizable to each other.

Deep in the shadows behind the columns, several couples were availing of the dark to neck—"necking" taking on quite a different meaning among the vampire teens. She could hear the deep, sucking sounds as vampires fed on their human familiars, the throbbing beat of blood and life force exchanged from one being to the next. Afterward, the vampires glowed even more, their features sharper and more distinct, while the humans looked vacant and listless.

One day, Schuyler knew, she would have to do the same. She would have to perform the Sacred Kiss with a human familiar. The thought both excited and terrified her. The Sacred Kiss was not a joke. It was a serious bond between vampire and human, one that was respected by the Blue Bloods. Human familiars were to be treated with affection and care for the service they provided.

The genteel atmosphere at the Four Hundred Ball had given way to a rowdier, more boisterous behavior. Several teens were dancing body-to-body to the hard beats of the house music the DJ was spinning, and a riotous, anything-goes atmosphere prevailed, as girls began dancing sexily with each other, or grinding their pelvises against their male partners. The party was soon packed with sweaty teens throwing their hands in the air and declaring they were getting mega-crunked tonight. (Crazy-ass drunk—on blood.)

Schuyler remained at the fringes. She didn't fit in with this crowd. She had no friends here.

She sighed. The Venetian mask she was wearing covered her entire face. She wished she could take it off; it was itchy and making her face hot.

She made her way to a small alcove hidden behind the speakers, so she could sit down while she debated her next move.

A boy followed her inside the room. How funny, Schuyler thought. How you knew who the girls were because they were wearing different dresses, whereas the boys were truly disguised since they all looked the same in their penguin suits. Just like this one, in his black silk mask that covered his eyes, nose, and hair, giving him a rakish air like an urban pirate.

"Don't you like parties?" he asked, when he noticed her sitting by herself on a ruined stone bench.

Schuyler laughed. "I hate them, actually."

"Me too."

"I never know what to say, or what to do."

"Well, it looks like dancing is involved. And drinking. Of all kinds."

He was a vampire, then. Schuyler wondered who he was, and why he was bothering to speak to her.

"Undoubtedly," she agreed.

"But you choose not to choose."

"I'm a rebel," she said sarcastically.

"I don't think so."

"No?"

"You're here, aren't you? You could have chosen not to come at all."

He was right. She didn't have to be there. She had come for the same reason she had chosen to attend the ball. For the chance to see Jack again. She had to face it: every time she saw Jack Force, something inside her quickened and came alive.

"To be honest, I came to see a boy," she said.

"What boy?" he asked in a teasing tone.

"It doesn't matter."

"Why not?"

"Because. It's complicated." Schuyler shrugged.

"Now, now."

"It is. He's . . . he's not interested," she said, thinking of Jack and Mimi, and the bond between them. Whatever she was feeling for him was irrelevant. He had made that clear at her grandmother's funeral. He had responsibilities to his family. She couldn't escape the image of the two of them holding their hands aloft. *Azrael and Abbadon*. The magnetic charge between them was electric. The whole ballroom had tingled with excitement at the announcement. *Two of our most powerful vampires. They have been revealed to us at last.* Who was she, Schuyler Van Alen, not even a pure-blood vampire, to come between them?

"How do you know he's not interested?" he asked in a serious tone.

"I just do."

"You might be surprised."

Schuyler realized that the boy was standing close to her as he spoke. His eyes behind the mask—she could detect a hint of green. Her heart skipped a beat. The boy moved closer.

"Surprise me," Schuyler whispered.

In response, the boy lifted her mask gently, so that her lips were exposed, and then he leaned down and brought his mouth to hers.

Schuyler closed her eyes. The only boy she had ever kissed was Jack Force, and this was like that—but different somehow. More urgent. More insistent. She inhaled his breath, felt his tongue in her mouth, rolling on top of hers, almost as if he wanted to devour her. It felt as if she could kiss him forever.

And then it stopped.

She opened her eyes, her mask askew from her face. What happened? Where had he gone?

"Hey!"

Schuyler turned. Mimi Force was standing in the foyer, wearing a dazzling Indian princess headdress, her "mask" expertly drawn on with makeup and face paint.

"Have you seen my brother anywhere?" Mimi had been upset at first to find her party overrun by human gate-crashers, but then she'd just chalked it up to her own irresistible popularity. So she wasn't fazed to find Schuyler, another non-invitee, at the party as well.

Before Schuyler could answer, Jack Force materialized by his sister's side. He was wearing an Indian headdress like his sister's. And his mask too, was made of face paint.

"Here I am," he said jovially. "Oh, hey, Schuyler. How was Venice?"

"Great," Schuyler said, trying to keep her composure.

"Cool."

"C'mon, Jack, the fireworks are about to start." Mimi said, pulling on his sleeve.

"See ya," Jack called.

Schuyler felt numb. She was so sure it was Jack she had been kissing. So sure it had been him behind that black mask. But his relaxed attitude, that casual friendliness, made her doubt her assumption. But if it wasn't Jack she had just kissed, then who? Who was the boy behind the mask?

With a pang, she realized tomorrow was the start of the Christmas holidays, and she wouldn't see Jack Force again for two whole weeks.

SEVENTEEN

Winter finally arrived in New York in earnest, unleashing several storms. The city was covered by a pristine blanket of snow for several days, until it turned to gray and yellow mush, creating impromptu snowbanks around the sidewalks and muddy puddles that hardy citizens either jumped across or grimly splashed through in salt-caked rubber boots.

Schuyler was glad for the cold, as the weather reflected her current mood. The holidays were a typically quiet time for the Van Alens. In the past, she and Cordelia would attend services at St. Bartholomew's across town, then have a modest repast at midnight on Christmas Eve.

As she did every year, she spent this Christmas Day with her mother at the hospital. Julius and Hattie had the day off to be with their families, so she had taken the bus all the way uptown by herself. The hospital was practically abandoned when she arrived. There was one sleepy guard at the front desk and a skeletal crew of nurses anxious to finish their shifts. She noticed the staff had tried to infuse the place with some Christmas cheer. There were wreaths on each door, and a lone Charlie Brown–like Christmas tree with brown branches stood in the middle of the nurse's station, along with a flickering menorah.

Her mother was asleep on the bed as usual. Nothing had changed. Schuyler placed another unopened gift by her mother's bedside. Through the years, Schuyler's presents collected more and more dust in her mother's closet.

Dusting off the snow, she removed her coat, and stuffed her wool cap and gloves in its pockets. If Cordelia had been there she would have set out their Christmas lunch, removing turkey and stuffing, ham and hot rolls from Tupperware containers Hattie had prepared. Hattie had made up the same meal for Schuyler to bring, but eating it without Cordelia correcting her on her table manners or snapping at the nurses to bring her porcelain, not plastic, plates just wasn't the same.

She turned on the television and settled in to eat her lonely lunch and watch another rerun of *It's a Wonderful Life*. The movie never failed to make her more depressed, since there was no happy ending for Allegra that she could see.

Oliver had invited her to spend the day with his family, but she had declined. Whatever family she had left in the world was in this lonesome hospital room. This was where she belonged.

Across town on the Upper East Side, the great houses and lavish apartments were empty of their residents. The Forces had already left on their Gulfstream IV for their annual sojourn, shipping their beachwear via FedEx to their villa in St. Barths, where they would spent the first week of the break, and sending their ski gear to their Aspen cottage for the second half of their vacation. The Llewellyns were off to Texas to visit family for Christmas and were meeting up with the Forces in Aspen for New Year's.

Even Oliver's family had made plans for a beach getaway to the family compound in Tortola, but he had opted to stay in the city to be close to Schuyler.

He planned to visit the Van Alen town house the day after Christmas with an abundance of presents. They always spent Boxing Day together. Oliver liked to bring over a crusty baguette, French butter—the real kind, he stressed, nothing like the bland American versions—several jars of premium Russian caviar from Petrossian, as well as a magnum of champagne from his parents' wine cellar for their post-Christmas feast.

But on the morning of the twenty-sixth, just as Oliver had packed the picnic basket with treats and was about to leave, he received a frantic call from Hattie, the Van Alen's maid.

"Mr. Oliver, you come, you come right now," she begged.

Oliver immediately jumped into a cab and arrived at the brownstone, to find Hattie frantic and incoherent, wringing her hands on her apron and close to tears. She led him up the stairs to Schuyler's room.

"Miss didn't come down for breakfast. I thought she was just sleeping in, until Beauty ran down the stairs and practically pulled me up here. Then I saw she was just lying there, and I couldn't wake her up. God help me, she looks so much like Miss Allegra, and I was so worried because she wouldn't move, didn't even look like she was breathing, so I called you, Mr. Oliver."

Beauty, Schuyler's bloodhound, was whimpering at the foot of her bed. The dog jumped up and licked Oliver's hands and face when he entered the room.

"You did well, Hattie," Oliver said, patting Beauty and then shaking Schuyler and checking for her pulse. There was none, but that didn't mean anything. His Conduit training had told him vampires could slow their heartbeat to a barely detectable rhythm to conserve their energy. Yet Schuyler was only fifteen years old and had only begun the transformation. It was too early for her to go into preservation mode. Unless . . .

Oliver suddenly had an awful thought: what if Schuyler had been attacked by a Silver Blood? His hands shook as he dialed his aunt, Dr. Pat, the human doctor who cared for

Blue Bloods. Dr. Pat discouraged Oliver from waiting for an ambulance or taking her to a proper hospital. "They won't know what to do with her. Just get her to my office now. I'll meet you there."

When Oliver arrived, holding Schuyler in his arms, Dr. Pat and her team were ready. They wheeled out a hospital bed, and Oliver gently laid his friend down.

"Tell me she'll be all right," Oliver pleaded.

Dr. Pat checked Schuyler's neck. There were no marks. No sign of Abomination. "She should be. It doesn't look like she's been attacked. She should be fine. They *are* immortal. But we'll see what's going on."

Oliver waited in Dr. Pat's outer room on a particularly uncomfortable plastic chair. His aunt had always been enamored of modern furniture, and the office resembled the lobby of a trendy hotel rather than a clinic: all-white plastic furniture, white flokati rugs, white space-age lamps. After a few anxiety-ridden hours, Oliver's aunt emerged from the inner office.

Dr. Pat looked tired and beat. "Come in," she told her nephew. "She's awake. I gave her a transfusion. That seems to have done the trick."

Schuyler looked even smaller and more fragile in the hospital bed. She was wearing one of those gowns that tied in the back, and her face was paler than usual. He could see her blue veins through her transparent skin.

"Well hello, Sleeping Beauty," Oliver cracked, trying to mask his concern.

"Where am I?"

"You're in my office, child," Dr. Pat said solemnly. "You went into hibernation. It's not something that usually happens until much, much later. It's another word for prolonged sleep, something vampires do when they are weary of immortality at the close of a cycle."

"My head feels weird. And my blood—it feels strange. Icky."

"I had to give you a transfusion. You had very low blood cell counts. It's going to feel strange for a little while as the new blood adjusts to the old."

"Oh." Schuyler shuddered.

"Oliver, can you excuse us?"

"Good to see you're okay," Oliver said, gripping Schuyler's shoulder tightly. "I'll just be outside."

Once Oliver was gone, Dr. Pat shone a light into each of Schuyler's pupils. She made a note on her chart, while Schuyler waited patiently for the diagnosis.

Dr. Pat examined Schuyler closely. "You are fifteen, yes?"

Schuyler nodded.

"Inducted into The Committee?"

"Yes."

"Like I said, you had very low red-blood cell counts. Yet your blue-blood cell counts are off the charts. In some ways, you already have the blood levels of a full-fledged vampire, and yet your body went into hibernation, which means you aren't producing the right levels of antigens."

"What does that mean?"

"It means the transformation is going a bit haywire with you."

"Excuse me?"

"The transformation is a process in which your blue-blood cells—your vampire DNA—starts to take over. You grow your fangs, your body switches from needing nourishment from food to needing nourishment specifically from human blood. The memories start to come back, and your powers, whatever they are, begin to manifest."

Schuyler nodded.

"Yet there's something odd in your blood analysis. The vampire cells are taking over, but it's not a normal, gradual process, wherein the human self is shed for the immortal—like a snake shedding its skin. I'm not sure, but it's almost as if your human DNA is fighting the vampire one. Resisting it. And so to overcompensate, your vampire DNA is fighting back, hard—sending your human blood counts way below where they should be. The shock sent your body into hibernation. Did something happen? Sometimes it's triggered by a traumatic event."

Schuyler shook her head. The night before had been uneventful.

"Sometimes, it can be a delayed reaction," Dr. Pat

surmised. "It must be your mixed blood," she added. Dr. Pat knew all about the circumstances of Schuyler's birth. She had been Allegra's obstetrician.

"No one has ever documented what happens when human DNA mixes with vampire blood. I'd like to put you under observation for a while."

EIGHTEEN

A week later, Schuyler still felt a bit woozy after the "episode," which is what she and Oliver were calling her emergency visit to Dr. Pat's office. Oliver had offered to pick her up in his car to take her to the first day back at school. Schuyler, who would usually resist such a gesture since she lived across town and out of the way, had meekly agreed to such an arrangement. Oliver was her Conduit—he was supposed to take care of her, and for once, she was going to let him.

The spring semester at Duschene was officially opened by an assembly, in which the Headmistress welcomed all the students back for another exciting term, followed by a tea of currant scones and hot chocolate in the belvedere. Oliver and Schuyler found their usual seats in the back pew of the chapel with the other sophomores.

There was a lot of cheerful greeting and exchanging

of vacation stories all around. Most of the girls looked tan and rested, trading cell phones to show pictures of themselves in bikinis on the beaches of the Bahamas, St. Thomas, or Maui. Schuyler saw Bliss Llewellyn walk in with Mimi Force, the two of them with their arms linked around each other's waists as if they were the closest of friends.

Mimi's hair had been made even lighter by the sun, and Bliss sported a few copper highlights of her own. Jack Force walked slowly behind them, hands jammed in the pockets of his Duckhead chinos. He had a bit of a ski-mask tan around his eyes, which only made him look more adorable.

Oliver noticed where Schuyler was looking and didn't comment. She knew how he felt about her crush on Jack Force.

Sensing her friend's pique, Schuyler leaned down and rested her head affectionately on his shoulder. If it hadn't been for Oliver . . . she might have . . . what? Passed out forever? Joined her mother in the comatose room uptown? She was still having trouble understanding everything. What did it mean that her vampire cells were fighting her human cells? Would she always be torn in two directions?

The hunger she had felt in Venice had abated somewhat with the transfusion. Maybe that was all it was. She had needed blood. Maybe she could just get transfusions instead of having to feed. She would have to ask Dr. Pat if that was a viable alternative. It was just too weird to always look at

Oliver and think he'd taste delicious. He was her best friend, not a snack.

Bliss Llewellyn looked around and met Schuyler's eye. The two girls waved shyly to each other. Bliss had been meaning to tell Schuyler about Dylan's return, to have the conversation she had started at the ball, but somehow the opportunity never seemed to come up.

The holidays had been an anxious time for Bliss. The blackouts and nightmares had returned in full force. Christmas Eve had been the worst night yet. She had woken up with a pain in her chest so excruciating that she couldn't breathe. She was drenched in sweat and the bedsheets were so wet they were pasted together. Gross.

Even more terrifying, the beast of her nightmares had begun to speak to her in her sleep.

Blisssss . . .

Blissssss . . .

Blissssss . . .

It only said her name, and yet it sent shivers down her spine. It was just a dream. Just a dream. Just a dream. There was no beast who could hurt her. It was just part of the transformation. Her memories waking up and talking to her, that's what The Committee said. Her former selves, her past lives.

She clenched her jaw and sat up straighter in her seat.

* * *

Next to her, Mimi Force yawned into her delicate palm. For Mimi, the two weeks off had been nothing short of heaven. She had picked up not one but two yummy human familiars on the trip, had had her fill of them, and felt like she could conquer the world. She was eager to start the new semester. A new season always meant another excuse to go shopping. Like Bliss, Mimi was anxious, too. Anxious to get to Barneys today before it closed.

Bliss forced herself to pay attention to the Headmistress's semiannual pep talk—*Another semester of excellence awaits you in the halls of Duchesne, blah blah blah*—when the chapel doors flew open with a bang.

Heads swiveled to look at what had caused the commotion.

A boy stood at the threshold.

A very, very handsome boy.

"Oh, er, sorry. Didn't mean to do that. Slip of the fingers, eh?" he asked.

"No, no, it's okay. Come on in, Kingsley. You can have a seat up here in front," the Headmistress said, waving him forward.

The boy grinned. He swaggered down the aisle, his walk a rolling, slouching gait. His black hair gleaming, a forelock saucily slanting over his left eye, he exuded a cocky confidence to go along with his model-perfect good looks. He wore a loose white oxford shirt and tight black jeans, as if he had just stepped off of a CD cover.

Like all of the girls assembled, Bliss couldn't take her eyes off him.

As though he could feel her stare, he turned around and looked at her directly in the eye.

And winked.

NINETEEN

His name was Kingsley Martin, and he was a junior. The female populace at Duchesne agreed: even his name was sexy. The minute he appeared, it was as if a wildfire had spread among the girls. Within a week, his accomplishments were legendary. Already, he had been tapped to start on the school's lacrosse, soccer, and crew teams. Just as impressive, he was an academic sharpshooter. He had slain the crusty AP English teacher with his presentation on Dante's *Inferno*, titled "Taco Hell," where he had compared the circles of hell to common fast-food establishments. In AP Calculus, he had solved a complicated problem set in record time.

It didn't hurt that he was what the girls called a kneetrembler. He was devastatingly handsome. The kind of handsome that combined Hollywood glamour with dapper European sophistication and a trace of mischief. The new boy looked *fun*.

And just like that, Jack Force became old news. The girls had all gone to school with Jack Force since pre-school. Kingsley presented a new, dashing, and mysterious alternative.

Mimi Force gave Bliss the rest of the scoop after lunch while they reapplied lip gloss in the girls' bathroom.

"He's a Blue Blood," Mimi said, making an O shape with her mouth as she slathered on the shine.

"No kidding," Bliss replied. Of course he was a vampire—she knew that the minute she laid eyes on him. She'd never met another vampire who flaunted his Blue Blood status so publicly. It was a surprise he hadn't bared his fangs in front of the whole school.

"I met him at the Four Hundred Ball," Mimi said. "His family just moved here from London, but he grew up every-where: Hong Kong, New York, Capetown. They're like, related to royalty or something. He has some sort of title but he doesn't use it."

"Should we curtsy?" Bliss joked.

Mimi frowned. "It's not a joke. They're like, *major*. Landed estates, advisers to the Queen, the whole she-bang."

Bliss refrained from rolling her eyes. Sometimes Mimi was so stubborn about her snobbery, it squeezed all the fun out of life.

They exited the bathroom and bumped into the object of their discussion. Kingsley was walking out of the boys' locker room, carrying a thick, leather-bound book. He looked rakish and wickedly charming. His eyes danced when he saw them.

"Ladies," he said, bowing.

Mimi smirked. "We were just talking about you."

"All good things, I hope," he said, looking directly at Bliss.

"This is my friend Bliss. Her dad's a senator," Mimi said, elbowing Bliss roughly.

"I know," Kingsley said, his smile deepening. Bliss tried hard to keep her composure. When he looked at her that way, it felt as if she was standing there with no clothes on.

The second bell rang, which meant they had five minutes to get to their next class.

"Gotta go. Korgan's senile but he can be an asshole," Mimi said, heading for the stairs.

"Ah, just make him shut up," Kingsley said. "Don't you know how to do that yet?"

"What are you talking about?" Bliss asked.

Mimi laughed nervously. "He's talking about using the glom on teachers. You know, mind control. Kingsley, you joker, you know we're not supposed to do that. It's against the Code. If the Wardens ever found out . . ."

Blue Blood teens were expressly forbidden from using their powers or showing off their superhuman strengths until they had reached adulthood. And even then, the Code of the Vampires was very clear on that policy: humans were not to be toyed with. They were to be respected. The Blue Bloods were supposed to bring peace and beauty and light to the world, not use their superior powers to dominate and rule.

"Wardens Shmardens," Kingsley joked with a dismissive wave. "They never know what's going on. Or do you still believe they can read your mind?" he teased.

"You're funny. We'll talk later," Mimi said, heading out.

"I should go too," Bliss said nervously.

"Wait."

Bliss raised her eyebrows.

"You've been avoiding me," Kingsley said simply. It was not an accusation, but a statement of fact. He shifted the book he was carrying to his other hip. Bliss glanced at it quickly. It didn't look like a textbook. It looked similar to one of those old reference books from the Repository that Oliver had used in their research on the Croatan.

"What are you talking about? I just met you."

"Have you forgotten already?" Kingsley asked.

"Forgotten what?"

Kingsley sized Bliss up and down, from her new Chloe ballerina flats to her highlighted hair. "I liked the green gown. And the necklace, of course. A perfect touch. But I think I liked you better wet and soaking. Helpless."

"You were the boy at the park," Bliss gasped. The boy who had rescued her had been Kingsley, not Dylan. Kingsley? How? Which meant, she thought with an ache in her heart, that Dylan was truly dead?

141

"You made a very pretty Lady of the Lake," Kingsley said.

Bliss's mind raced. So that meant she had danced with Kingsley at the after-party as well. He was the boy in the Pierrot mask.

"What happened to Dylan?" Bliss whispered, a dread creeping into her heart. She had been so sure Dylan was alive. But if he hadn't been the one who had rescued her in the lake, or who had danced with her at the party . . . then she had to face it. She was holding on to a dream. He was gone forever, and he wasn't coming back.

"Who's Dylan?"

"It doesn't matter," Bliss said, as she tried to process this new reality and absorb the information. "What did you mean, then, the night of the party, when you said you hadn't been gone for long. Do we—do we know each other?" she asked.

Kingsley looked serious for once. "Ah. I am sorry. You lot *are* a bit delayed here, yes? You do not recognize me yet. I truly am sorry. I had thought you knew me when we were dancing. But I was mistaken."

"Who are you?" Bliss asked.

Kingsley put his mouth to Bliss's ear and whispered softly, "I am the same as you."

The final bell rang. Kingsley wagged his eyebrows and grinned. "I'll see you around, Bliss."

Bliss slumped against the wall, her knees shaking, her

heart galloping in her chest. He had stood so close to her, she could still feel his breath on her cheek. Who was he really? What was he talking about? And would she ever discover what had truly happened to Dylan?

The minute Schuyler walked down to breakfast on Friday morning, she noticed something different about the living room—sunlight. The room was bright with sun, *drowned* in sun. The canvas covers on the furniture were removed, and the ray of sunshine through the windows was so strong it was blinding.

Lawrence Van Alen stood in the middle of the room, examining an old portrait that hung over the fireplace. There were old-fashioned steamer trunks stacked in the hallway, along with a large, battered Louis Vuitton footlocker.

Hattie and Julius stood around him, clasping their hands. Hattie saw Schuyler first. "Miss Schuyler! I couldn't stop him—he had a key. He said he owned this house, and he began to open the curtains and demanded we remove the drop cloths. He said he's your grandfather. But Mrs. Cordelia was a widow since I've known her."

"It's all right, Hattie. It's fine. Julius, I'll handle this," Schuyler said, soothing the staff. The maid and chauffeur looked doubtfully at the interloper, but they heeded Schuyler's words and excused themselves from the room.

"What are you doing here?" Schuyler demanded. "I thought you were keeping out of it." She tried to feel anger, but all she felt was elation. Her grandfather! Had he changed his mind?

"Isn't it obvious?" Lawrence asked. "I've returned. Your words wounded me deeply, Schuyler. I could not live with myself knowing how cowardly I had acted. Forgive me, it has been a long time since Cordelia and I had made the pact. I never expected anyone would come looking for me."

He walked over to the picture window overlooking the frozen Hudson River. Schuyler had forgotten that their living room had such a marvelous view. Cordelia had kept the curtains drawn for years.

"I could not let you go back to your old life, alone. I have been in exile long enough. It is time for New York to remember the power and the glory of the Van Alen name. And I have come to raise you. You are, after all, my granddaughter."

In answer, Schuyler buried herself in her grandfather's arms and hugged him tight. "Cordelia was right about you. I knew she would be."

But before she could say anything more, the doorbell chimed loudly several times, as if someone were pressing it in a highly agitated manner.

Schuyler looked at her grandfather. "Are you expecting someone?"

"Not at the moment. Anderson is joining me in a week, after he has closed up my homes in Venice." He looked grave. "It appears my return to the city was not as secret as I had hoped."

Hattie moved to answer the door, but Lawrence waved her away. "I'll handle this," he said as he opened the door. Charles Force and several Wardens from The Committee stood on the doorstep, looking grim and determined.

"Ah, Lawrence." Charles Force smiled thinly. "You have honored us with your presence once again."

"Charles." Lawrence nodded.

"May we come in?"

"By all means," Lawrence said graciously. "Schuyler, I believe you know everybody. Charles, Priscilla, Forsyth, Edmund, this is my granddaughter, Schuyler."

"Yeah, um. Hi," Schuyler said, wondering why her grandfather was acting as if the Wardens had simply dropped in for a friendly visit.

They ignored Schuyler.

"Lawrence, I'm sorry about this," Priscilla Dupont said in her gentle, mellifluous voice. "I was overruled."

"It's quite all right, my dear. I must say, it delights me to see you so well. It has been a long time since Newport."

"Too long," Priscilla agreed.

"Enough of this," Charles interrupted irritably.

"Lawrence, I do not recall your exile being revoked. You must appear before the Conclave to formally testify. If you will come with us, please."

"What's happening?" Schuyler cried, as two Wardens took a hold of Lawrence's arms on either side. "Where are they taking you?"

"Do not fear, granddaughter," Lawrence said. "If I do not have a choice, I shall go willingly. Charles, you will find no contest from me. Schuyler, I should be back soon."

Charles Force snorted. "We shall see about that."

Schuyler watched as they led her grandfather out the door and inside one of the black cars in front of the building. She felt like crying. Just when she thought help had finally arrived, it was taken away as quickly as it had come.

"Has he gone?" Hattie asked, storming in from the kitchen. "Thank the Lord."

"He'll be back," Schuyler said. She walked over to the portrait Lawrence had been studying. It was a painting of a wedding, hidden underneath an acid-free cloth for years, dating from the early eighteenth century. There was Cordelia in her wedding dress, looking comely and prim. The man standing beside her, wearing a crisp morning suit and ascot, had the unmistakable, hawkish features of a young Lawrence Van Alen.

FEBRUARY 10, 1872
MARRIAGE ANNOUNCEMENT

INVITATIONS HAVE BEEN ISSUED for the marriage of Miss Caroline Vanderbilt, daughter of Admiral and Mrs. Vanderbilt, and Alfred, Lord Burlington, on Thursday evening, February 24, at six o'clock, at the home of the bride elect's parents, 800 Fifth Avenue. The Reverend Mr. Cushing of this city will officiate. Miss Vanderbilt will be attended by her younger sister, Miss Ava Vanderbilt, and the Marquis of Essex will act as best man. There will be a reception after the ceremony. The bride's family is prominent in society, and among the eight-hundred invited guests will be the governor of New York and the mayor of this city. Lord Burlington is an exchange broker, doing business in London and New York, and is the eldest son of the Duke and Duchess of Devonshire. The bride and groom will then leave for an extended tour of the Indian subcontinent.

———

The boy stood precariously on the railing of the balcony off the third-floor library. When the weather was warm, the balcony was nicknamed "Club Duschene" since students routinely took their lunches there, tanning, rolling up jeans into shorts, girls unbuttoning their blouses as low as they dared, and boys going as far as to take off their shirts.

But it was the middle of January, and the windows that led out to the balcony were usually locked. Not today. Today, someone had opened the window, letting an arctic blast inside the library, and that someone was now outside, balancing on a slim, four-inch iron rail.

Jack was on his way back from the music building when he came upon a lively crowd gathered in the cortile, the courtyard behind the main school. He saw Schuyler slip through the side entrance, her face lined with concern as she spoke to her friend Oliver, the Red Blood.

He tore his eyes away from her, wishing he were the one she would turn to for comfort, and looked up to where several people were pointing, and noticed the boy. He was a freshman, a Red Blood, and he stood on the railing with a blank, dazed look on his face.

"Jump!" Soos Kemble screeched, collapsing in giggles.

"What does he think he's doing?" another girl asked, horrified and titillated at the same time.

Jack noticed that the crowd was amused by the situation. Half of them were eagerly, if unconsciously, rooting for the boy to fall. Classes would be canceled for the rest of the day for sure.

"C'mon! Get it over with! I have a Pre-calc quiz I don't feel like taking this afternoon!" someone called.

In one corner, hidden behind a hedge that surrounded a stone bench, Jack's supersensitive hearing picked up the sound of Kingsley Martin, the new boy, laughing with Mimi.

"Make him do a pirouette," Mimi said.

Kingsley waved his hand, and the boy on the ledge executed a ballerina turn. The crowd gasped. But the boy landed on his feet. He looked shocked at what had just happened, almost as if he had no control. . . .

No control . . .

Jack glanced sharply at Kingsley. He knew in an instant

what was happening. Kingsley was using the glom to control the boy's mind, as a puppet master would pull the strings.

At Committee meetings, they had been told there would be strict punishments for using their powers on the Red Bloods without provocation. Jack felt a deep rage rise within him. The stupid, arrogant fool. Kingsley was going to put them all in danger.

"Release him!" Jack commanded, holding up a palm, his eyes shooting daggers at Kingsley.

The crowd turned to see who was causing the scene.

"Aw, we were just having a bit of fun, mate," Kingsley said, and with another flick of his wrist, the boy stopped turning.

The boy screamed to find himself alone on top of the balcony. He wobbled; his left foot slipped off the edge. . . .

"Martin! Bring him down! NOW!"

"If you insist," Kingsley said, looking bored already. The boy regained his balance and safely stepped off the railing onto the terrace.

"Modo caecus," Jack whispered, sending a blinding spell over any of the humans who had congregated, to make them forget what they had seen.

"That was foolish and dangerous, not to mention cruel and petty," Jack said, confronting Kingsley. He had never felt so angry in his life. And to see Mimi standing there next to him was even worse. Was he actually jealous? Or was he just angry and disappointed to find his sister engaging in such low behavior?

"Stop being a spoilsport, Force," Kingsley said. "No harm done, eh?"

"Yeah, Jack, get off it," Mimi said. "It's just a frosh. Nothing would have happened."

"That's not the point, Mimi," Jack said. "The Wardens will hear of this."

"Oh, the Wardens." Kingsley laughed. "Listen, why don't you come after me yourself?" he taunted. "Or are you too much of a Red Blood lover you've forgotten your Blood is blue?"

Jack blushed to the roots of his fine blond hair.

"You Forces—or whatever your call yourselves these days—would be nothing without my family, without the sacrifices we made," Kingsley said darkly. He turned on his heel and started to walk away. "Any time you want to eat your words, Force, you know where to find me."

"Jack, it's just a joke," Mimi said, trying to mollify her brother.

"Drop it," Jack said, shrugging off her hand from his shoulder.

He walked away quickly, and Mimi followed him, a cross look on her face. "Jack, wait, c'mon."

But Jack didn't turn around. His ears were burning from embarrassment at lashing out like that in public. Had that been wise? He'd had to stop Kingsley, hadn't he? Or was he just being humorless like his sister had said? And anyway, what was Kingsley talking about? What sacrifices had the Martins made?

He would have to ask his father about this.

TWENTY-TWO

Oliver had saved her a seat next to his in Chem lab. He handed Schuyler her goggles, and she put on her lead apron. "What are we doing today?" she asked, fitting the goggles over her nose. Oliver was already wearing his. The whole class looked like a team of welders. Across the room, Mimi loudly complained that the goggles gave her an ugly red mark on her nose, but no one paid much attention.

"Making candy again?" Schuyler asked.

Oliver checked the Bunsen burner and turned it on slowly, so it emitted a small, red flame. "Yup."

In the past, Duchesne had had one of the most inventive and charismatic science teachers on the subject. In fact, Chem lab was so popular among the students that both juniors and sophomores were allowed to take it as an elective. But Mr. Anthony, the boyish, enthusiastic, and recent Yale grad, had been discharged from the school over winter break due to an unfortunate affair with one of his students, who had gotten pregnant. Mr. Anthony was fired, and the student expelled. This was not Degrassi Junior High, after all. This was Duchesne.

Which was all well and good, except that with Mr. Anthony and his advanced, yet exciting, lab experiments gone (last semester they had turned copper into gold, or at least gold plate), the students were stuck with boring old Mr. Korgan, whose syllabus included a series of experiments each duller than the next. Calculating density. Determining the composition of water. Identifying a solution as acid, base, or neutral. Yaawwwn. Mr. Korgan was so slow that for two weeks the class was involved in creating a chemical reaction in hydrogen and fructose—otherwise known as turning sugar and water into candy.

Schuyler was ready to place a beaker filled with water above the burner, when Mr. Korgan announced they were going to do something different that day.

"I would like you to—*cough*—switch lab partners every week. The class has grown very disruptive of late and so I must—*cough*—separate you from your friends. Will the partner on the left please step down to the next table, and so on, and we will keep this rotation every week."

Oliver and Schuyler looked pained. "See you after class," Oliver called as Schuyler collected her things and moved over to the next table, where Kingsley Martin was standing.

If anything, the large plastic goggles on his face only served to enhance his beauty by highlighting how nothing could put a damper on his good looks—not even bug-eyed plastic shades. Kingsley could wear polyester pants and a Groucho mustache and still look hot. Schuyler hadn't seen much of Kingsley since he arrived, although she had heard all the raves about him, and had witnessed his arrogant performance at the cortile that morning.

"Shame about your grandfather," he said as a greeting.

Schuyler tried not to show her shock. But then, Kingsley was a Blue Blood. His parents were probably high-ranking members of the coven.

"He'll be all right," she said tersely, waiting for the water in the beaker to boil.

"Oh, I'm sure. I just wish I were there to see Lawrence and Charles battle it out. Just like the old days."

"Uh-huh." Schuyler nodded, not wanting to get into the conversation. She hadn't even told Oliver about Lawrence's return. She felt superstitious about it. What if The Committee just sent him back to Italy posthaste? Then there wouldn't even be anything to tell.

"Tell me, are you still hung up on that boy?"

"Excuse me?" Schuyler asked, holding a test tube.

"Nothing." Kingsley shrugged innocently. "If that's how you want to play it," he said teasingly.

When Kingsley wasn't looking, Schuyler studied his profile. He had been at the Four Hundred Ball, she'd heard.

Could he—could he have been the boy behind the mask she had kissed at the after-party? Schuyler subconsciously put a hand over her lips. If he was the boy she had kissed, did that mean that even though she found him repulsive, there was actually something about him that she found attractive? Oliver was always quoting from Foucault, saying that desire stemmed from revulsion.

A random thought flew into her head: what if the boy behind the mask had been *Oliver*? There had been Red Bloods at the party . . . and Oliver hated being left out of anything fun. He would have been able to find out about it, she was sure. Had she felt drawn to the boy in the mask because he was her best friend? Had they kissed? Was that why he was so nice to her lately? Treating her with so much tenderness?

She peeked across the room at him, watching him grimace as Mimi Force, his lab partner, burned the fructose so that it melted into a sickeningly sweet–smelling disaster.

If she had kissed Oliver, did that mean they were more than friends now? Would they have to start dating? Was she even attracted to him? She looked at his chestnut hair flopping over his eyes, and thought of how, in Venice, she had wanted nothing more than to taste his blood. Did that equal attraction? And who knew how he felt about her?

Schuyler placed the perfectly molded candy squares on the table, and caught the eye of another boy across the room.

Jack Force. Her stomach immediately tied up in knots.

Suddenly Schuyler knew she was just kidding herself. She might toy with the idea of liking Kingsley or Oliver. But really she knew she nursed a not-so-secret hope about the identity of the boy she had kissed: she wished for one name and one name only.

Jack.

TWENTY-THREE

When Schuyler arrived home from school, Lawrence still had not returned. She asked Julius to bring her grandfather's luggage up to Cordelia's room. It looked forlorn and lonesome in the entryway. Hattie had prepared supper, and Schuyler took a tray up to her room, eating her meat loaf and mashed potatoes in front of her computer. Cordelia would never have allowed such a thing. Her grandmother had been vigilant that Schuyler eat dinner properly at the table every night. But then, Cordelia wasn't around to enforce her rules anymore.

Schuyler fed Beauty scraps from her plate as she checked her e-mail and made a halfhearted attempt to finish her homework.

Afterward, she brought her tray down to the kitchen and helped Hattie load the dishwasher. It was after nine o'clock. Her grandfather had been gone for more than twelve hours already. How long could the meeting have lasted?

Finally, at a little past midnight, Lawrence's key turned in the lock. He looked exhausted. The lines on his face were haggard. Schuyler thought he looked as if he had aged several decades.

"What happened?" she asked, alarmed at his condition. She flew up from the window seat where she had been dozing. The living room, removed of its heavy drapes and covers, was a surprisingly comfortable place. Hattie had lit a fire in the hearth, and Schuyler couldn't get enough of the river view.

Lawrence set his crushed fedora on the rack and sank into one of the antique couches across from the fire. Dust flew as he shifted in his seat. "I do think Cordelia could have put some money into keeping this place a little cleaner," he grumbled. "I left her with quite a nest egg."

Cordelia had always given Schuyler the impression that they had run out of money, and what little they had went to financing the bare necessities: Duchesne tuition, food, shelter, the skeletal staff. Anything aside from that—new clothes, money for movies or restaurants—was grudgingly parceled out dollar by dollar.

"Grandmother always said we were broke," Schuyler said.

"In contrast to how we lived once, surely. But we Van Alens are far from bankrupt. I checked the accounts today.

Cordelia invested wisely. The interest has been collecting interest. We should be able to bring this house back to where it should be."

"You went to the bank?" Schuyler asked, a little startled.

"I had to run a number of errands, yes. It's been a long time since I was in the city. Marvelous how the world has changed. One forgets that in Venice. Ran into several friends. Cushing Carondolet insisted I dine with him at the old club. I'm sorry, I would have come back earlier, but I had to find out what Charles has been up to in my absence."

"But what happened with The Committee?"

Lawrence took a cigar out of his pocket and carefully lit it. "Oh, at the hearing?"

"Yes," Schuyler said impatiently, mystified by Lawrence's casual attitude.

"Well, they brought me into the Repository," Lawrence said. "I had to speak in front of the Conclave—the coven's highest leadership. Wardens, Elders. Enmortals like me." Enmortals were vampires who kept the same physical shell over the centuries, who had been given permission to be exempt from the cycle of sleeping and waking, otherwise known as reincarnation.

"Never seen such a sorry bunch," Lawrence said, pursing his lips in distaste. "Forsyth Llewellyn is a senator—did you know that? Back in Plymouth he was just Michael's lackey. It's a disgrace. And completely against the Code. It wasn't always so, you know. We have ruled before. But after the disaster in Rome, we agreed that taking positions of power in the human sphere was forever out of the question."

Schuyler nodded. Cordelia had told her as much.

"And they've kicked out the Carondolets from the Conclave, Cushing told me all about it. Because he had proposed a *Candidus Suffragium*."

"What is that?"

"The White Vote. For the leadership of the coven," Lawrence said, kicking off his banker's cap-toes and waving his stockinged feet in front of the fire.

"But I thought Michael—Charles—was Regis. Forever."

"Not quite," Lawrence said, flicking his ashes into an ashtray he had removed from his jacket pocket.

"No?"

"No. The coven is not a democracy. But it is not a monarchy either. We had agreed that leadership can be questioned if the coven feels the Regis has not led us properly. So the White Vote is called."

"Has there ever been a White Vote?"

"Yes." Lawrence sunk so low into the chair that only the smoke from his cigar was visible. "Once, in Plymouth."

"What happened?"

"I lost." Lawrence shrugged. "They banished Cordelia and me from the Conclave. Since then, we have held no power on the council. We bowed to their rule, and later on, around the time of the Gilded Age, we decided we had to separate."

"Why?" Schuyler asked.

"Cordelia told you we suspected that a high-ranking member of the Conclave was harboring the Silver Blood. I thought it would be safer for her if I disappeared for a while, so I could continue our investigation without The Committee knowing about it. We thought it was clever of us. But alas, it meant that I was not here when Allegra succumbed to her heartsickness. Or when you were born. And my work so far has been fruitless. I am no closer to confirming my suspicions than I was before."

"But what happened—why did they let you go free? I thought you were exiled."

Lawrence chuckled. "So did they. They had forgotten I went into exile *voluntarily*. I don't think any of them ever expected me to come back. They didn't really have much of a choice. I havn't broken any rules of the Code. There was no reason to prohibit my return. Still, because I have been gone for so long they demanded that I testify."

"Testify to what?"

"Oh, to promise not to question the Coven's leadership as I had once done. You know, call for another White Vote. They even reinstated my position on the Conclave, as long as I promised not to bring up the Silver Blood menace again. According to Charles, the Croatan threat has been contained, if it ever existed at all."

"Just because no one's died in the last three months," Schuyler said.

"Yes. They are blind as usual. The Silver Bloods are

back. It was just as Cordelia and I had warned, so many years ago."

"But everything else is all right, then," Schuyler said happily, not caring about the Croatan threat for the moment. "You're back, and they can't do anything about it."

He studied the fireplace sorrowfully. "Not quite. I have some bad news."

Schuyler's smile faded.

"Charles has informed me he is making plans to adopt you."

"What? Why?" Charles Force—adopt her? What gave him the right? What kind of sick joke was this?

"Unfortunate as it is, he is, nonetheless, your uncle. When Allegra, his sister, revoked their bond and refused to take him as her partner in this cycle, he turned his back on the Van Alen family. Actually, he did everything he could to destroy this family. To destroy your mother. He could never forgive her for marrying your father and giving birth to you. He hardened his heart against her. He even changed his name."

Schuyler thought of the many times she had found Charles Force kneeling by her mother's bedside. He had been her mother's constant visitor, and she had overheard him begging Allegra for *her* forgiveness.

"Hence, he is your last living blood relative, aside from me, of course. But there is no record of my existence in this cycle—in fact, according to the papers, I'm legally dead. I died in 1872. Thank goodness for Swiss banks. Our accounts are merely numerical codes, otherwise I would not have been able to touch them. Charles has decided that I am not fit to raise you. He wants to raise you himself."

Her uncle. Cordelia had intimated as much, and yet Schuyler had refused to acknowledge this fact of her twisted family tree. "But they can't . . . I mean, he's not . . . I don't even know him."

"Do not worry, I won't let that happen. Allegra would want nothing more than to keep you away from him," Lawrence said.

"Why does he hate you so much?" Schuyler asked, a glimmer of tears in her bright blue eyes. Lawrence had finally returned, and again the forces—or make that, the Forces—were conspiring to take him away from her. Schuyler thought of what adoption might be like: having to live with Mimi and Jack, her cousins. Mimi would *love* that, she was sure. . . . And Jack, what would he think?

"'They will be divided, father against son, son against father,'" Lawrence said, quoting from Scripture. "Alas, I have always been a disappointment to my son."

SEPTEMBER 30, 1872
DISAPPEARANCE STILL A MYSTERY

Maggie Stanford has given no sign in two years.
Father dead of grief, mother demented.

THE MYSTERY SURROUNDING the disappearance of Maggie Stanford, now eighteen years old, who disappeared on the night of the annual Patrician Ball two years ago, has yet to be solved. The police never found a ransom note or any indication of kidnapping or foul play in relation to the case, and have suggested the girl ran away of her own volition. Mrs. Dorothea Stanford, of Newport, has reportedly become mentally unbalanced from the shock of her daughter's disappearance. Mr. Stanford died from grief shortly after Maggie went missing.

Strange hallucinations continue to afflict the mother, who claims that her neighbors and friends are concealing the truth about her daughter's whereabouts and keeping her from coming home. The *Herald* visited Mrs. Stanford in her home, and from what could be made of Mrs. Stanford's speech, she is still laboring under the impression that someone has her girl in custody and refuses to release her.

The *Herald* has discovered that Maggie Stanford had been living at the St. Dymphna Asylum in Newport for a year before she went missing, receiving treatment for an unknown condition. Anyone having any information on her disappearance is urged to come forward.

TWENTY-FOUR

Chic magazine was located in a snazzy new steel-and-glass building in the middle of Times Square. It was just one of the high-profile media properties owned by the Christie-Best organization, a conglomerate that also counted *Flash*, *Kiss*, *Splendid*, and *Mine* among its many other one-word-only glossy titles. Its lobby was a serene, marbled space with a dribbling zen fountain and an army of blue-jacketed security guards who manned the onyx reception desks.

One afternoon after school, Bliss stood patiently in the lobby while waiting for the guard to call up to *Chic*'s model booker for entrance. Farnsworth Models had sent her for a go-see, an appointment to see if the magazine would like to hire Bliss for their next photo shoot.

Bliss was wearing her standard go-see outfit: tight, tight dark-wash Stitched for Civilization jeans, Lanvin flats, a loose white blouse. Her face was freshly scrubbed and free of makeup, as advised by her agency. Bliss had been much in demand since she had booked the Stitched campaign, and the photos of her in the dazzling Dior dress had been reprinted all over the globe—crowning her the new young socialite (and displacing Mimi in the international best-dressed list). She had shot a shoe ad, a Gap ad, and had already done a five-page editorial spread in *Kiss*. *Chic* was the mother lode, the top of the glossy heap, and while Bliss thought modeling was a bit of a lark, she also wanted the gig very much.

"Schuyler Van Alen," she heard the girl at the next station tell the guard.

"Schuyler! Are you here for the *Chic* go-see?" Bliss asked, pleasantly surprised to find Schuyler there as well.

"I am." Schuyler smiled back. Ever since her grandmother's passing, she had turned down the modeling opportunities that had come fast and furious after her Times Square Stitched for Civilization billboard. But Linda Farnsworth had convinced her to keep the *Chic* appointment, and Schuyler had agreed, if only to keep her mind off the distressing news that Charles Force wanted to adopt her.

As usual, Schuyler looked like a ragamuffin in her tattered sweater, empire-waist tunic, footless tights, and Jack Purcell sneakers, with several layers of plastic beads draped around her neck. Although, it should be noted that several fashion editors who had spotted her in the lobby had quickly noticed her unique style, and three months later, the pages of *Kiss*, *Splendid*, and *Flash* would all feature an outfit eerily similar to the one Schuyler was wearing.

"You girls can go up," the guard told them, beeping them through the automatic turnstiles.

The *Chic* office was on the tenth floor, and Schuyler and Bliss felt a little intimidated by the immaculate surroundings. The interior waiting area was lined with poster-size blowups of the most famous *Chic* magazine covers—a virtual tour of the most celebrated beauties of the twentieth and twenty-first century.

A grandmotherly receptionist advised them to take a seat on one of the white Barcelona chairs.

The girls chatted quietly about neutral topics: school gossip, tests, why the cafeteria was suddenly serving hot dogs. They both studiously avoided the topic of Dylan's death—Schuyler, because she feared it would hurt Bliss too much, and Bliss, because she felt there was nothing more to say, since the boy in the lake had turned out to be Kingsley.

"You've been hanging out with Kingsley a lot," Schuyler said, when Bliss mentioned he had taken her to a party at the hot new club, Disaster.

"Yeah." Bliss bit her thumb. She was sitting forward on the edge of the chair, not quite comfortable enough to take up too much space. She held her black, modeling portfolio on her lap. "He's cool."

Bliss still hadn't figured out who or what Kingsley had been in her past, although she had to admit he made the present pretty fun. He seemed to have it in his mind that Bliss was his girlfriend, and the two of them spent most of their free time together. Kingsley always seemed to have the latest invitations to the best parties, and with him at her side, Bliss no longer felt like a wallflower, but more like a social butterfly. Besides, her own growing fame was making her increasingly confident among the glittering denizens of New York nightlife. Even Mimi had sourly mentioned how sick she was of seeing Bliss's name in boldface in the newspaper columns.

"How's Oliver?" Bliss asked.

"Fine," Schuyler said abruptly. In truth, Oliver had been a tad distant lately, after being so commiserative before. Maybe it was a reaction to her pulling away from him, or his own reservations about the changing nature of their relationship. The transition from best friend to human Conduit was not an easy one to maneuver.

They stopped talking when a willowy brunette walked through the glass doors. She was wearing a loose peasant blouse belted at the hips, skinny denim shorts, patterned tights, and wedge heels. The effect was quirky and offbeat, as if she'd thrown the outfit together at the last minute, when in reality it had probably taken hours of studying runway shots and careful calculation of each element's relationship to the outfit as a whole—weighing the options as meticulously as a an artist mixing paints.

"Bliss? Schuyler?" she called.

"Chantal?" Schuyler asked.

"No, I'm Keaton, Chantal's assistant."

"As in Diane or Buster?" Schuyler joked.

Keaton ignored her. "Chantal's late at an accessories meeting, but she told me to bring you in," she said condescendingly.

Keaton led them through the white carpeted hallway, where girls dressed in similar fashionable eccentricity glided through the maze of cubicles in four-inch heels. Rolling racks of clothing were parked against the wall, with cards and notations on hangers that read "JAN—FRONT OF BOOK," "REJECTS," "GO," "BRANNON MTG," "RETURNS," and "INDEX."

Chantal's office was a mess of modeling portfolios, and one solid wall was filled with hundreds of models' glossy eight-by-tens and Polaroid pictures. There were blue pages of next month's cover, mock-ups of the February issue, and a little teacup-size terrier yapping in the corner.

"Wait here," Keaton ordered. "Don't move."

Schuyler and Bliss did as told, even though Bliss really wanted a glass of water and Schuyler was dying to use the bathroom. But the atmosphere at *Chic* was so intimidating, and Keaton so humorless, neither of them wanted to risk it.

An hour later, Chantal finally arrived. Bliss expected another tall glamazon, but Chantal was a small, short, pinched-looking woman with a pixie haircut and cat's-eye glasses. She wore a loose APC sweatshirt and baggy trousers, as well as comfortable (but limited edition and therefore, punishingly expensive) Japanese sneakers.

"Hi girls," she said briskly, then immediately called out, "Keaton! My Polaroid! Didn't I tell you to bring it?"

She sat at her desk and flipped through each of their portfolios quickly. "Yes, saw that. Nice. Ooh. Not bad. Like that one, not so much that," she muttered. She slammed both books closed and instructed them to pose against the one blank wall in her office as she took several shots of each girl with her camera. Bliss went first.

It was all business as usual until Bliss suddenly fainted as the flashbulb exploded in her face.

"Oh my God. She's not anorexic, is she? I mean, it's fine if she is, God knows all the girls are. But I can't have her doing that on the shoot," Chantal said, more annoyed than concerned, as Bliss crumpled to the floor.

"No, that's not it," Schuyler said, worried. She knelt down and put a hand on Bliss's forehead. "It's a little hot in here."

Bliss was making odd groaning sounds and dry-heaving. "No . . . Go away . . . No . . ."

"It'll be hotter on location," Chantal said darkly. "God help me if she vomits on my carpet."

Schuyler glared at her, annoyed that the booking editor seemed to care more about her office than Bliss's health.

"Bliss? Bliss? Are you okay?" she asked, helping her

friend to her feet. Bliss blinked her eyes open. "Schuyler?" she said throatily.

"Yeah."

"I need to get out of here," Bliss implored.

"Keaton will walk you out. I'll let Linda know," Chantal said as she picked up the ringing telephone. It was obvious the booking editor had moved on to other concerns once the threat of projectile regurgitation had subsided.

Schuyler helped Bliss out of the office. "Steady. Easy." She pressed the down elevator button and glared at a Christie-Best girl, who gave them a curious look.

"I blacked out," Bliss said. "Again."

"Again?"

"It happens all the time now." Bliss told Schuyler about the nightmares she was having and the dizzying experiences of waking up and finding herself in places where she had no memory of going. "I'll just wake up and I'll be somewhere else, with no idea where I am. I guess it's all part of the transformation," Bliss said.

"Yeah, it's happened to me too. Not as dramatic as what you've described, but a couple of weeks ago I blacked out. More like a hibernation, Dr. Pat said." Schuyler explained her condition as she led Bliss inside the elevator.

"Mine are pretty short, and it's part of the memory flashbacks, except I don't seem to remember anything," Bliss explained, looking relieved that she wasn't the only one who suffered from the episodes.

"I guess we just need to deal with it."

"Kingsley said there are tricks to coping with it. He's going to show me how."

The elevator arrived in the lobby, and as the doors opened, Jack Force entered. He was wearing a black Christie-Best "guest" sticker on his lapel with 10TH FLOOR written on it.

"Oh, hey," he said, looking somewhat embarrassed.

"Don't tell us . . ." Bliss said, grinning. "Jack Force, super-model! Can you show us Blue Steel?" she joked, quoting from *Zoolander*.

"Shhhh," Jack said, smiling sheepishly. "It's not my idea. But they need guys for some upcoming shoot. Chantal's a friend of my mom's, and well, here I am."

"We just saw Chantal," Bliss said, keeping the conversation afloat since Schuyler was too shy to speak to him directly.

"So I guess I'll see you guys at the shoot." Jack grinned.

"Yeah right," Bliss said. "I don't think so. I fainted when she took my picture, and Schuyler didn't even get a Polaroid. I don't think there's any chance of either of us getting picked."

It was difficult to determine who looked more disappointed—Jack or Schuyler—as the elevator doors shut.

O n the first floor, past the Temple of Dendur, among the sarcophagi in the Egyptian antiquities section, there is a gold and lapis snake bracelet that once belonged to Hatshepsut. I would like you to bring it back to me," Lawrence said, holding up a stopwatch. Schuyler and her grandfather were standing in his study, one of the many rooms that Lawrence's return had opened.

Already, her grandfather had commissioned contractors and architects to restore the mansion to its former glory, and the sound of construction on the facade—drilling, pounding, hammering—was a daily disturbance. But the inside of Lawrence's study was as soundproof and quiet as a tomb.

It was the third day of her training. A week ago, Lawrence had been appalled to discover that The Committee had done almost nothing to teach the newest crop of vampires how to control and use their powers. Schuyler told him that the most they ever did was read a bunch of books and meditate.

"No one has undertaken a *Velox* test?" he had asked, raising his eyebrow in consternation.

Schuyler shook her head. "What's that?"

"Or learned the four factors of the glom?"

"No." Schuyler shook her head.

"Then none of you have any idea how to counter a Silver Blood attack," Lawrence said testily.

"Um. No."

Lawrence was greatly disturbed, and with the clock ticking—Charles Force's adoption petition was winding its way through the family court bureaucracy—who knew how much time they would have together? Vampire lessons had formally begun. "If you want to know how to defeat the Silver Bloods, and find out who or what is responsible for their return, you will have to learn how to use your Blue Blood knowledge and abilities first."

Her grandfather had decided to begin with the *Velox*, or speed test.

"Being swift is not enough," Lawrence lectured. "You must be so fast that you are undetectable. So fast that you do not set off alarms. So fast that no one can see you. Most Red Bloods think of this as "invisibility." But this is not a real trait. In fact, there is no such thing as invisibility. It is just that we are so fast, we are undetectable to the human eye. Once you master the art of *Velox*, you will be able to be any-where you want in a blink of an eye. The Silver Bloods are swift—that is one of their greatest powers. So you must be faster than they, if you are to survive."

He gave her the instructions on how to find the bracelet in the Metropolitan Museum of Art.

Snake bracelet. Gold and lapis. First floor. Egyptian antiquities. Among the sarcophagi.

"Go," Lawrence said, holding up the stopwatch. Schuyler disappeared.

Before it had even clicked to the next second, Schuyler had reappeared.

"Better," he said. Several days ago, it had taken her two minutes to complete the task.

Schuyler held up the bracelet. She had picked the lock on the case so expeditiously that the alarm had not had time to register a disturbance.

Lawrence allowed a small smile to play on his lips. "Now return it."

The next day, Schuyler was exhausted from the effort yester-day's lesson had required, yet she managed to hide it. There was little time for weakness; she wanted to forge ahead without Lawrence worrying about what it was costing her. She was eager to learn the tenets of *animadverto*, or "intelligent sight."

"The vampire trait of *animadverto* is another one that is

founded in myth and misunderstanding," Lawrence lectured. "Humans think that we have the capacity of infinite knowledge, when in fact all we have is a perfect photographic memory. If you exercise this ability, you will be like me, able to quote verbatim from every book you have ever read in your entire lifetime.

"The library of Alexandria has been lost to humankind for centuries, but thankfully, I was a voracious reader even then," Lawrence said, pointing to his head. "It is all in here."

"Why would we need to know all this? How is this helpful to defeating the Silver Bloods?" Schuyler asked.

"The Silver Bloods put no value on learning, and those who do not learn history are condemned to repeat it. It is imperative that we find traces, clues, to their operations by immersing ourselves in the history of the world. Perhaps then one of us will successfully figure out the mystery of their continued existence."

He gestured to the entire thirty-book *Encyclopaedia Britannica*. "Take a mental snapshot of each page. Catalog it in your memory. With your speed, this should take you less than five minutes. But I will give you an hour." Lawrence left the study and closed the door behind him.

At the appointed hour, Lawrence came back to find Schuyler splayed on the couch, napping.

"Finished?"

"Fifty-five minutes ago." Schuyler grinned.

"Fine. Give me their definition of the Egyptian reanimation rite."

Schuyler closed her eyes and spoke in a slow, measured voice, almost as if she were reading from the page. "The rite to prepare the deceased for afterlife, performed on statues of the deceased, the mummy itself, or statues of a god located in a temple. An important element of the ceremony was the ritual opening of the mouth so the mummy might breathe and eat. The rite, which symbolized the death and regeneration concept of the Osiris myth, in which the dismembered . . ."

"Excellent," Lawrence praised. "You are doing very well for your age. Very well indeed. It is impressive. I had thought that with your mixed blood, the vampire strength would be diluted, but instead it is even more tenacious."

"Grandfather?" Schuyler asked hesitantly as she helped him put the encyclopedia volumes back on their proper shelf.

"Yes?"

"If vampires can do this. Why do we need to go to school? I mean, is it really necessary?"

"Of course," Lawrence replied. "What we are doing here is merely rote memory. School teaches a different skill set entirely: socialization, debate, learning to mix with humans. One must not alienate oneself from the mainstream. Blue Bloods must understand their place in the world before we can attempt to change it. You may be able to call up the entire encyclopedia, but a brain with no heart and no reasoning . . . well, nothing is more meaningless."

Schuyler began to look forward to the tests every afternoon. Lawrence presented her with the hardest one yet at the end of the week.

"You have heard of the glom," Lawrence said. "The ability to control human minds."

"Yes." Schuyler said. "One of the most dangerous arts, Priscilla Dupont said. Best that we do not attempt it until we are of age."

"Ridiculous. You need to learn it now, to protect yourself from its seductive effects. Because the glom also works on Blue Bloods. It is a pernicious Silver Blood technique."

Schuyler shuddered.

"So you must learn how to control it, and defend yourself against it. We shall try the first one, before I can prepare you for the second." Lawrence decided. "There are four factors to the glom. The first one is merely telepathy. The ability to read minds. To read another's thoughts, one must concentrate on their energy—and strive to understand its source. A mind is like a puzzle; you must unlock it to read its hidden secrets."

"Anderson, come in here, please."

The white-haired gentleman entered the room. "Yes?"

"Anderson has been trained to resist the glom. He must,

if he is going to be a good Conduit. One cannot have a vampire's assistant corrupted."

For the next three hours, Schuyler sat on one end of a table, Anderson sat at the other. Lawrence would hold up a flash card to show Anderson, and Schuyler had to guess what was on the flash card.

What is he thinking? She focused on his signal, but all she got was static, a dense gray fog.

"Queen of hearts?" Schuyler asked.

Lawrence showed her an ace of spades.

"Ten of clubs?"

Three of diamonds.

And so it went. The gray fog did not lift. Schuyler felt depressed. After her success on the *Velox* and the *aminadverto*, she was certain mastering the glom would be just as straightforward.

Anderson was excused, and Schuyler was left alone with her grandfather.

"It is a hard one." Lawrence consoled, shuffling the cards and stacking them back in their case.

Schuyler nodded. "But it seems so easy," she said, mentioning how she could read Oliver's thoughts with no trouble.

"He is unprotected. Remind me, we will have to train him as well if he is going to be an effective Conduit."

Schuyler nodded. The effort to master the glom had taken a lot of her energy, and she felt dizzy and tired all of a sudden.

"Are you all right?" Lawrence asked, concerned.

She waved her hand away. Schuyler never admitted it to her grandfather, but sometimes after completing the tests, she was so weak she could barely stand.

TWENTY-SIX

*T*heir meeting in the Repository had been purely accidental. Schuyler was there to read as many books as possible on Lawrence's instructions and had been pleasantly surprised to find Jack studying at one of the desks.

"Oh, hey." He grinned, raking a hand through his hair and motioning for her to take the seat across from him. "What are you reading? *The Trial*?" he asked, showing her his copy.

She nodded. They had been assigned the Kafka tome in their AP English class. It was one of the several books she had in her stack.

"Silly love story, don't you think?" he asked, paging through the yellowed leaves in his book, which Schuyler noticed was well worn and dog-eared.

"Love story?" She made a face. "Isn't the book about the tyranny of justice? The absurd nature of bureaucracy? We never know what he's on trial for, after all."

"I disagree. And since Kafka never wanted the book to be published, who's to say what it's really about?" Jack asked in a slightly teasing tone. "I read that it's about his failed courtship and engagement to Felice Bauer. Which means it's not about the law at all, but about a man who's frustrated in love. . . ."

"Oh, Jack . . ." Schuyler sighed. She wasn't sure if he was pulling her leg or not, but she was enjoying their banter. It hadn't been clear until then whether they would ever be able to mend the budding friendship, or whatever it was that had started between them and then ended so abruptly last semester. But it looked as if Jack might not be too put off from trying again. Not that it meant anything. He was still Mimi Force's brother.

"Maybe my book has something yours doesn't," Jack said, pushing his copy over. "Here, let me take yours." He said. "Yours has a better cover anyway."

Schuyler picked up his book, inhaling its mildewy scent. She found the page where she had left off and began to read.

Boring old place, Mimi thought, as she followed Kingsley down the stairs into the Repository of History, The Committee's headquarters and the coven's main library located underneath Block 122, the superexclusive nightclub open to Blue Bloods and their guests only.

Kingsley had become a friend, someone who shared Mimi's sense of wickedness. The incident with the boy on the balcony had been the start of their alliance. Kingsley represented everything Mimi admired in a vampire—the desire to use power. Privately, she agreed with Kingsley: The Committee was much too cautious, and she chafed against its stringent rules. Why not use their strength to dominate humans? What good was reading someone's mind if you couldn't use it for material or emotional gain? Why not feed on more than one familiar at a time? Why not flaunt their superior status instead of trying to blend in with the mortal world?

He had asked her to come with him to the Repository so he could show her something cool, and he had disappeared into the stacks to find it.

She looked around the cavernous old room. Several pathetic humans, former Conduits no longer attached to vampire families, were working diligently in their carrels.

Mimi took a seat at one of the large reading tables in the middle of the room, drumming her fingers impatiently.

The soft sound of conversation drifted to her ears from behind a row of books.

"There's nothing about love in here, Jack," a girl was saying. "Maybe you're the one being absurd."

"Are you sure? You should look harder, maybe you're not reading it closely enough," he countered.

Mimi gritted her teeth. That was the Van Alen mouse again, talking to her brother. She stood up and cleared her throat, peering over the low shelves at the two of them.

Jack and Schuyler immediately moved away from each other.

"I'll, uh, see you later," Schuyler said, taking her books and walking over to a different desk, not realizing she still had his copy.

"Oh, hi," Jack said, turning in his seat to smile at his sister. "I didn't even know you knew the way to this place."

"Don't you underestimate me, Benjamin Force. For your information, I'm a huge reader," Mimi sniffed.

Jack grinned. *Liar*, he sent.

You're the liar, she sent back.

He made a conciliatory gesture. *Forgive me.*

Always. Mimi's face softened.

I'm off. I'll see you at home.

Bye.

Mimi watched him leave, but even with his gentle thoughts imprinted on her mind, she couldn't help but feel troubled. Why was Schuyler still a factor? There was something about that girl that was keeping her brother off balance, she could feel it. She could sense his desire to commit himself to their bond, but it was almost as if he were convincing himself to fall in love with her against his will. Why? It had never been like this before. In every cycle, the two of them had reaffirmed their bond without any complications.

For a moment, the supreme, smug self-confidence left Mimi's face, and she looked like a lost and scared little girl. What if he leaves me? What if he doesn't renew our bond when the time comes? What will happen to us?

Mimi shuddered as she thought of Allegra Van Alen, lying in her hospital bed, practically dead to the world.

She could not let that happen, to either of them.

"You look like you've seen a ghost," Kingsley said, setting a thick book in front of Mimi.

Mimi flashed him her most disarming smile. "I wish." She looked down at the leather-bound tome.

"What is that?"

"It's something we shouldn't be looking at. It's an old reference book of forbidden spells. You've heard about this Croatan thing, right—the Silver Bloods?" Kingsley asked.

"Yeah," Mimi said warily. "But they're not supposed to exist."

"Right," Kingsley smirked. "Only because they're not so obedient anymore."

"What do you mean?"

"Silver Bloods used to be the Blue Bloods' slaves. When we were doomed to spend our immortal lives on earth, those who still followed Lucifer were subdued by Michael and Gabrielle, for a time. We controlled them, but they rose up against us and stopped doing our bidding. They hunted us, we hunted them, the war raged on for centuries. Now supposedly they're gone. But there is a way to bring them back."

"What do you mean?" Mimi asked, thinking Kingsley

was being way too cavalier about this sort of thing. The Silver Bloods weren't some kind of joke, after all. Most Blue Bloods couldn't even talk about it.

"Call one from the Dark. You know. Make it do whatever you want," Kingsley said.

"I don't know if I like the sound of that," Mimi said, shuddering. "Too serious for me."

"C'mon, I think it would be fun," Kingsley said. Kingsley used "fun" to describe all manner of mischief. It was apparent that to him, a dark and dangerous old spell was equal to driving a Ferrari at two hundred and fifty miles an hour: probably not a great idea, but one that had to be undertaken just to say you had done it.

"Nah." Mimi shook her head. But even if she wasn't interested in that, there might be something else she could find in the book that might prove useful.

Materia acerbus. Dark matter.

She turned to the first page and began to read.

TWENTY-SEVEN

*A*llegra Van Alen was awake. She was sitting up in bed, her fine blond hair cascading over her shoulders and hospital gown.

Her green eyes open, wide and bright.

In a low, haunted voice she spoke. "Beware, Schuyler. Beware."

Schuyler woke with a start. She found herself in her mother's hospital room at Columbia Presbyterian, but she had no recollection of how she had gotten there. It was past midnight, and the last thing she remembered was falling asleep while reading a book. She had no memory of leaving her bedroom, taking the bus up to 168th Street, and arriving at the hospital. She must have been sleepwalking, or had blacked out—just as Bliss had described.

She looked down at her mother. Allegra was sleeping

underneath the covers, silent and peaceful as ever. Was it just a dream? But it seemed so real. Her mother was awake, was speaking to her. She had told her to beware. Beware of what?

"Mother," Schuyler said, stroking Allegra's cold cheek. The pain of missing her never quite went away. Schuyler kissed her mother's forehead and left the room, turning out the lights.

At dinner the next evening, Lawrence invited Schuyler to dine with him at his old club. The Adventurers Club was an elite organization founded by the Blue Bloods in the early part of the eighteenth century as a meeting place of like-minded globe-trotters who were eager to document and share their research and theories on natural and geographic phenomenon. It was located in a well-appointed town house on Fifth Avenue, across from the Knickerbocker Club and minutes from the Metropolitan Museum—two Blue Blood associations that had to effect a more inclusive policy in recent years and accommodate Red Bloods into their ranks.

But the Adventurers Club was still a vampire stronghold, if only because humans didn't seem to be as interested in environmental issues as social ones, and there was no cachet to be had by joining the stodgy old Adventurers circle.

The dining room was filled with members of the old families: the Carondolets were there, as well as the Lorillards and the Seligmans, whom, like the Van Alens, had more illustrious histories rather than present-day fortunes.

Lawrence was welcomed by the maître d' and walked around the room, shaking hands and chatting before he and Schuyler were finally able to sit down.

The menu at the Adventurers hadn't changed since the nineteenth century. Sole *meunière*. Steak Diane. Roasted rabbit.

Schuyler ordered the sole, Lawrence opted for the steak.

Their food arrived underneath silver covers.

"Voilà," the waiter said, uncovering both at the same time. *"Bon appétit."*

As she cut into her fish, Schuyler told Lawrence what had happened the night before. "I had a blackout . . . I woke up and I was at the hospital, in Mom's room," she confessed.

"Blackouts? How do you mean?" Lawrence asked, chewing on his steak.

"You know, when you slip out of time and then you wake up and you don't know how you got there."

Lawrence put down his fork. "I know memory flashbacks. But vampires are always in control when they relive their memories."

"Really?" Schuyler asked.

Lawrence nodded. "What you're describing is highly unusual."

"Unusual?" Schuyler paused. But it happened to Bliss all the time, so it couldn't be that uncommon. She relayed to her grandfather what Bliss had told her.

Lawrence digested the information. "Perhaps this crop of vampires has something new in their genetic makeup that causes it. I don't think it's anything to worry about, but let me know if it ever happens again." Then he sighed and put down his fork. "Now, I must tell you something."

Schuyler steeled herself for the news she had been dreading since the day her grandfather had returned.

"The judge has agreed to hear Charles's petition to adopt you. The hearing is in a month."

PATIENT RECORD
St. Dymphna Home for the Insane

Name: Margaret Stanford

Age: 16

Admitted: April 5, 1869

CAUSES:

Showing the probable causes of insanity in the patient admitted.

MORAL:

Religious excitement

Love affairs

PHYSICAL:

Self-abuse

Accident or injury

Epilepsy

Suicidal. Patient found with wrists slashed a week prior to admittance by family member.

Delusional ravings

FAMILY HISTORY:

No sign of dementia or hysteria in any family member. Only child of both parents still living.

PREVIOUS HISTORY:

Epileptic fits. Patient complains of headaches, nightmares. Blackouts. Patient has no memory of certain actions. Love affair with inappropriate young man cited in hysteria. Patient was not pregnant upon admission, however.

PRESENT CONDITION:

Excerpt from admission interview with patient:

"It seems so real. I cannot escape it. I wake up and I can feel it in my bones. It's coming, it says in my dreams. It knows my name. It says it is part of me. That's all I can remember. Help me doctor, help me. I need to get away. I need to get away from it."

TWENTY-EIGHT

*T*he inspiration for the photo shoot was "Talitha Getty in Marrakesh." Lots of gauzy, linen djeballas, jeweled caftans, and the occasional turban—oh, and the tiniest string bikinis possible. But somehow the fashion assistant in charge of travel had misunderstood and booked them to Montserrat instead, so the Caribbean island would have to stand in for the North African enclave.

Not that anyone seemed to mind—everyone loved a beach.

Bliss had gotten the call from Farnsworth Models on Thursday, she was on a plane on Friday, and had arrived at the beach at sundown. Schuyler had been chosen as well, after *Chic*'s first choice of models—two Russian beauties— had discovered that their visas had expired and they wouldn't be able to return to their country.

The fashion director of *Chic*, Patrice Wilcox, was a stern, no-nonsense woman dressed in head-to-toe black, even in the tropical heat. She welcomed the models and crew with a smile as thin as her figure. "This isn't a vacation, people. This is work. I expect everyone to be on set at eight o'clock tomorrow morning."

However, even with Patrice's dire warnings, there was no denying it—the photo shoot was a vacation. While she was giving her lecture on punctuality, Jonas Jones, the famously incorrigible Blue Blood photographer, winked behind her back. "Margaritas at the bar in five minutes," he mouthed.

By midnight the entire crew, aside from the fashion director, including Jonas's two assistants—cute guys from the Rhode Island School of Design—a gaggle of models—none of whom were over eighteen—and Schuyler and Bliss were at the beachfront bar, knocking back shots.

Bliss and Schuyler impressed the Red Bloods among the gang with their ability to drink everyone under the table. Vampire genes, natch.

Schuyler looked out at the dark beach, the full moon shining over the long shoreline, and the gentle rumbling of the surf. It was gorgeous. She had arrived early, half expecting to be greeted by Jack Force. But he was not among the male models, and she felt a pit of disappointment at his absence.

But as she wished him there, she felt a soft nudge on her elbow, and there was Jack standing at the stool next to hers.

"What are you drinking?" he asked. "Nothing too absurd, I hope," he said, as if it had been just yesterday that they had spoken in the Repository.

"It's a pretty awful concoction. Some kind of coconut rum and pineapple juice, but it isn't a piña colada. Taste?" she offered, handing him her glass.

Jack took a sip and made a face. "It's awful."

"Told you."

"I'll have one," he told the bartender.

"Brave man," she said, saluting him with her glass.

Jack stirred his drink. "How's Lawrence?"

"He's well." Schuyler wondered if Jack knew about his father wanting to adopt her. She didn't want to bring up such an awkward subject.

"Do you still believe they've returned?" Jack asked, meaning the Silver Bloods.

"I have to," Schuyler said simply. "It's the only explanation for Dylan—for what happened to Cordelia."

Jack looked down at his glass and shook it so the ice cubes clattered. "The Committee doesn't believe it. The crisis in Rome was abated, Lucifer was destroyed by Michael himself. There's no way they could come back."

"I know." She looked down at the dregs of her drink. "But I think The Committee is wrong."

Jack looked as if he was about to reply, but a hoarse voice called from the other side of the bar, where a raucous drinking game was underway.

"Schuyler! Jack! We need two more oars for Viking Master, c'mon!"

The next day, the whole team trekked to a hidden nature reserve on an isolated side of the island. The crew had set up makeup tents to shield the models from the heat. Bliss emerged from her cabana wearing a zebra-striped bikini with cowrie shells on its string ties, a transparent silk caftan, and jeweled thong sandals.

"Where're the parrots?" Jonas asked behind the camera.

The shot called for Bliss to hold two large, brilliantly plumed Scarlet Macaws on each arm, in homage to the ones Talitha had owned.

The animal trainer released the birds, but neither cooperated with any of his commands. One perched on Bliss's head while the other flew around her, squawking loudly.

The trainer was finally able to free Bliss from the bird's clutches, and Jonas compromised by staging the shot with Bliss underneath a tree, next to the birds.

"Thank God that's over with," Bliss groused as she walked carefully in the tall grass back to the haven of the makeup tent.

Schuyler was called next. She was wearing a black Gucci maillot, a one-piece that could only be described as two strips of fabric down the front, culminating in a tiny V at the bottom. The stylist had taped the fabric to her chest, but she still couldn't help but feel way too naked.

"I'm going for a Blue Lagoon type of thing here," Jonas explained. "I want hot. Smoldering. Sexy. But innocent."

Schuyler eased into the cold pool underneath the water-fall.

"Ready?" Jack Force asked from the other side of the pond.

She nodded. She had known they were going to be part-nered for the photo, but the sight of Jack's toned, athletic body, in his low-waisted Vilbrequin board shorts, was mak-ing her blush.

Especially when Jonas admonished them to stand closer together. "Didn't you hear me? It's Blue Lagoon! You're obsessed with each other! Try to show it! Jack, put your hand on her thigh. Schuyler, arch your back, move so that your body is next to his. There. That's more like it."

"Sorry," Jack said, as he drew Schuyler closer.

"All part of a hard day's work, I guess," Schuyler said, trying not to let him know how much his presence affected her.

The camera snapped.

"Next!" Jonas yelled.

That night, when Jonas took out the entire crew for dinner at an outdoor restaurant, Bliss found herself seated next to Morgan, the seriously cute photo assistant. Morgan had been paying her a lot of attention all weekend. He was a sophomore at RISD, nineteen, and had an arsenal of bad jokes that kept Bliss giggling despite herself. He poured her drink after drink, not realizing that Bliss was immune to alcohol's effects.

Bliss leaned back on her wicker chair and draped her feet over his lap. After months of winter in New York, she felt free here, with the cool ocean breeze blowing through her hair, no parents to nag her, and even better—no nightmares since she'd arrived on the island.

"Wanna take a walk?" he suggested.

Bliss nodded. A "walk on the beach" sounded pretty suspicious. Wasn't that just a nice way to say "Wanna hook up?"

They walked hand in hand on the beach, Bliss dipping her feet into the rolling waves and feeling the cold water over her skin.

The lights of the hotel grew fainter and fainter.

"Morgan's a girl's name," she teased.

"Oh yeah?" he asked, hugging her and pulling her to the ground.

Bliss pretended to struggle as he pinned her arms down.

"You're not getting away from me," he said.

"No?"

The boy began to kiss her, and Bliss kissed him back. This was different from kissing Dylan, or from kissing Kingsley, she thought. This was a human. A Red Blood. She could feel his heart thumping in his chest, smell his ripe human scent. And suddenly, she knew what she was about to do.

He lifted up his shirt and tossed it to the side. Bliss helped him unbutton her blouse. Her whole body tingled as he slipped a hand underneath her bikini top and untied the strings. He was moving so fast . . . but then, so was she.

She rolled him over so that she was straddling him, her knees pressed on the sand on either side of his hips.

"Nice," he said, ever the frat boy, admiring Bliss sitting astride, topless in the moonlight.

"You think?" she asked coyly. Then she bent her head down, kissing upward from the dark line of his torso, up to his chest, then to his neck, to the warm spot underneath his chin. She kissed him slowly with her tongue.

He sighed and held her head with his hands, pressing her closer to him.

And that's when she bit him with her fangs and began to feed. . . .

*T*he Committee maintained that all one needed to learn about one's past lives was to sit in a chair, close your eyes, and meditate, letting the mind wander down the endless hallways of memory, perusing a catalog of a thousand lifetimes.

In the dark privacy of her bedroom, Mimi snuggled on her princess divan, put a fur mask over her eyes, and began to concentrate.

The visions couldn't be clearer. Every iteration of her past showed her the same story: she and Jack together, happy, bonded, in love. She analyzed the history of their recent past: Plymouth, Newport, but neither time nor place offered a hint of a clue.

Try as she might, she couldn't find a reason for his withdrawal, for his doubt, for his hesitation. Or could she?

With a shock she remembered the look on his face at

the Four Hundred Ball. That look of total and complete adoration. At the time she had tried to dismiss it as mere infatuation. Nothing more than mere curiosity, even. That was stupid of her. She had allowed herself to be blinded by her pride. She had been too long in denial.

The answer had been in front of her all along.

Schuyler Van Alen.

The little half-blood. Or more correctly, a Blue Blood without a past. A new spirit. This was the anomaly in their universe. This was the unknown factor that was keeping Jack off balance.

How could she have not seen it before?

Schuyler had never existed in their world until now. Only now . . . in this cycle. And only now, in this cycle, was Jack and Mimi's bond under question.

He was drawn to Schuyler—as he had once been drawn to Gabrielle. Mimi tore off her eye mask in a snit and threw it across the room, almost hitting her chow, Pookie, who whimpered in annoyance.

Gabrielle. It was always Gabrielle. Even before the Fall, it had been so. Gabrielle, the Virtuous, the Messenger, an archangel of the White, the one who would brings news of salvation. Mimi and Jack were Angels of the Underworld, their destiny one of darkness and justice, to remind man of their mortality. And yet Jack, Abbadon, had always been drawn to the Light. Had always been drawn to the power of the White.

And everybody said *she* was the social climber? Mimi thought.

Through the centuries, Mimi knew Jack had been unsatisfied with his lot, had been uncomfortable with his title and position—the Angel of Destruction. Jack would never shy from his responsibilities, Mimi understood her twin too well. She just wished he would accept the world as it was made instead of aspiring for something greater. That was what got them into trouble in the first place. They had followed Lucifer upward during his ascent, Jack thinking that if he could shine like the sun Gabrielle loved so well, he would win her hand. But Gabrielle had spurned him then, and even when she had abandoned Michael on Earth she had turned to a human rather than to Abbadon of the Dark.

There were no secrets between the Force twins. Mimi had learned to live with the fact that Gabrielle's face had haunted Jack's dreams for over a millennia. But now the power of attraction had transferred from mother to daughter, and that she could not accept.

Mimi knew now what she had to do. To save their bond, to save themselves.

She had to destroy Schuyler Van Alen.

THIRTY

*T*he banging on the door was insistent, shaking the thin rattan walls of the beachside hotel. The sound broke the silence of the dawn. It was almost five in the morning.

"Schuyler! Schuyler! Wake up!"

Schuyler stumbled out of bed and opened the door a crack. She saw Bliss standing in the outdoor hallway looking panicked, still wearing her outfit from the night before, her hair in disarray.

Schuyler unlocked the door chain and opened the door fully.

"What?"

"Oh my God, Schuyler, you have to help me, I'm in huge trouble, oh shit, it's bad, I think he's dead," Bliss said, shaking uncontrollably.

Schuyler immediately woke up. "Dead? Who's dead?"

"Morgan—the assistant—I . . . come quick."

As Schuyler ran down the beach with her, Bliss told her the story. "I did it. I did the *Caerimonia Osculor*. The Sacred Kiss. I don't know, I just felt like it. I wanted to get it over with, you know? I was hating being the only one in our year who hadn't done it. And it was great, it was fine, he seemed to really get into it—but then, I don't know, I think I went too far. Oh shit, Schuyler, if The Committee finds out, I'm in huge, huge, huge trouble."

Bliss led Schuyler to the spot where she and Morgan had made out, in a secluded area underneath palm trees, behind a sand dune.

The boy was lying faceup in the sand, blood still dripping from the two small punctures on his neck.

"He's not breathing," Bliss said nervously. "I think I went too far."

Schuyler knelt down and took his pulse. "There's no pulse."

"Oh my God, they are going to kill me! No human has ever been killed in a *Caerimonia*! Ever!"

"Shhh . . . Let me think. . . . Jack. We need to get Jack," Schuyler decided.

"Jack? Why?"

"Because he's done this before. Morgan might not be dead. Maybe this is what happens to Red Bloods after the ritual. Maybe Jack will know something we don't."

* * *

Jack was at the door, fully dressed and wide awake before Bliss had even finished knocking. Schuyler marveled at his speed. She bet he would be a natural for the *Velox* test. She hadn't thought to use the vampire speed in such a fashion—she was still wearing her pajamas. Jack listened to Bliss's story and was at the boy's side in seconds.

He knelt on the sand and took Morgan's pulse by pressing two fingers against his neck. "It's there . . . You can sense it, very faint, but it's there."

"Oh thank God," Bliss said, sinking to the ground in relief.

"So he'll be okay?" Schuyler asked.

"He'll be okay." Jack said. "He might not remember what happened, but when he awakes, he'll be looking for you. He'll be drawn to the one who marked him as her own."

"Why?"

"The Sacred Kiss creates a bond. It means he's yours. No other vampire can take him. When you took him, your blood mixed with his, and it will be poison to any other Blue Blood."

Bliss and Schuyler absorbed this new information.

"So he's like my boyfriend?" Bliss asked, not sure if she really wanted that.

"If you want," Jack allowed. "It's not a casual thing, you know. It means something. For both parties."

Bliss blushed. "I . . ."

"It's okay," Jack said. He lifted the boy up. "Let's just take him back to his room. He'll probably just think he has a really bad hangover in the morning."

"Thanks, Jack," Schuyler said, when both Morgan and Bliss were safely stowed in their rooms. She put a light hand on his forearm to show how much his actions that evening had meant to her.

Jack smiled, his green eyes shining in the dim light. Schuyler thought she had never seen anyone so calm under pressure. He had been such a stabilizing influence, a natural leader, assuaging Bliss's anxiety and taking such respectful care of Morgan. He put his left hand on top of Schuyler's. "Any time. And tell Bliss not to worry. We all make mistakes."

His skin felt warm and smooth to her touch, and Schuyler thought they could stand like that forever, framed in the doorway to her room. But Jack released his hand first, and she reluctantly took hers back as well.

"Well . . . good night," Jack mumbled, nodding to the sunrise that was slowly breaking through the clouds. He began to walk away, his footsteps soft on the wood floor.

"'Night," Schuyler whispered. "Sweet dreams?"

"You bet," Jack replied.

Schuyler laughed softly to herself as she unlocked the door to her room. She hadn't meant for Jack to hear her last words, but there were no secrets from a vampire with extrasensitive hearing.

* * *

Later that morning, Schuyler and Bliss shared a taxi to the airport. Their flight was scheduled at eight, and both of them had had only two hours' sleep after all the ruckus.

"You okay?" Schuyler asked.

"God, I need a cigarette," Bliss said, fumbling for her purse. She brought one out and lit it, while rolling down the window at the same time. "Want one?"

Schuyler shook her head.

"I'm not sure," Bliss admitted. "I kind of wish I had waited. I don't know, I just felt like doing it. You know? Because Mimi talks about it all the time—and all those other girls, they always brag about their familiars. And I felt like such a stupid, I don't know, *virgin* or something."

"So what was it like?" Schuyler asked.

"Honestly?"

"Yeah."

"It was awesome. It's like you devour their soul, Schuyler. I could taste his . . . being. And then I felt great, you know. It's a high. A rush. I know why people do it now." Bliss confessed.

The taxi whizzed along, and the girls looked out at a view of the flat, untroubled waters of the Caribbean. It was a spectacular sight, but both of them were glad to be going back to the dirty, gray streets of New York.

"I haven't done it yet," Schuyler confessed, taking a deep breath.

"You will," Bliss said, flicking her ashes out the window. "But take it from me—when you do take a familiar, make sure he matters something to you. I feel a pull toward Morgan, and I don't want to. I hardly even know the guy."

Name: Margaret Stanford

Age: 16

Admitted: April 5, 1869

PREVIOUS HISTORY:

Recommended isolation therapy, April 30, 1869

Patient unresponsive. Isolation therapy no longer recommended, May 23, 1869.

Patient continues to have delirium, delusion, nightmares.

Suicidal tendencies more pronounced.

Patient is violent, danger to self and to others.

Recommend transfer to full-security facility.

PRESENT CONDITION:

A week before patient was to be transferred, patient started responding to treatment. Patient stayed and was allowed to remain in our facility for several weeks, in which no signs of delusion, hysteria, or dementia were observed. Patient responds well to questions and appears to have fully recovered. Recommend release to family in three months if progress continues.

THIRTY-ONE

Every Valentine's Day, the student council sponsored a holiday fundraiser by selling roses that would be delivered in class. The roses came in four colors: white, yellow, red, and pink, and the subtleties of their meaning were parsed and analyzed by the female population to no end. Mimi had always understood it thus: white for love, yellow for friendship, red for passion, and pink for a secret crush. Every year on Valentine's Day, Mimi was the recipient of the biggest and most elaborate bouquets. One of her human familiars had once bought five dozen red roses to declare his undying devotion.

Mimi perched on her stool in Chem lab, her first class that morning, and waited for the floral tidal wave.

The student council flunkies arrived with their buckets of flowers. "Happy Valentine's Day!" they chirped to a harried Mr. Korgan.

"Go ahead, get it over with," he complained.

Many of the girls received several small bouquets—most were yellow roses, which meant the girls had spent their money on each other, in the way girls do to make themselves feel better about not having a Valentine on that holiest of holidays.

Schuyler, sitting at her usual table—they had rotated around so that she was back with Oliver again—accepted a pretty yellow bouquet. Oliver had sent her one last year as well, and sure enough, the accompanying card had his precise handwriting on it.

"Thanks, Ollie," she smiled, inhaling the fresh blooms.

"And here's one for you, Mr. Hazard-Perry," the freshman delivery girl said, handing him a bouquet of pink roses.

Oliver colored. "Pink?"

"A secret crush!" Schuyler teased. She had decided to send him the pink flowers since they always traded yellow roses, and it was getting too predictable. Why not spice it up a little.

"Ha. Right. I know they're just from you, Sky," Oliver said, plucking the card from the top. He read it aloud: "Oliver, will you be my secret valentine? Love, Sky." He placed it back in the envelope and couldn't look at Schuyler for a moment.

Schuyler wanted to peer inside his mind. She had been successful in accomplishing the first factor of the glom—telepathy—but Oliver had been taking lessons as well, and as soon as he had mastered the antidote to telepathy—*occludo*, which meant closing your mind to external influence— Schuyler couldn't get a read on him anymore.

Bliss, who was sitting with Kingsley, received two red bouquets of similar size. "Ah, I have a rival I see," Kingsley drawled.

"It's nothing. It's just from some guy I don't even know that well," Bliss mumbled. Sure enough, the second bouquet was from Morgan, who had ordered the flowers all the way from his dorm room in Rhode Island.

"You are always on my mind. Love, M." his card read.

Kingsley handed his bouquet to her personally. "I wish these were green, they would suit you better. The color clashes with your hair."

"It's fine," Bliss muttered. She still didn't know how she felt about Kingsley. Being with him seemed like a betrayal to Dylan's memory.

Having handed out all the middle-size bouquets, the floral messengers were now bringing out the big guns. The three or four dozen mega-arrangements, roses of the deepest scarlet, all of which seemed to have Mimi Force's name on their cards. Soon, the area around her desk looked like a funeral parlor.

"Looks like that's it," Mr. Korgan grumbled.

"Wait—we have one left," the runner said, bringing out what was surely the most expensive bouquet of all: a three-foot-tall arrangement of two hundred white roses, in the palest ivory color. All the girls swooned. Almost no boys bought white roses *ever*. It was too big a sign of commitment. But this one practically trumpeted a captured heart.

The runner set the bouquet in front of Schuyler.

Mimi raised an eyebrow. She had always won the roses lottery. What was this all about?

"For me?" Schuyler asked, awestruck by the size of the thing.

She took the card from the tallest stem.

"For Schuyler, who doesn't like love stories." It was not signed.

Mimi glared at her red bouquets; the flowers seemed to wilt a little at her stare. She didn't have to guess who had sent the dazzling white flowers to the little beast. White for light. White for love. White for forever.

The time for her plan was at hand.

When she walked by Schuyler's desk, she pretended to trip, and caught a strand of Schuyler's dark hair under her fingertips as she steadied herself on Schuyler's chair.

"Ouch!" Schuyler yelped.

"Watch it," Mimi sniffed, the strand of hair securely in hand.

It wouldn't be long now.

fter mastering the first principle of the glom,
Schuyler had moved on to the second principle: suggestion. The second tenet was the ability to plant a seed of
an idea in another mind.

"It is how we push the Red Bloods to strive for excellence, art, and beauty," her grandfather revealed. "We use
the suggestion. It is a useful tool. Most people don't like to
think their ideas are not theirs, so we suggest them instead. If
we did not, the humans would have never had the New Deal,
Social Security, or even Lincoln Center."

Suggestion was even more complicated than telepathy.
Lawrence explained that one had to do it subtly, so the
human would not feel as if they were being manipulated.
"Subliminal advertising was invented by one of our kind, of
course, but when the Red Bloods discovered it, they immediately forbade its use. A pity."

The night before, Lawrence had asked her to suggest something to Anderson. After several hours of Schuyler attempting to not only find the target signal, but to send something to it, Anderson suddenly stood up and said that he felt like a cup of tea, and did anyone else want one?

When he left, Lawrence looked over at his granddaughter.

"That was you, wasn't it?"

Schuyler nodded. It had taken almost all of her strength to send one simple request.

"Good. Tomorrow we will move from afternoon delicacies to more important matters."

The next day at school, the effort it had taken to perform the suggestion took its toll on Schuyler. As she walked down the back hallways after third period, she suddenly began to feel woozy. She swooned and would have tumbled down the back stairs, had Jack Force not been there to catch her.

"Hold on," he said. "Are you okay?"

Schuyler opened her eyes. Jack was looking at her, concerned.

"I just lost my footing . . . I fainted."

The girls on the stairway behind her exchanged knowing smiles. Fainting was a regular occurrence at the school, and a telltale sign of anorexia. Of course Schuyler Van Alen was suffering from an eating disorder. Everyone could tell the bitch was too skinny.

"Let me take you home," Jack said, lifting her to her feet.

"No—Oliver—my Conduit—he can . . . and really, it's nothing, just—I've been working too hard on the glom," she said, half delirious.

"I believe Oliver is currently giving a presentation in English class," Jack said. "But I can call for him if you'd like."

Schuyler shook her head. No, it wasn't fair to ask Ollie to take a bad grade just because she felt ill.

"C'mon, let me put you in a cab and get you home safe."

Lawrence was writing in his study when Hattie knocked on the door. "Miss Schuyler is back, sir. It seems she had an episode at school."

He walked down the stairs to find Jack Force holding Schuyler in his arms. Jack explained that Schuyler had fallen asleep in the cab on the way home. "I'm Jack Force, by the way," he said as an introduction.

"Yes, yes. I know who you are. Just put her down on the couch, there's a good lad," Lawrence instructed, leading Jack into the living room. Jack placed Schuyler gently on a velvet-upholstered divan, and Lawrence covered her with an afghan blanket.

Schuyler's skin was so pale it was transparent, and her dark lashes were wet against her cheek. She was breathing in irregular, tortured gasps. Lawrence put a cool hand on her hot forehead and asked Hattie to bring a thermometer. "She's burning up," he said in a tense voice.

"She fainted at school," Jack explained. "She seemed all right in the cab, and then she said she felt sleepy, and . . . well . . . you can see."

Lawrence's frown deepened.

"She's been working on the glom, she said." Jack looked sharply at Lawrence out of the corner of his eye.

"Yes, we were practicing." Lawrence nodded. He sat next to his granddaughter and gently inserted a thermometer between her parched lips.

"That's against Committee rules," Jack noted.

"I don't recall you ever caring very much for rules, Abbadon," Lawrence said. Neither of them had acknowledged their former friendship until then. "You, who stood with us at Plymouth at great cost to your own reputation."

"Times change," Jack muttered. "If what you say is true, then she has been weakened by your own hand."

Lawrence pulled the thermometer out of Schuyler's mouth. "One hundred and twelve," he said matter-of-factly. A temperature that would certainly spell imminent death or permanent damage to a mortal. But Schuyler was a vampire, and it was still within an acceptable range for her kind. "A tad high, perhaps," Lawrence pronounced. "But nothing a good rest won't cure."

A few minutes later, Schuyler woke up to find Jack and her grandfather looking at her keenly. She shivered underneath the wool blanket and pulled it around her shoulders tightly.

"My dear, has this happened before?"

"Sometimes," Schuyler acknowledged softly.

"After lessons?"

Schuyler nodded. She hadn't admitted it, because she wanted the lessons to continue.

"I should have seen this. The first time this happened—when you went into hibernation—that was several days after you chased me in Venice, was it not?"

Schuyler nodded. She remembered what Dr. Pat had said: *Sometimes it's a delayed reaction.*

"I have figured out why you are so weak," Lawrence said. "I chastise myself for not realizing the problem earlier. It's simple. By exercising your vampire powers, your blue-blood cells are working overtime, and since your red-blood cells aren't high to begin with—because of the mixed nature of your blood composition—your energy flags. There is only one solution to keep your blood counts in the normal range. You must take a human familiar."

"But I'm not even eighteen," Schuyler protested, citing the age of consent for the Sacred Kiss. "I was kind of planning on waiting."

"This is serious, Schuyler. I've already lost your mother to a coma, I don't want to lose you as well. While you possess certain special powers that vampires your age wouldn't even dream of having, in many ways, you are also much weaker than the average Blue Blood. You cannot escape from the progress of the transformation, but you can control

220

some of its more adverse effects. You *must* take a familiar sooner than eighteen. A human boy. For your own sake."

Jack cleared his throat, and Schuyler was surprised to see him there. He had been so quiet during her grandfather's lecture. "I think I'll take your leave, Lawrence. Schuyler."

The door to the room opened just as Jack was about to exit.

Oliver Hazard-Perry stood in the doorway, looking flustered at seeing Jack. "I heard Schuyler had to go home from school. I was worried, I came as soon as I could."

The three vampires looked at him, all with the same thought on their minds.

Oliver was a human boy. A Red Blood. And Schuyler needed a familiar. . . .

"What?" Oliver asked, when no one replied. "Do I smell or something?"

It was time to try her plan. The roses had been the last straw. It was not only that—her brother was becoming bolder and bolder in his pursuit of the half-blood. He hardly ever tried to disguise the fact that he lingered in hallways outside Schuyler's classroom, or had taken to hanging out in the library at school or the Repository to catch a glimpse of her. Mimi had even caught the two of them shamelessly flirting in public! The other day a friend told her she had seen Jack actually walk out of the school with Schuyler in his arms! Not that Mimi even believed that one.

Mimi drew the pentagram as the book had instructed, with a small white chalk on the pale blond hardwood floor. Then she placed the necessary ingredients together in a small steel bowl on her dressing-room table: verbena leaves, bay leaves, a cluster of tiger lilies, marjoram, a toad heart, and a bat wing. The array looked out of place among the many crystal bottles of perfume and expensive French lotions.

She lit a candle and drew a flame from it with a stick of rosemary. She blew out the candle as directed and threw the burning herb into the bowl.

A tall, violet flame erupted.

Mimi glanced at herself in the mirror and was surprised to find that the room, which only moments before had been filled with afternoon sunlight, was now pitch black, save for the light shooting up from the bowl.

Her hands trembled slightly as she opened a small, glassine envelope that contained Schuyler Van Alen's hair. She shook out the contents and held it in her hand.

The book instructed her to throw the hair into the flame, while saying the words that would vanquish her enemy. Mimi closed her eyes and tossed it into the fire.

"I, Azrael, command the spirits. Annul the power of my rival.

"I, Azrael, command the spirits. Annul the power of my rival.

"I, Azrael, command the spirits. Annul the power of my rival."

"MIMI!" The door flew open. Charles Force stood at the entryway. With a wave of his hand, he extinguished the bright violet flame.

Mimi opened her eyes and gasped. She tried vainly to wipe off the traces of the pentagram with her foot. "I was just curious," she explained. "The Committee never lets us do anything. . . ."

He walked over to her side and poked a finger into the burning embers. "It is understandable. We are made from dark magic—we who are condemned to walk the earth forever. But these incantations are very strong. If you do not know how to control them, they can control you. That is why it is forbidden to the young until you are ready."

Charles picked up the book on her desk. "Where did you get this? I know. The Repository. But this is kept under lock and key. It is a dangerous book for those who are not yet of age."

He tucked the book under his arm. "Darling, why don't you find something else to do with your time?"

When her father left, Mimi picked up her white princess phone and dialed a familiar number.

"Kingsley," Mimi asked. "Can I talk to you for a minute?"

"Sure, baby, what's on your mind?"

"You know that thing you said? About calling up a Silver Blood from the Dark?"

"Yeah."

"Do you think it would work?"

THIRTY-FOUR

here's something different about you," Kingsley
said, one afternoon while they were supposedly doing
homework in Bliss's bedroom. "Supposedly" because that's
what Bliss liked to think was going to happen, but Kingsley
always had other ideas. BobiAnne insisted that Bliss leave the
door open to her room whenever she had a boy over—that
was one of her rules. But BobiAnne wasn't there that afternoon. It was her weekly spa appointment, and she would be
gone for hours. Jordan was at ballet rehearsal, which ran until
midnight. Bliss was alone in the apartment, save for the staff,
who were on the first floor, far away in the servants' wing.

"I got a haircut," Bliss offered, looking up from her
German essay. She knew that wasn't what Kingsley was after.
Ever since the double-bouquet delivery, Kingsley had been
harassing her to find out the identity of Bliss's so-called
"mystery man."

"No, that's not it." Kingsley smiled. He was stretched out on her bed like a lazy cat, his black hair so long that it curled onto his shirt collar. His notebooks and binders were scattered around him, including that dark leather-bound book he was always reading. But in the past hour, he had done absolutely no homework and instead had been needling her all evening.

"I don't know what you're talking about," Bliss said stubbornly.

"I think you do," Kingsley drawled. "It's written all over you."

"What?"

"You did it. You took a human during your little vacation or photo shoot, whatever you call it. *Vou drank hees blaad,*" Kingsley said, affecting a Transylvanian accent. "Whoever gave them the idea that we were some provincial hicks from Eastern Europe was brilliant."

"So what if I did?" Bliss asked.

"Oh, goody. Now we're getting somewhere. Did you like it?"

"You're not jealous?" Bliss asked.

"Jealous? Why would I be jealous?" Kingsley looked shocked. "I don't think you understand—it's like being jealous of your hairdresser. Familiars perform a service, that's all. We don't get emotionally attached to them."

"We?"

"You know what I mean."

Kingsley walked over to Bliss's side and began massaging

226

her back. "C'mon, relax. . . . Are you still having those flash-backs? Those blackouts?"

Bliss nodded.

"Did you try doing what I suggested?" he asked.

She shook her head. She was too scared to do what he had proposed.

"Well, you should, it works. Worked for me." Kingsley's fingers kneaded her sore muscles expertly, and Bliss was soon swooning under his touch. It was like being hypnotized. . . .

Red eyes with silver pupils, and a voice that whispered in a hiss . . .

Soon . . .

Soon . . .

Soon . . .

The beast had come again, chasing her down mazelike corridors. She felt its hot, foul breath on her cheek. She was trapped against a corner, and she could not wake up. She looked it in the eye. Do it, do it, she thought. Do what Kingsley said.

Talk to it.

What do you want? Bliss asked. *I demand a palaver.*

The crimson eyes blinked.

When Bliss woke up, she found she had scratched herself in fear. There were ugly red bruises all over her arms.

But Kingsley had been right. It had worked. The beast had gone.

Schiz·o·phre·ni·a (n.) Greek for "Shattered mind." Mental disorder characterized by impairments in the perception of reality. Persons having schizophrenia suffer from auditory delusions, visual hallucinations, disorganized speech (incoherence), disorganized behavior (crying frequently).

Continuous sign of disturbance must occur for more than six months in order for the patient to be diagnosed as such.

—*Dictionary of Mental Disorders*,
American Academy of Mental Health Professionals

*T*he Mercer had been Oliver's idea. He'd nixed Schuyler's room or his, thinking it would be too weird to do "it" in the same place where they had spent so many innocent hours reading magazines and watching television. So he'd booked a suite at the downtown hotel.

He had convinced her to have a few drinks with him in the library bar before they went up to the room. "You might not need a drink, but I definitely do," he'd said. Schuyler watched patiently as Oliver downed one Manhattan after another. Neither of them said much. The library bar was off-limits to non-hotel guests, and the two of them sat in a private corner. The only other patron was a movie star giving a magazine interview across the room. The movie star had her feet on the couch and she was laughing too loudly, while the reporter looked nervous and starstruck. A small silver recorder sat on the cocktail table between them.

"All right, let's do it," Oliver said, pushing away his half-finished third drink.

"God, you look like I've asked you to go to war," Schuyler said, as they walked toward the elevator.

The one-bedroom suite had a stunning view of downtown, and was decorated with a hip modern edge: dark Makassar ebony furniture, lamb's wool throw pillows, black epoxy floors polished to a high gloss, an onyx bar that glowed from within, a flat-screen television, and stainless steel walls that looked cold to the touch but actually felt smooth and warm, like butter.

"Cool," Schuyler said as she sat on one edge of the king-size bed, while Oliver sat on the other.

"Are you sure you want to do this?" Oliver asked, sitting forward and putting his face on his hand.

"Ollie, if I don't, I'll pass out in a coma and I won't ever wake up. This morning I couldn't even get out of bed."

He gulped.

"I hate to ask you this—but it's just, I don't know, I don't want my first time to be with someone I don't even know, you know?" She'd told him about what had happened to Bliss in Montserrat. "And you're my best friend."

"Sky, you know I'd do anything for you. But this is against the Code. Conduits aren't allowed to be familiars to their vampires. We are supposed to be objective. It's not part of the relationship. Things like the *Caerimonia*, it complicates things, you know," Oliver explained.

When Schuyler had first asked Oliver a week ago if he would consider becoming her human familiar, he had told her he would think about it. The next day, he hadn't brought it up, and Schuyler assumed he was too polite to tell her no, so he was just going to act like she'd never asked him at all. Several days went by, and neither of them mentioned it. Schuyler was beginning to think she would have to find an alternate solution. But that morning, she had found an envelope stuffed into her locker. It was from the Mercer Hotel, and held a plastic door key for their suite. "See you there tonight," Oliver had written. "Chomp! Chomp!"

It wasn't as if Schuyler didn't have mixed feelings of her own—she hated putting Oliver in this position—but she felt she had no choice. If she had to take a familiar, at least she would take one who was, forgive the pun, already familiar to her. And she'd felt drawn to Oliver since Venice. Maybe that was a sign it was going to be all right. That this was something that was supposed to happen.

"Just say the word, Ollie, and we won't do it, okay?" she offered, her hands gripping the edge of the bed, pulling out the sheets from their corners.

"Okay. Let's not do it," he said promptly. He sighed and lay down on the bed, waving his arms over the downy comforter. His long legs dangled from the edge but his torso was totally horizontal. He closed his eyes, as if the prospect was simply too much to bear, and put his hands on his face again, as if to shield himself from something.

"Do you mean it?" Schuyler asked a little fearfully.

"I don't know," Oliver groaned behind his hands, which were now folded over his mouth.

"It's just, you know, I'll be really careful, if you're scared, I mean. You have to trust me." She was still sitting upright so that her words were spoken to the wall of windows, while Oliver seemed to be talking to the ceiling.

"I trust you," Oliver said in a strained, sad voice. "I trust you with my life."

"I know it'll change our relationship, but we're best friends. It can't change that much, can it? I mean, I already love you," Schuyler said. Every word she said was true, she was very fond of Oliver. She couldn't imagine life without him.

She turned around to look at him. Oliver had removed his hands from his face and opened his eyes. She noticed how his chestnut hair framed his handsome face, and how his neck looked inviting under his stiff Oxford collar. "Don't you love me?" She knew she was being manipulative, but she couldn't help it. She needed Oliver to say yes. Otherwise . . . who would she do it with?

Oliver tried not to blush and couldn't quite meet Schuyler's eyes. He lifted himself to a sitting position once again. "All right," he said, almost more to himself than to her.

Schuyler moved closer to him and leaned against his body, and with a few small movements, she was sitting on his lap. "Okay?"

"You're heavy," he teased, but he was smiling.

"Am not."

"All right, you're not."

"You're cute, you know? I mean, really cute. Why do you spend all your time with me? You should date," she said matter-of-factly as she brushed the hair out of his hazel eyes. They were the kindest eyes she had ever seen, she thought. She would always feel safe with Oliver.

"Yeah, me, date." Oliver laughed. He put his arms around her waist.

"Why not? It's not unheard of."

"Yeah?" Oliver asked.

"Uh—" But Schuyler didn't finish, because Oliver was putting a warm hand on her chin and drawing her toward him, and soon they were kissing. Soft, tentative kisses that turned more vigorous as they opened their mouths to each other.

"Mmm . . ." she sighed. So this was what it was like. Kissing Oliver. It wasn't anything like she'd imagined. It was better. It was as if they were made for each other. Schuyler pressed herself against him, and Oliver put his hand through her hair. This was new. This was a turning point. Then she started kissing his chin and his neck.

"Sky . . ."

"Mmmm?"

Suddenly, Oliver pushed her away, took her hands from behind his back, and abruptly shoved her off his lap.

"No," he said, panting heavily. His cheeks were aflame with embarrassment.

"No?" Schuyler asked, not understanding. It seemed like it was going well—this was what was meant to happen, wasn't it?

"No." Oliver stood up and started pacing. "The Sacred Kiss means something. It did to your mom. And you know what? You'll have to find another guinea pig. I'm not going to do it out of obligation."

"Ollie."

"Don't, Schuyler."

He never called her Schuyler unless he was really mad.

Schuyler shut up.

"I'm going. I can't be with you . . . You're not yourself." Oliver said, putting his coat on and slamming the door of the hotel room as he stormed out into the night.

*I*n a hidden alcove deep within the underground stacks underneath the Repository of History, Mimi Force was leaning over an old leather-bound book. The same book her father had confiscated several weeks ago. The Repository might keep it under lock and key, but it was only a matter of figuring out which key was used to liberate it, and that had taken minimal effort—the human librarians being no match for the rage of an angry vampire.

The book was open to the final page, a black page, whose words were etched in a luminous blue—the same color as the blood that ran in Mimi's veins.

Kingsley Martin stood next to her, and the two of them read from the page by the light of a lone tapered candle. Around them, the stacks—rows and rows of six-foot-tall bookcases that seemingly stretched to infinity—were silent and shrouded in darkness. The Repository held approximately ten million books. It was the largest library in the world, and the stacks went far under Manhattan, several stories below the sidewalk. No one was even sure how far down the old, rickety caged elevator went.

They had decided to perform the incantation on the sub-basement level. The spell had mandated a "location of primal power," and Kingsley had suggested the Blue Blood headquarters.

"It says only one who is of like mind can call it," Mimi said, reading from the text.

"That means it has to want what you want, because only then can it answer your call," he explained.

"Okay."

"First you have to draw your victim," Kingsley said.

Mimi drew a pentagram around the two of them, making sure they were within the chalk lines.

"Dark Prince of the Silver Bloods, heed my call; I Azrael, command you to bring my enemy forward," Mimi ordered in a loud, clear voice.

On the top level of the Repository, Schuyler Van Alen arrived in the main reading room, looking for Oliver. After sitting in the hotel suite for an hour, she decided she couldn't just hang around and do nothing, or wait for him to calm down. She had to find Oliver and apologize. What she had asked for was wrong. She knew it now. She had asked for too much, and she wanted to ask for his forgiveness. He usually spent his weekend nights holed up in his cubicle at the Repository, which was the first place she decided to look after he didn't pick up his cell phone or answer his BlackBerry text messages.

Bliss Llewellyn was sitting on one of the shabby couches in the main reception area.

"Hey," Schuyler said. "Have you seen Oliver?"

Bliss nodded. "I think he's back there. He just arrived a few minutes ago."

"Cool."

After what happened in Montserrat, Bliss had been a little embarrassed around Schuyler. "I'm, uh, waiting for Kingsley," Bliss said. "He asked me to meet him here."

Schuyler nodded, even though she hadn't asked Bliss to explain her presence. She left Bliss by the entrance and walked quickly through the quiet room to find her friend. The Repository was crowded for a weekend night. Almost all the carrels were filled. Librarians were cataloging books on the shelves, and several senior members of The Committee were walking in for their weekly meeting. Schuyler saw Priscilla Dupont's elegant white head among them, the Chief Warden was talking animatedly to a fellow Conclave member. The Elders disappeared into a private conference room, and Schuyler noticed Jack Force was sitting in his usual chair by the fire, reading a book.

Inside the pentagram, the flame on the candle flashed, and

showed Mimi a vision of the Repository upstairs. Yes. Just as the spell had promised. There was Schuyler Van Alen, standing in the middle of the room.

Her victim had been drawn to the site.

Mimi felt a gladdening of the heart. This was it. This was really going to happen. She was going to be rid of that little cockroach once and for all. Schuyler had of course made a beeline for Jack as soon as she had entered. But no matter—it wouldn't be long now.

Kingsley handed Mimi a silver knife.

It was the only way the spell would work: blood for blood. Mimi held out her right wrist; the blade felt cold on her skin. Her heart was thumping and she felt the first quivers of fear. Even though she was immortal, and the blood sacrifice would not hurt her, she still felt queasy thinking about what she had to do.

But the sight of Schuyler Van Alen reminded her what was at stake. The bond. Jack. Abbadon. She had to stop this before it was too late.

"I give thee my blood for your blood. O, Prince of Darkness. Hear me, hear my call. Destroy my enemy, once and for all," Mimi chanted.

"NOW!" Kingsley called.

Mimi took a deep breath and slashed her wrist with the knife, opening up a vein and spilling her blood upon the candle, causing a black flame to shoot upward.

* * *

The last thing Bliss remembered was a massive explosion that ripped through the floor of the library, splitting it in two, a crack in the earth itself, and her nightmare came to life. Right in front of her was a dark mass with crimson eyes and silver pupils, roaring, struggling, leaping into life, covering the entire space with the buzzing of a thousand hornets, the agonies of a thousand tortured souls, and the ugly laughter of a deranged lunatic.

Bliss screamed and screamed and screamed.

Then everything went black.

THIRTY-SEVEN

*T*he smoke was suffocating. It was a dark, violet smoke, and smelled faintly of sulfur and acid. Schuyler opened her eyes to find them burning. Tears were falling from her cheeks although she was not crying. Something had happened—an explosion—it sounded like a rip in the universe. She looked around: the Repository was in disarray, whole shelves of books were toppled, and papers were strewn all about, as if a bomb had destroyed the place. There was debris from the ceiling, plaster and dust everywhere, shattered glass and broken pieces of wood.

"Jack! Jack, where are you?" Schuyler asked, panicking. She had been standing right there, next to his chair, but his chair was nowhere to be seen. She felt blood dripping into her eyes and put a tentative hand on the crown of her head. Something had cut her, but it wasn't a deep wound. The palms of her hands were scratched and bloody, and there was a tear in her jeans, but thankfully that was the extent of her injuries.

There was a cough, and Schuyler crawled over to the sound. Jack was lying underneath the reading table, momentarily stunned.

"I'm all right," he said, struggling to sit up and wiping the smoke from his eyes. "What the hell happened?"

"I don't know," Schuyler said, coughing and covering her mouth and nose with her hands.

"Jack! Are you all right? Can you hear me? Jack!" Mimi's frantic voice could be heard from the hidden alcove that led to the underground stacks. She emerged from the corner, looking dazed but unhurt.

"I'm here."

"Oh thank God! Jack! I was so worried!" Mimi cried, throwing herself into her brother's arms. She began to sob uncontrollably. "I thought . . . I thought . . ."

"It's all right, I'm all right," Jack soothed, gently stroking her.

Schuyler took a step back to let them have their privacy, feeling a tangled weave of jealousy and pity and embarrassment at witnessing their intimacy.

There was a groan beneath a toppled bookshelf. "Help," a strangled voice called. "Help!"

Jack, Mimi, and Schuyler ran to the sound, and helped lift the heavy weight from the boy.

Kingsley thanked them. "Fucking-A. What was that?"

All around them, librarians and Committee members were picking themselves up from the rubble, counting heads, and making sure friends had survived. The smoke enveloped everything, and it was hard to see through the haze.

"Over here!" A familiar voice called. Schuyler left the Force twins and Kingsley to find Oliver kneeling next to an injured librarian. There was a cut on his chin and a bruise on his forehead, and he was covered in a thick layer of plaster dust.

"You're all right," Schuyler said. "Thank God."

"Schuyler, what are you doing here?" Oliver asked.

"Looking for you."

He nodded briskly. "C'mon, give me a hand."

Renfield, one of the crotchety human historians, was doubled up against one of the overturned copy machines, groaning. He had been thrown against the wall by the explosion, and the force had broken his ribs.

They helped him lie down by a stack of books, promised to send help as soon as possible, and walked around to see if there were any other trapped or injured parties.

So far, everyone they came across had survived. There were minor scratches and a few concussions, but people were surprised to find themselves more or less intact. Oliver stopped to administer first aid to a Blue Blood girl with a broken arm by ripping his shirt sleeve and creating an impromptu sling.

Schuyler picked through the mess and came across the

prone body of a girl, facedown and covered with dust and plaster.

She turned the girl over and gasped. "Bliss, oh God, Bliss . . ." There were two punctures underneath her chin, and her blood, sticky and blue, was running down her neck.

"STAY WHERE YOU ARE!" a loud voice commanded from the entry. The group froze.

Schuyler kept a shaky hand on Bliss's neck to staunch the blood. Oh, Bliss . . .

The violet smoke cleared, and Charles Force and Forsyth Llewellyn were soon standing by her side, holding gleaming swords aloft.

Charles knelt down next to Bliss and put a hand on her head. "This one is still alive."

This one? Schuyler wondered. There was a scream from the other side of the room, and Schuyler soon understood what he had meant. There, by the entrance to the Coven headquarters, splayed on the archway steps, was Priscilla Dupont, the Chief Warden.

Lying in a pool of blood.

THIRTY-EIGHT

*O*liver took Schuyler home, both of them still feeling shaken up. The awkwardness of what went on between them earlier at the Mercer had completely disappeared in the face of this new calamity. They were back to their normal selves, and Schuyler was glad to have her friend by her side.

Hattie made a fuss over the two of them when they arrived, placing bandages on Schuyler's head and the cut on Oliver's chin. The loyal maid prepared steaming cups of hot chocolate and wrapped them snugly in cashmere blankets by the fire.

"Where's Lawrence?" Schuyler asked, taking a cookie from a tray that Hattie was holding out to them.

"He ran out of here just a few minutes ago; said he had an emergency meeting of some kind," Hattie said. "He told me to take good care of you when you got here. To get the first-aid kit out. I think he knew something happened."

Once Hattie had left the room, Oliver asked, "Do you think it was a Silver Blood?"

Schuyler shrugged. "It has to be. It's the only explanation. But it doesn't make sense. Lawrence told me that Silver Bloods hunt by themselves. They take their victims when they are alone, without their canine protectors. The attack happened in a public space, where there were many witnesses."

"Do you think she's dead?" Oliver asked again.

"Who? Bliss? No. Charles Force said she was alive," Schuyler replied. Still, it was hard to believe. The Texan girl had two deep puncture wounds on her neck, and the floor around her had been swimming with her blood.

"No, I mean . . . Mrs. Dupont," Oliver clarified.

"I don't know." Schuyler shuddered. It had certainly looked that way from where she was standing, and she had overheard members of the Conclave discussing the situation from across the room as they gathered around the body.

Full consumption . . . Impossible . . . But the blood has been drained . . . Which means . . . She is gone . . . She has been taken . . . Not Priscilla! Yes . . . This is dire indeed.

Dr. Pat's ambulance team had taken Bliss away on a stretcher, with an oxygen mask on her face and her father by her side. But the second stretcher, the one that carried Priscilla Dupont, had been covered with a white sheet over the body. Which only meant one thing . . .

Schuyler scooted up next to Oliver so that the two of

them were leaning against the couch legs. She put her head on his shoulder and closed her eyes, and he put an arm around her to draw her closer. They took comfort in each other's company.

Lawrence returned close to dawn. He saw Schuyler and Oliver sitting side by side on the rug against the couch.

"You should both be in bed. Especially you, granddaughter. Surviving a Silver Blood attack is not to be taken lightly," he said, waking them gently.

Schuyler waved the sleep from her eyes, and Oliver yawned.

"No. Not yet. We want to know what happened," Schuyler insisted. "We were there."

Lawrence sagged onto the opposite leather chair and put his feet up on the ottoman. "Yes, and I'm only glad that nothing worse happened to either of you."

"It wasn't after us," Schuyler said.

"Thank heaven for that," Lawrence replied. He took out his customary cigar and cigar cutter.

Schuyler knew this was a sign that her grandfather would explain everything, or at least as much as he himself knew. She leaned in closely.

"What did Cordelia tell you about the Croatan?" He asked, puffing on his cigar.

"That they were an ancient danger that became a myth to the Blue Bloods. Because the last known attack was four hundred years ago," Schuyler said. "During Plymouth."

"Yes. Roanoke was their most violent and crushing victory. They took out an entire settlement. But she did not tell you about Venice, or Barcelona, or Cologne."

Schuyler raised an eyebrow questioningly.

"What is not known, or at least, what has been suppressed, is that ever since their so-called defeat in Rome, Silver Bloods have returned to feed on the Blue Blood young at the turn of each new century. We had tried to convince the Conclave of this pattern, this ever present danger. But the years after Roanoke were peaceful, and there was only one other instance of an attack in the New World."

"Here? In America?" Schuyler asked. Cordelia had never mentioned this.

"Yes." Lawrence set a thick file folder, burned at the edges, on the coffee table and pushed it toward Schuyler. "This is the file Priscilla Dupont was working on. She was going to present some evidence to The Committee, testify to what Cordelia and I had warned them about, so long ago."

She opened it, and several newspaper clippings fell out. She and Oliver looked through them. "Who's Maggie Stanford?"

"She was a Blue Blood who disappeared. We had no idea that she had been committed to an asylum. Red Blood doctors had thought it was a mental disease, but it was actually evidence of Silver Blood corruption. She was a victim."

Lawrence tapped on the papers with his cigar. "When

Maggie was never found, Cordelia and I knew the Silver Bloods were behind it, but that we would never be able to prove it. That was when we decided to separate, so that I could continue the investigation without The Committee being the wiser. Priscilla had told me she had found something in the archives that would shed some light on their actions, but I have looked through this file. There is nothing I haven't seen before."

"What happened after Maggie?" Schuyler asked, noting how pretty the young debutante had looked in her picture.

"Nothing. The Silver Bloods retreated back into the shadows again. Until last year, when Aggie Carondolet was killed. And since Aggie, there have been four Blue Bloods slain at the beginning of their Transformation. Four. That is the most since Roanoke. That means they are getting stronger, more confident.

"Priscilla's death, however, is the most troubling. To know that they have overcome a vampire at the height of her powers—this means their strength has grown. They are becoming more aggressive.

"The Committee must wake up to this danger. We can no longer sit back and wait while the Prince of the Silver Bloods marshals his forces against us and takes us one by one."

"You really think Lucifer has returned?" Schuyler asked.

Lawrence said nothing for a long moment, his cigar burning steadily, the ashes at the tip growing longer and longer until they fell, sizzling into the Aubusson rug and leaving a small hole. "Oh, rats," he cursed. "Cordelia will never forgive me for that. She never let me smoke in the house."

"Grandfather, you haven't answered my question." Schuyler said sharply.

"Maybe it doesn't need to be answered," Oliver said nervously. All this talk of Lucifer and Silver Bloods was making him feel queasy. Maybe he shouldn't have drank so much hot chocolate or eaten that fifth cookie.

"Only the most powerful of Silver Bloods would be able to cause a massive destruction in such a protected place," Lawrence finally said.

"Protected?"

"The Repository of History is one of the safest of our strongholds. It has wards all over it, spells to keep out such an invasion, to keep out Abomination. It is an ominous sign for all of us that the wards did not hold."

"What are you going to do?" Schuyler asked.

"The only thing I can do—Call for the White Vote. It is time Michael is challenged as Regis."

THIRTY-NINE

They were arguing about her. Through the morphine haze, Bliss could hear her father and Charles Force arguing about her behind the closed hospital door. What had happened?

She dimly remembered the black, purplish fire that covered the entire library in a thick, impenetrable fog, and she knew something bad had happened to her. There was the gauze around her neck. Had she been bitten? By a Silver Blood? The thought made her forehead perspire. If she had been attacked by Abomination, why was she still alive?

Bliss tried to lift her hands up to her neck so she could check on the wound, but she was paralyzed. She panicked, until she realized her hands were tied down to the bedposts. Why?

The room was as lavish as a hotel suite, with the modern white plastic furniture she knew so well. She was in Dr. Pat's clinic, the Blue Blood hospital. With her extrasensitive hearing, she concentrated on what her father and Charles Force were arguing about in whispered tones in the hallway.

"She has not been corrupted, Charles—you know the signs as well as I do—you've seen her neck! There wasn't enough time," her father was saying.

"I understand, Forsyth, I do, but you know how it looks. I can't get Lawrence off my back about this. She's going to have to be tested, just like everybody who was there that night."

"She's a victim! This is an outrage! I won't let you!"

"You don't have a choice," Charles said, and his tone brokered no further argument. "I know how worried you are, but as you said, she appears to be safe."

There was a long silence, and then the two men returned to Bliss's room. Bliss immediately closed her eyes and pretended to be asleep.

She felt her father's hand on her forehead as he whispered a short prayer in a language she didn't understand.

"Hey," she said, opening her eyes.

Her stepmother and Jordan walked into the room and crowded by the foot of the bed. BobiAnne was wearing another haute-hideous outfit—a cashmere sweater with VERSACE emblazoned on its chest—and carried a small handkerchief, which she kept pressing to the side of each eye, although no tears were visible.

"Oh, honey, we were so worried! Thank God you're okay!"

"How are you feeling?" her father asked, his hands clasped behind his back.

"Tired," Bliss replied. "What happened?"

"There was an explosion at the Repository," Forsyth explained, "but don't worry, it was so deep underground the Red Bloods didn't even notice it on the sidewalk. They think it was just a small earthquake."

Bliss hadn't even thought to worry about humans discovering the Blue Bloods' most secret place.

"What happened to me?" she asked.

"Well, that's what we're going to find out," he said. "What do you remember?"

She sighed and glanced out at the window, which looked into an empty office in the building next door. Rows of computers were switched on, blinking, even though it was past office hours. "Not much. Just a lot of black smoke . . . and . . ."

Eyes, crimson eyes with silver pupils. The beast, come to life. It had spoken to her . . . It had said . . .

She shook her head and closed her eyes tightly as if to ward off the evil presence. "Nothing, nothing . . . I don't remember anything."

Forsyth sighed and BobiAnne sniffed again. "Oh, you poor, poor child."

Jordan, her sister, remained silent, watching Bliss from the corner of her eye.

"Bobi, can you and Jordan leave us alone for a minute?" her father asked.

When they were gone, Forsyth turned to Bliss. "Bliss, what I'm about to tell you is very important. You were attacked by a Silver Blood, one of the Croatan," her father said.

"Noooo," Bliss whispered. "But The Committee says they're just a myth. . . ." she said weakly.

"The Committee was wrong. We realize that now. In fact, Priscilla Dupont had gathered enough evidence to . . . but I won't talk about that now. The fact is, somehow the Silver Bloods have survived, and we must face up to that reality."

"But how?"

"Sadly, it means one of us is culpable. The Silver Bloods would not be able to thrive unless someone from our circle was hiding them. Helping them. It would have to be one of the very old families, powerful enough to cover up such black evil that Michael could not notice a change in the balance."

"But what does it mean for me?" Bliss asked, her voice quavering.

"There are very few who have lived after a Silver Blood attack, and there is always the danger of corruption."

"Corruption?"

"Sometimes, the Silver Blood will not take his victim to full consumption; instead it will instill a hunger . . . drawing enough blood so that the vampire is left weakened. But Red Blood becomes poison to the victim, and he will hunt his own kind for survival."

That's what happened to Dylan, Bliss thought. He had been *turned*. Corrupted. Transformed into a monster, and then killed before he could reveal its secrets.

"The crisis in Roanoke, we believe, happened because several of our people in that settlement had already been corrupted when they left the Old World."

"How do you know if you've been corrupted?" Bliss asked nervously.

In answer, Forsyth began lifting the gauze from Bliss's neck. He unwrapped the bandage.

Bliss looked at her father anxiously. What was he going to show her? Had she been turned into a monster?

Her father handed her a small hand mirror from the nurse's table.

She brought it up to her neck, dreading what she would see.

But her neck was smooth, as clear and unblemished as before.

"What does it mean?"

"There are no marks, which means the poison was not strong enough to hold. Your Blue Blood, the *sangre azul*, was able to rehabilitate your chemistry on its own. Heal itself, and protect you from corruption. The Croatan did not make you one of its own."

She nodded, grateful and relieved. She had survived. . . . She wasn't sure how, but she had lived.

"There will be other tests," Forsyth warned. "One of the Elders will administer them to you. They will ask you to share your memories, to commune with them. To show them what you saw. But I am confident you will pass their judgment."

Her father was about to leave the room, but Bliss called out another question. "But, Dad, if one had been corrupted . . . how could you tell?"

"It's hard to say, but we have noticed that those who have befallen corruption tend to be drawn to the Dark Matter, and to start exhibiting curiosity concerning the Black Spells."

Later that evening, Nan Cutler, one of the high-ranking Wardens, arrived to visit Bliss. Nan was one of the bird-thin, elegant society women in Priscilla Dupont's circle; she had a shock of white hair with a raven stripe in the middle. The city knew her as an indefatigable fund-raiser and shopper of high-end couture. But when she came into Bliss's hospital room that evening, all traces of the public facade were gone. Here was a formidable, centuries-old vampire. Bliss could see the faint blue blood lines on her face.

She introduced herself to Bliss, then took a seat at her bedside.

By evening, sensation had returned to Bliss's limbs, and she was feeling much better already.

"Take my hands, child," Nan said softly. Bliss placed

Melissa de la Cruz

both of her hands in the old lady's soft ones. Nan's hands were smooth and unwrinkled.

"Now close your eyes and take me back to yesterday evening. Show me everything you saw."

The glom. Nan would use the glom to read her mind, Bliss knew. She had to open her mind and let the old woman see.

Bliss nodded.

She closed her eyes.

Together, they saw what had happened. Bliss, waiting in the reception area for Kingsley. They saw Renfield bring a list of files to Priscilla Dupont. They saw Schuyler walk in and ask if she had seen Oliver. They saw several girls from Duchesne check out books for the next Committee meeting.

Then all went black. A dark, noxious smoke engulfed the entire area. . . .

Bliss waited for the beast to appear, but all they saw was the thick, black smoke.

When she opened her eyes, Nan was scribbling in her notebook.

"Good," Nan said. "Now, if you please, lift your hair and show me the back of your neck."

The back of my neck?

Bliss did as told. Nan nodded. "You may put your hair down."

After the Warden left, her father walked in and hugged her tight.

Whatever test it was, it looked as though she had passed.
The back of her neck . . .

Part of the test . . .

She thought of how Kingsley's hair was so long, it always covered the back of his neck. A fashion statement? Or was he hiding something?

Kingsley . . . who carried that book around with him all the time, the *materia acerbus*. Kingsley, who had taught her to palaver with the beast of her nightmares.

Kingsley Martin, who was part of an old, old, Blue Blood family. One of the most powerful, and the most prestigious . . .

Bliss closed her eyes. She saw the beast again, the beast had spoken to her. It had said one word . . .

Now.

*S*chuyler was brushing her teeth when her cell phone rang. She rinsed, gargled, and spit, quickly wiped her face, and ran to pick it up. It was early in the morning, and she was getting ready for school.

"Yeah?"

"Is that any way to answer the phone?"

"Oh, Bliss. Hey. Sorry. I thought it was Oliver. He always calls in the morning."

"Sorry to disappoint."

"No, not at all. How are you?" Schuyler asked. She had been meaning to visit Bliss in the clinic, but the past several days had been hectic, what with trying to keep up with a full class schedule, vampire lessons, and deal with the fact that her grandfather was getting ready for the battle royal of his life. The White Vote had been called, and the election was imminent.

"Better," Bliss said. "You, uh, know what happened to me, right?"

"Yeah," Schuyler said. "My grandfather said it was a Croatan, but that you were safe."

Bliss told Schuyler about the test, opening her mind up to Nan Cutler, and how the marks on her neck disappeared.

"The same thing happened to me," Schuyler said. "Remember? The night we modeled for that shoot?"

"Yeah."

"I was attacked, but the marks disappeared. And I couldn't remember anything."

"She also wanted to see the back of my neck. Isn't that odd?"

Schuyler nodded, even though Bliss wasn't able to see her. "Actually, that's another kind of test, my grandfather said. Nan came over here, too. To check me out."

"Really? I'm not the only one?"

"No, of course not. Everyone there that night has to be tested."

"Cool."

"So, what's up?"

"Listen, I found out something from my dad. You know how The Committee always said there was no such thing as the Silver Bloods?"

"Uh-huh."

"Well, I guess they're coming around."

"Yeah, I heard that too," Schuyler said. Lawrence had

filled her in on the politics of the Conclave. Now that a full-grown vampire had been taken, the Conclave was up in arms and primed for revolt. The Silver Bloods were a grim reality they would have to face.

"Anyway, my dad said that it has to be one of us—someone high up, an old family," Bliss said.

"That's what Cordelia always said too."

"You might think this is crazy," Bliss said, "but I think I know who did it."

"Who did what?"

"I mean, I think I know who's harboring the Silver Blood, or Silver Bloods," Bliss said. "I think Kingsley has something to do with it."

Bliss told Schuyler her suspicions, and how they matched up with what her father had told her about corruption—his intense curiosity about the Dark Matter, the odd book she always saw Kingsley reading, the way he was so familiar with Silver Blood history and mythology.

Schuyler whistled. "I don't know . . . it sounds suspicious . . . but don't you think you're jumping to conclusions?"

"Maybe, but I'm stuck in here for another week," Bliss said. "Do you think you and Oliver could look into it?"

Later that week, Schuyler and Oliver dug up a few interesting facts about the new boy. The Repository had been restored to somewhat usable condition (the *Velox* factor came in handy). All the dust and plaster had been cleared, and nothing remained of the explosion except for a small, hairline crack in the middle of the marble floor. It was amazing what vampires could do when they set their minds to it.

Tracking Kingsley's whereabouts was easy with Oliver's network of connections in the private-school circuit, as well as some clever computer sleuthing.

Schuyler called Bliss at the clinic to let her know what they had found. "The Martins moved to New York the same night that you said Dylan was murdered," she said. "And we found out Kingsley spent summer school at Hotchkiss, where that girl was killed, and he'd spent a week at Choate visiting a friend, where a sophomore had been found dead right before school started. He was here in New York the night of Aggie's death at Block 122, and he was also at the party where Landon Schlessinger died."

"I knew it!" Bliss said.

"There's other stuff: Kingsley was the last person to visit Summer Amory. Oliver said the gossip was that he was dating her. So that places him at the scene of all the crimes. But I'm not sure, it could just be coincidence. Lots of other Blue Blood kids spent summer school at Hotchkiss, go to Choate, were at Block 122 that night, and knew Landon Schlessinger. And Summer Armory was dating a bunch of people. I'm sure if we wanted to, we could find several other people who fit the bill."

"No, it has to be him. I know it is," Bliss said emphatically.

"Are you going to tell your dad about this?"

"I'm not sure. He's kind of an adviser to Kingsley's family. I mean . . ."

"I'll tell Lawrence." Schuyler offered. "He'll know what to do."

When Schuyler presented their case to Lawrence at dinner, with all of Bliss's suspicions and the incriminating evidence, her grandfather hardly looked up from his rib-eye steak.

"Interesting," he said absentmindedly.

"Interesting, that's it?" Schuyler asked. "But don't you think we might have something here?"

Lawrence took a sip from his wineglass. "Perhaps."

That was all he would say on the matter, and Schuyler could not get anything out of him for the rest of the evening.

he Committee's investigation on the incident at the Repository called for a public hearing, wherein all the witnesses to the attack were called to testify before The Committee. The hearing took place inside one of the massive courtrooms underneath the Repository. The members of the Conclave sat in a row on a high platform, facing the crowd, Charles Force in the middle. Lawrence Van Alen was seated to the far right, and was already puffing on his customary cigar. The new Chief Warden, Edmund Oelrich, a famous art historian and gallery owner in his public life, ran the proceedings from his seat up on the platform. There was a small podium to the side where witnesses were called, and the inquisitor, The Committee's official prosecutor, stood across from it.

The seats in the courtroom were filled with almost all the Blue Blood families, and tension ran high as Schuyler, Jack,

Bliss, and Oliver described their version of the events one by one. They were seated next to each other in the front row. Mimi was seated next to Jack, and was still waiting for her turn. She was nervous about the investigation, but figured there had to be some way to bluff her way through it. After all, it wasn't like she had wanted Bliss to be hurt or Priscilla Dupont dead—not in the least! She couldn't have cared less about the old bag. It was just an unfortunate accident. They had to understand that, right? If there was no motive, they couldn't find her guilty, could they? She reached over to grab her brother's hand, and Jack gave it a warm squeeze.

The inquisitor called Kingsley Martin to the stand.

"State your name for the records."

"Kinsgley Drexel Martin."

"And your position."

Position? Mimi raised an eyebrow. What was this all about?

"I am a Truth Seeker. A *Veritas Venator*. I was commissioned by The Committee to investigate the deaths of several Blue Bloods: Aggie Carondolet, Dylan Ward, Summer Armory, Natalie Getty, Landon Schlessinger, and Grayson St. James."

A murmur ran through the crowd. Older Blue Bloods knew *Venators* as the highest order of The Committee's secret police, fearless warriors in the fight to keep the Blue Bloods safe from harm and discovery.

"And your mission?" The inquisitor prompted.

"I was sent to the Duchesne School to accumulate any evidence that might lead to the detection of the enemy," Kingsley said evenly.

Another murmur, this time more agitated. A *Venator* had been sent to one of their safest sanctuaries—Duchesne! What was The Committee thinking, sending one of their powerful assassins to spy upon school children?

"Who were the suspects?"

"Madeleine Force. Bliss Llewellyn. Schuyler Van Alen."

This time there was an audible gasp from the crowd. Kingsley was an undercover agent! A latter day Johnny Depp on *21 Jump Street*, an undercover vampire working the teen beat.

Schuyler gaped, Bliss couldn't help but laugh, and Mimi only gnashed her teeth. That little prick.

"And what did your findings show?"

"I immediately crossed off Schuyler Van Alen. She was a victim of two Silver Blood attacks and did not show any indication of being drawn to the Dark Matter," Kingsley said, taking out a small notebook from his jacket pocket and flipping through his notes.

"Bliss Llewellyn was a more promising subject. She has complained of nightmares and delusions, similar to those suffered by Maggie Stanford before her demise. But due to these delusions, I had to conclude that Bliss was a possible victim and not a perpetrator."

"And Madeleine?"

"I have concluded that Madeleine Force harbors the Silver Blood that has been attacking our community," Kingsley said, his tone of voice almost casual.

"Quiet! Quiet in the court!" The Chief Warden admonished, as the crowd became even more angry and agitated. Several vampires stood from their seats, and there was hissing and booing at Kingsley's testimony. Mimi Force—the Regis's daughter—Silver Blood accomplice? Was this some kind of joke?

"And the basis for your evidence?" The Chief Warden grunted from the high platform.

"She expressed a desire to learn more about the Dark Matter. Specifically, she wanted to know how to perform the *Incantation Demonata*. The call for the Silver Blood."

"And why did she say she wanted to do this?"

"She said she wanted to finish off an enemy," Kingsley said, looking straight at Mimi.

Mimi quavered in her seat. Lies, lies. All lies! Stop talking! Shut up! Shut up! You were my friend! Traitor!

"And that was Bliss Llewellyn."

"No."

"No?" The inquisitor looked mildly surprised.

"No."

"Who was the intended target?"

"Schuyler Van Alen."

There was another angry buzz among the audience.

266

Schuyler felt herself freeze. So she wasn't just paranoid—Mimi *did* want to destroy her. She remembered her dream in which her mother was awake and speaking to her. What had Allegra said? *Beware.*

"Why did you allow her to perform the incantation?" The Chief Warden asked.

"I needed the evidence. I thought I could control it, stop her before it happened. But I could not. It was obvious she had done this before. Many times."

"Thank you, *Venator*."

Kingsley stepped down. Now that his identity was known, he looked much older, the cocky adolescent boy had been a facade, merely a pose. He walked gravely to his seat in the front row next to the Duchesne kids, and they gave him a respectful berth.

"The investigation now calls Charles Force to the stand," the Chief Warden announced.

The head of the coven staggered down to the podium from his seat on the high platform. His own daughter, harboring a Silver Blood! The shame of it was written all over his face. His silver hair looked white under the light, and there were heavy bags under his eyes. He looked like a broken man, not the indefatigable leader of the vampires.

"State your full name for the record," The inquistor ordered.

"Charles Van Alen Force."

"Have you witnessed your daughter meddle with the Black Spells?"

"Yes, but . . ." Charles answered, wiping his brow with a silk handkerchief.

"Incantations. Forbidden spells."

"Yes, but . . .

"That will be all. Thank you," the inquisitor said, cutting off his testimony.

Charles looked as though he wanted to say something more, but his words died on his tongue. He looked ashen and disheartened. He stepped down and walked back to his seat with the Conclave.

None of the members of the Conclave would look at him, and several in the crowd began to boo and hiss.

"As final evidence against Madeleine Force, we present the Mark. I believe you will find it on the back of her neck," the inquisitor declared.

"That's absolutely ludicrous. I don't bear the Mark of Lucifer any more than the rest of you," Mimi said. She wanted to scream. This was a travesty. She was being set up!

"Lift your hair, please," the Chief Warden directed.

Mimi gathered her hair and lifted it. She had done this for Nan Cutler the night before, when she had come to perform the test. Nothing had happened, and she was certain she had been cleared.

There was an agitated murmur from the Conclave.

"What?"

Your neck, Mimi, there's something on your neck.

Jack, you're scaring me.

She felt the back of her neck with the tips of her fingers. Raised flesh. A tattoo. More like a burn, like a cattle brand.

Judgment was swift and resolute. Mimi was the perpetrator. She was found guilty of conspiring with a Silver Blood. She would be taken to their ancient prison in Venice, where her blood would be burned, her memories destroyed, with no hope of reincarnation. Bail was set for one million dollars, which her father promptly paid, so that Mimi could be released to his custody.

Mimi looked at Jack. *This can't be happening . . . I didn't do it. You know I didn't.*

I know. I know. Jack put an arm around his sister, but his face was lined with anxiety. This was serious. Sentenced to burn! Mimi!

The Force twins waited for Charles to walk down the platform to their side. He still had the same shell-shocked look on his face.

"Father, what can we do now?" Mimi said. "Surely . . ."

Charles Force was aghast. "There is nothing . . ."

"Nothing?"

"There is only one way to refute the Mark of Lucifer. You must submit to an even more ancient custom. The blood trial. But only Gabrielle—Allegra Van Alen—is able to perform this."

"Gabrielle?" Mimi asked, with a sinking feeling.

"Yes."

A whole lot of good that was going to do her. Allegra was in a coma and would never wake up.

"So there is nothing I can do to prove my innocence?" Mimi asked.

"Nothing."

The audience from the hearing dispersed to the Repository upstairs, and Schuyler waited for her grandfather by the entrance. Oliver had already gone ahead, citing an afternoon Trig quiz he couldn't miss. They had been given special dispensation to attend the hearing that morning. Schuyler knew she should have gone back with him, but she wanted to hear her grandfather's take on the whole situation.

He was leaving the Conclave headquarters, with Edmund Oelrich and Nan Cutler at his side.

"We'll take your leave, Lawrence," Edmund said, bowing. "It is a travesty what has happened to this community."

"We assure you, you will have our votes when the time comes," Nan added, patting Lawrence on the arm. "We should have listened to you four hundred years ago. To think that the Abomination has reached the royal family!"

"Thank you." Lawrence nodded. He turned to Schuyler. "So. What do you think of Kingsley Martin now?"

They began walking up the stairs, toward the side doors of the vampire-only club, Block 122, and out onto the sidewalk.

"It was Mimi all along," Schuyler marveled. "Mimi . . ." It was still hard to believe, especially with all their lingering suspicions about Kingsley. "Did you know about Kingsley being a *Venator*?"

Lawrence nodded. "Yes."

Schuyler remembered what Kingsley had said to Jack that one morning. *You would be nothing without us, without the sacrifices we have made.*

"But you were right, granddaughter. Kingsley is a Silver Blood," Lawrence said, waving Julius over in the town car.

"How do you mean?" Schuyler asked as she stepped inside, Lawrence holding the door open.

"His family is an old one. One of the ancient warriors. They were corrupted by Lucifer himself. But they came back into the Blue Blood fold, repenting their actions, and they have learned how to control the Abomination, the hunger, the voices in their heads," Lawrence said, closing the door. "Duchesne, please, Julius. We shall drop off Schuyler first and then home for me," he said, tapping on the glass that separated the driver from the passengers.

They drove through the streets of Chelsea to the West Side Highway. It was another gray New York day.

"But how can we trust them?"

"We have trusted them for thousands of years. Kingsley Martin is a Silver Blood only by default. His blood is as blue as yours and mine. They have sworn off their allegiance to Lucifer, and have been very helpful in our search for the conspirator." Lawrence sighed. "And yet . . ."

"And yet?"

"And yet . . . something about this case bothers me. Do you believe Mimi Force is guilty?"

"Yes," Schuyler said unequivocally. "She's an awful person, grandfather."

"And to know that you were her target is extremely troubling, yes. But . . ."

"But what?"

"But if you were the target, why was Priscilla taken? And the Llewellyn girl? Something doesn't add up."

Schuyler shrugged. Maybe she shouldn't rush to judgment, but wasn't that what The Committee had done? And she couldn't find it in her heart to pity Mimi. The girl had sent a Silver Blood to kill her, after all.

"You heard what Kingsley said. And he's a *Venator*. Doesn't that mean he has to tell the truth? At all times?"

Lawrence nodded. "Yes. Charles has always trusted them. He was the one who recruited them back to our cause. But I do not know. I have always harbored my doubts about the Martins."

The car pulled up to the gates of the Duchesne School.

Schuyler hopped out of the car, but not before giving her grandfather a kiss on the cheek.

"Your grandmother always said never to trust shiny surfaces. They hide a multitude of flaws."

As she walked into the school, Schuyler bumped into Jack Force, who was coming in from the side door. Jack was still wearing his dark gray suit from the hearing, and his eyes were red-rimmed, as if from crying. Schuyler felt a stab of pity. While she had no love for Mimi, Jack was a reminder that not everyone felt the same way.

"She didn't do it, you know," he said preemptively.

Schuyler flushed, thinking, She wanted to destroy me! She admitted it herself! But to Jack she said coolly, "That's not what the court found."

"Mimi's selfish . . . but she's not evil," Jack implored. The afternoon bell rang, signaling the end of the lunch period and the start of classes. Students began streaming out of the cafeteria, up the stairs, and crowding the marble foyer, where Jack and Schuyler were standing. Several whispered to each other as they noticed Jack and Schuyler huddled in conversation. Some Blue Bloods who had attended the hearing looked sympathetic when they saw Jack, while others glared, and one went so far as to hiss at his presence. A special Committee meeting had been scheduled that afternoon to alert junior members on the latest discoveries.

"She would never truly hurt another person." Jack

continued to press his sister's case. "She doesn't hate you. Not really." He wished he could explain. *It's not you she hates, Schuyler. It's me. She just turned her anger outward because she couldn't bring herself to hate whom she loves. And she does hate me for what I have done—for loving you.*

Schuyler looked at him skeptically, but remained silent. Mimi Force. Azrael. The Angel of Death? Wasn't that Mimi's job? To bring about the end of life? To her surprise, Jack seemed to be able to read her mind.

"You don't understand—it is part of the balance. We are who we are. Death is as much a part of life. It is the gift of the Red Bloods. Mimi is part of the grand plan," Jack said.

Schuyler shrugged. "I'm not so sure," she said. "Goodbye, Jack."

*L*awrence was poring over archives from the Repository, and noticed that one clipping had been completely burned—except for the date on the top. November 23, 1872. He was still puzzling over it when Schuyler returned from school. She told her grandfather about Jack Force being able to read her mind that afternoon.

"I thought I was safe from telepathy, and yet he was still able to read my thoughts. Why?" she asked.

"Abbadon has always been one of our most gifted seers," Lawrence said. "It will take more than a simple *occludo* exercise to close one's mind from him. But it sometimes happens that those who are drawn to each other can share a kinship of some kind."

"Drawn to each other?" Schuyler asked.

"You must have noticed he is drawn to you," Lawrence said.

276

Schuyler blushed. She had hoped but she had never thought of it as a reality. And yet, even with his bond with Mimi, he had sought her friendship and hinted that maybe he would be interested in something more. . . . He had kissed her once, so long ago. And the boy behind the mask . . . Could it have been him?

"But he is bonded," Schuyler said. "It cannot be."

"No. Not among our kind. Abbadon has always been this way. You were not the first to tempt his fidelity," Lawrence said. "But it will pass. Thank goodness you are not drawn to him. Otherwise it will spell disaster for both of you."

She looked down at the carpet, wondering if her grandfather was testing her, or if he merely assumed that Schuyler would choose the right path simply because she was his granddaughter.

"Yes," she said. "Thank God for that."

She felt a sudden light-headedness, and her vision became pixilated and blurry; her knees buckled, but before she could collapse, Lawrence leaped to his feet and steadied her. "You have not done as you were told," he said grimly. "You have not taken a human familiar. You are weakening."

She shook her head.

"This is not a trivial matter, Schuyler. If you do not take a familiar, there is a very real danger you will succumb to a coma like your mother."

"But I . . ."

Lawrence cut her off with a curt directive. "You must

hunt, then—use the seduction. The call. That is the only way now."

The *Caerimonia Osculor* was a ritual between vampire and human that was usually a development within an existing relationship. That was why human familiars were traditionally lovers and friends of Blue Bloods. But the Code also allowed for the use of the powers of Seduction if the vampire was desperate. The vampire would use The Call to draw the human to him, hypnotizing the human and drawing its blood.

"I have taught you the words from the sacred language that would induce it," Lawrence said. "I will be going to the club tonight. When I return, I will trust that you have performed what is necessary."

Her grandfather departed soon after that, leaving Schuyler upstairs in her room. I don't want to, she thought stubbornly. I don't want to do it with a stranger. I don't want to do it with someone I don't know. I'm not desperate! Or am I?

Then, almost as if drawn by the call, someone knocked on Schuyler's bedroom door.

"What is it, Hattie?" Schuyler asked.

The door opened. "It's not Hattie, it's me," Oliver said, slouching in the doorway.

"I didn't hear the front door open. What are you doing here?" Schuyler asked defensively.

"Your grandfather told me you wanted me to come over," Oliver explained.

Ah. So Lawrence had performed a call of his own. Only, this one merely involved the use of a telephone. Very clever, grandfather, Schuyler thought.

Oliver walked over to sit on the footlocker across from Schuyler's bed. He looked at her pensively. "I was thinking . . . if you still want to do it, we can."

"You mean?"

"Yeah."

"Here?" Schuyler asked, looking around at her room, at her Evanescence posters, the pink Barbie dream house, the row of *Playbill* covers—*Rent, Avenue Q, The Boy from Oz*—taped on her wall during the time when Cordelia regularly took her to Broadway musicals. It was still a childish bedroom and painted Mountain Dew yellow. It didn't look like the lair of a vampire.

"As good a place as any," Oliver shrugged. "Besides, it'll save me the cost of a hotel room."

"You're sure about this?" Schuyler asked, reaching for his hand.

"Yes." Oliver exhaled. "I know what's going to happen to you if you don't, and between you and me, I'd prefer it if you weren't a vegetable. I hate vegetables," he joked. "Especially broccoli . . . So how do we . . ." Oliver said. "Should I stand? Or . . ." He stood up and looked around. He was so much taller than she was.

"No, sit down," Schuyler said, pushing him gently by the shoulders onto her bed. "This way I can reach down." She stood between his legs. He looked up at her. She thought he had never looked so handsome, or so vulnerable.

Oliver closed his eyes. "Be gentle."

Schuyler leaned down, kissed the hollow at the base of his neck, and then, ever so gently, she elongated her fangs and stuck them in.

Oliver whistled between his teeth, as if in pain.

"Should I stop?"

"No . . . go on . . ." he said, waving a hand.

"I'm not hurting you, am I?"

"No . . . It feels . . . good, actually," he whispered. He put a hand on her head and guided her to his neck again.

Schuyler closed her eyes and sank her fangs back into his neck. As she did so, her senses heightened, and his mind became open to her. The blood memory came flashing out. It was just as Bliss had said: she was devouring his soul, his very being . . . and, what was this? His mind was an open book to her now, his blood mixing with hers, reviving hers . . . and she could read every thought he'd ever had in his life . . . could access every memory.

Oliver was in love with her.

He had been in love with her all along. Ever since they'd met. For years and years and years.

She had long suspected this but had repressed it. But now it was confirmed. She couldn't deny it.

Oh, Ollie. I shouldn't have done this. Schuyler despaired. The Sacred Kiss would only increase his love, not dispel it.

Now they were bound to each other in a new and more complicated way.

This was more than she'd bargained for. Their friendship would be jeopardized, she knew that now. There was no going back from here. They would only be able to go forward. As vampire and familiar. Entwined by an ancient ritual of blood.

She finished. She was satiated. She withdrew her fangs and felt the life-giving energy flow through her body. It was as if she had ingested twenty-four gallons of high-octane coffee. Her cheeks flushed with color, and her eyes sparkled.

Oliver's head flopped down. He was already asleep. Schuyler gently laid him on her bed, where he would have to rest for the next several hours, and covered him with her blanket.

What have I done? she wondered, even as she felt her vision clear and her senses heighten. Would they be able to keep this a secret from The Committee? What if Oliver were banished because they found out a Conduit had become a human familiar? She remembered Cordelia telling her that Allegra had married Schuyler's father, her human familiar, against the Code of the Vampires. Her mother had exchanged one bond for another.

And what about Jack?

* * *

When Oliver woke, Schuyler was sitting at her desk, watching him.

"Well," he said, scratching his neck where the bite marks were still raw, "I guess that's what you call friends with benefits."

They both cracked up.

Schuyler threw a pillow at him. She walked Oliver to the door and thanked him again. He kissed her on the lips as he left. A quick kiss, but still, a kiss on the lips.

She closed the door behind him, her heart anxious and troubled.

This was a mistake.

*A*llegra Van Alen's hospital suite was on the top floor of Columbia Presbyterian, in a private wing where the rich and famous convalesced. The room was decorated in a style suited to the city's best hotels, with white Italian linens on the bed, sumptuous carpeting, and crystal vases filled with fresh flowers. Every day, a team of nurses massaged and manipulated Allegra's limbs to keep her muscles from the dangers of entropy.

Not that Allegra would ever notice. Once the city's most celebrated beauty, she slumbered, oblivious to the world around her: a woman with a glorious and tragic past, but no future. The heart monitor next to the bed showed a steady pulse, and for a long time, there was no sound in the room but the steady beeping from the machine.

Lawrence Van Alen sat in a chair opposite Allegra's bed. He had come to visit his daughter for the first time since he had returned. It was a visit he had been postponing due to the emotional weight of seeing his child reduced to such diminished capacity.

"Oh, Gabrielle," he said finally. "How did it come to this?"

"She can't hear you," Charles Force said as he entered the room, bearing another vase of flowers. He placed it on the sideboard next to her bed. He didn't seem surprised to find Lawrence there.

"She chooses not to hear," Lawrence said. "You have done this."

"I have done nothing. This is her own doing."

"Be that as it may, it was still your fault. If you had not—"

"If I had not saved her, you mean, in Florence? If I had let the beast have her? Then she would not be in a coma? But what was the alternative? To let her die? What was I to do? Tell me, Father."

"What you did was against the laws of the universe. It was her time, Michael. It was her time to go."

"Do not speak to me of time. You have no idea what happened. You were not there," Charles said bitterly.

He put a hand on Allegra's cheek and stroked it gently. "One day she will awake. She will awake out of love for me."

"It is sad that you still do not understand, Michael. She will never love you the way she did before. She herself did not understand the choice you made. You should have let her die. She will never forgive you."

Charles Force's shoulders shook. "Why do you talk to me as if I were still a boy? She only left Heaven out of love for you and Cordelia when you were banished."

"Yes. We had been doomed, we who were loyal to Lucifer. But your sister brought us hope. It was her choice to become one of the undead."

"Just as it was my choice to follow her."

Lawrence ruminated on their ancient history. How long ago it seemed now: Lucifer's ascent to the throne, the Prince of Heaven in all his glory, his bright shining star rising as beautiful as the sun, as powerful as God, or so they had thought, to their own detriment. How they had suffered. The cruel exile from Paradise, and Gabrielle, the Virtuous, who had volunteered to join the ranks of Lucifer's minions to bring hope and salvation to her kind. She had turned her back on Heaven for love of them, and Michael had followed her out of Paradise because he could not bear to be separated from her. The two of them were called the Uncorrupted because they did not bear the sin of banishment. They had left on their own accord. Out of love and duty.

"So you have won, Lawrence. After all these years, you finally have what you want. The coven."

The White Vote had been called that morning, and Lawrence had been installed as Regis in an almost unanimous election. Charles had been stripped of his title and responsibilities immediately. His reputation had been badly tainted by Mimi's conviction. He had tendered his resignation from the Conclave as soon as the news had been announced.

"I never wanted to displace you, Charles. I only wanted us to be safe."

"Safe? No one is safe. All you will do is sow fear and weakness. You will have us retreat once again. Back to the shadows. Back to the darkness, where we will hide like animals."

"Not a retreat, a tactical exercise in which we will be able to prepare. Because war is coming, and there is nothing you can do to stop it this time. The Silver Bloods are ascendant and the future of this world will be decided once and for all."

Charles Force remained silent. He walked toward the window and looked out at the Hudson river. A slow barge moved across the surface, and a seagull honked its lonely cry.

"But I have hope. It is said that Allegra's daughter will defeat the Silver Bloods. I believe Schuyler will bring us the salvation we seek," Lawrence said. "She is almost as powerful as her mother." He told Charles of Schuyler's astonishing abilities. "And one day she will be even more powerful."

"Schuyler Van Alen . . . the half-blood?" Charles mused. "Are you certain that she is the one?"

Lawrence nodded.

"Because Allegra had two daughters," Charles said in a light, almost playful tone. "Surely, even you have not forgotten that."

imi's condemnation, the formal process for her execution, was coincidentally scheduled during Duchesne's Ski Week in March, so she allowed herself to pretend the family was just going on vacation to Venice. The whole prospect of what was to come—her blood burned, her imminent destruction—seemed absolutely ludicrous.

She believed her father would find some way to rescue her from her fate, and she spent the flight from New York paging through fashion magazines, marking off the clothes she would buy when she returned to the city. But once they arrived in Venice, Mimi's bravado cracked a little. Especially when members of the Conclave escorted them to their hotel. They had traveled to the ancient prison as well, to witness the final rites.

It was hard to believe in death and burning in her comfortable bedroom, where she could still watch TiVo'd *My*

Super Sweet Sixteen and *Tiara Girls*. But stepping foot on the waterlogged sidewalks of Venice seemed to bring the past to life, and her memories screeched with images of the hunt: bringing death to Blue Blood foes, the black robes of the condemnation worn by the corrupted traitors, the screams of the guilty.

Mimi shuddered.

Tradition called for the accused to voluntarily surrender to the jailor, and on the evening of their arrival, Mimi left their hotel and made the historical walk across the Bridge of Sighs, where thousands of Blue Blood prisoners had walked before.

The bridge was so named because it was the last vantage point from which the condemned could view the city. She walked on it lightly. Jack was at her side, silent and grim. A few paces behind them, Elders and Wardens from the Conclave followed in a procession. Mimi could hear the heavy footsteps from the mens' boots, and the softer stiletto clack from the ladies' shoes.

"Don't," she said to her brother.

"What?"

Don't act like I'm dead already. I, for one, am not giving up.

She stuck out her chin, defiant and unbowed. "I'm not worried! They'll see I've been set up!"

"Nothing gets you down, huh?" Jack asked with a ghost of a smile. He was amused to find his sister as bratty and confident as ever. Her bravery was admirable.

"I laugh in the face of death. But then again, I am Death."

They stood in the middle of the bridge, the two of them remembering another walk, another time, in their shared past. A happier memory.

An idea occurred to Mimi.

She turned toward her brother. They stood in front of each other, forehead to forehead, as they had all those centuries ago.

"I give myself to you," she whispered, linking her fingers into his. Those were the sacred words that began the ceremony. That was all the bond entailed. All he would have to do was repeat them back to her, and the bond would be resealed in a new lifetime. In this lifetime.

Jack held her delicate hands in his. He brought them up to his lips and kissed them passionately, deeply. He closed his eyes and held her trembling fingers, feeling with his mind her love, her desire, her whole soul, waiting on a precipice for his response.

"No. Not yet," he sighed, keeping their hands linked tightly and opening his eyes so he could look deep into her eyes.

"If not now, when?" she asked, the threat of tears in her voice. She loved him so much. He was hers. She was his. It was the way of their kind. This was their immortal story. "Time might be running out for me. For us."

"No," Jack promised. "I would never let that happen." He looked away and released his hands from her.

Mimi crossed her arms, furious, and glanced to see what had distracted him.

Schuyler Van Alen was walking with her grandfather a few steps behind them. Seriously! Couldn't the wretched girl leave her in peace? She had won, hadn't she?

"Wait," Jack said. "It's not what you think. I need to talk to Schuyler."

Mimi watched as Jack walked over to her rival. On the night of her condemnation, couldn't she even catch a break?

Schuyler was startled when Jack Force appeared by her side. She had traveled to Venice with Lawrence at her grandfather's request. The thought of being witness to Mimi Force's demise wasn't an experience she was looking forward to, although, like Mimi, she couldn't quite believe it was truly happening.

"You know about the blood trial," Jack said.

She nodded. "Yes. My grandfather told me it's the only way to prove what really happened that night. The only way to overturn a ruling by the Conclave in session."

What Schuyler didn't say was that Lawrence had told her something else about the blood trial. Her grandfather had briefed her on her mother's history during their vampire lessons and confided that Gabrielle was the only vampire who was able to do it: as one of the highest-ranking *Venators*, she could tell blood memory from false.

"As Allegra's daughter, you may have inherited this ability," Lawrence had said. "You may be able to clear Mimi Force."

"Grandfather," Schuyler pleaded, "I'm not . . . I can't . . ."

"Listen to me closely, the blood trial will mean you will have to drink Mimi's blood to discover the truth of what happened that night. Only the Uncorrupted have the power to ascertain real memory from false in the blood memory. But it is a great risk: drinking the blood of another vampire means there is a chance you may give in to the temptation that afflicts the Silver Blood, kill Mimi, and become doomed in the process by becoming Abomination yourself. It is a risk only you can decide to take."

"And if I choose not to?" Schuyler asked.

"Then punishment will be rendered."

The thought that she held Mimi's life in her hands oppressed Schuyler. To risk her own life to save her enemy's! How could she volunteer for such a task? She had visited her mother in the hospital for guidance.

Allegra slumbered peacefully in her bed.

"I don't know what to do. If I don't do it, Mimi will die. But If I do, then I could become a monster. . . . Tell me what to do, Mother. Help me."

Yet, as usual, there had been no sign from Allegra.

And now Jack was studying Schuyler carefully. What did Jack mean by bringing this up now? Shouldn't he stay by Mimi's side and help her to accept the inevitable?

Jack looked over at Lawrence, who was watching the two

of them keenly. He returned his gaze to Schuyler. "You are your mother's daughter. Only you can perform the blood trial."

She took a step back.

Lawrence cleared his throat, but held his tongue.

"Lawrence, you said so yourself, that Schuyler has powers none of us have. Schuyler, please. I'm begging you." Jack said, with tears in his eyes. "You're her only chance. They *will* destroy her."

Suddenly, Schuyler understood what was at stake. This wasn't a game the Conclave was playing. This wasn't make-believe or a play put on for their amusement. They had conducted an investigation and pronounced judgment. Punishment had been recorded in the *Book of Laws*. They had traveled across the ocean to Venice, to the ancient prison, to fulfill the sentence.

Mimi was going to burn.

Schuyler looked askance at Jack. Your sister tried to destroy me! She wanted me dead—taken by a Silver Blood! How can I . . .

But she knew what she had to do. This was the sign she had been seeking all along. She looked deep into Jack's anxious green eyes.

"Okay," she said, taking a deep breath. "I'll do it."

*T*he condemnation was held in one of the ancient rooms deep inside the Ducal Palace and began with a formal pronouncement of the sentence. Mimi Force was led to the front of the room in shackles. A black robe had been placed on her shoulders, and her blond hair was covered by its hood.

The Conclave of Elders stood in a semicircle around her. The Chief Warden had finished describing the process when Lawrence halted the proceedings.

"As Regis, I have cause to call for a blood trial to refute or confirm the findings in the Conclave session."

"Blood trial?" Edmund Oelrich, the Chief Warden, asked. "But surely, there is no way. Allegra is still asleep, is she not?"

Charles Force, who was seated in the front next to his son, leaped up. "I second the motion for the blood trial."

"Lawrence, is this wise? What are you talking about?" Nan Cutler asked.

"Allegra's daughter, Schuyler Van Alen, has volunteered to perform the ritual." Lawrence called for Schuyler to come forward.

"The half-blood?" Forsyth Llewellyn exclaimed. "I oppose this! How do we know she is worthy?"

"Allegra's daughter?" another Elder asked.

"She is gifted with powers far beyond the norm, and I am confident she will be able to carry out this task."

The Conclave murmured, and a stay of execution was granted while they convened on this new development in another room. A few hours later, the Conclave returned. Finally, the Chief Warden spoke.

"The blood trial will be borne out."

Mimi and Schuyler were led to a small cell next to the courtroom. Lawrence patted Schuyler on the back. "Be safe, and remember what I told you."

When they were alone, Mimi pulled the hood off her head and looked at Schuyler with distaste. "You."

"Me."

"I don't need you. I'd rather die."

"Would you? Because that's certainly the other option," Schuyler snapped.

Mimi flushed. "My brother put you up to this, didn't he?"

"Yes. It's him you'll have to thank for your life, if indeed you are proved innocent," Schuyler replied.

Mimi crossed her arms and studied her cuticles. She rolled her eyes. "Fine. Let's just get this over with."

Mimi lifted her chin and closed her eyes. Schuyler stood on her tiptoes and put her mouth on Mimi's neck. She sank her fangs in . . . and just as with Oliver, she was transported into the past . . . seeing what was inside Mimi's memories . . . flying back to the night of the attack.

The dark underground of the Repository. Mimi and Kingsley laughing over the book. Standing inside the pentagram, the candle flickering and casting their shadows against the stone walls.

Mimi slicing her wrist, sending the blood over the flame and calling the words.

But then . . . nothing happened.

Mimi had fainted, but the spell had not worked.

She had been unable to summon the hatred needed to bring out the Silver Blood.

But Mimi had not been rendered unconscious, just disoriented. She had witnessed the events that unfolded next, but the memory of it remained in her subconcious, which is why she had not been able to recall it to prove her innocence. Now, through the blood trial, Schuyler was able to see what had really happened.

Kingsley cursed and picked up the knife. He sliced his wrist and called out the summons in a strong, deep voice.

There was a rip in the ground: the earthquake, the flame that shot out. Smoke filled the air, and suddenly there was a hulking dark mass going straight for Bliss Llewellyn and then killing Priscilla Dupont.

In the resulting confusion, Kingsley helped Mimi stand, and put a hand on her shoulder.

Schuyler felt a cold pressing on the back of her neck just as Mimi had experienced.

Then Kingsley pushed Mimi out of the alcove and ran to the Repository, pretending to be pinned by a bookcase.

It was Kingsley all along.

Schuyler gurgled, feeding on Mimi's blood. She knew she should stop, but she couldn't. She wanted to *see*, wanted to devour all of Mimi's memories. She saw something else: the night of the Four Hundred Ball. The after-party at the Angel Orensanz Foundation. Jack Force, putting on the black mask worn by the boy who had kissed her that evening.

So it had been Jack who kissed her after all.

The realization made her lose her hold on Mimi, and she stepped away, disengaging her fangs. The call of the blood had been strong—she had been tempted to take Mimi to full consumption, to *become* Mimi, to absorb all her memories and her being. But the shock of seeing Jack in the mask had saved her from becoming Abomination.

Schuyler staggered against the wall, feeling faint and delirious, while Mimi swooned and fell onto the nearest chair.

* * *

When she found her bearings, Schuyler returned to address the Conclave.

"Mimi is innocent," she said, and just as Lawrence had shown her, she held their minds in her own and showed them what she had seen in the blood memory, projecting the vision of Kingsley Martin calling up the Silver Blood to everyone in the room.

Mimi was released to her family, and Schuyler waited with her grandfather at the entrance of the Ducal Palace for their speedboat to arrive.

"Are they going to arrest the Martins?" Schuyler asked.

Lawrence looked up to the sky. "Yes, a team of *Venators* was already sent to their town house. But they won't find them there."

"Why not?"

"Because they will already have disappeared," Lawrence said. "It will not be easy to catch them."

"Did you know?"

"Not until you read the truth in the blood memory. I suspected, but I did not know. It is not the same thing."

"So why did you do nothing?"

"Nothing?" Lawrence asked with a smile. "I saved an

innocent girl from death. I wouldn't call that nothing."

"But you should have sent someone to Kingsley's . . ."

"Not without proof."

"But you waited—and they are gone."

Lawrence nodded. "Yes, they are gone. But at least we know we were on the right track. Priscilla Dupont was killed not just as a show of their growing power, but because she had come close to discovering who was harboring the Silver Blood on the Conclave. In fact, she was about to confront the perpetrator when the explosion happened."

"She was going to name the Martins?"

"I believe so."

"So what does that prove?"

"It proves Cordelia and I were right all along."

"But with the Martins gone . . ."

"The Martins were not the only suspects," Lawrence said. "They were merely foot soldiers, pawns, made to do the bidding of their masters. If what she told me is true, there is another family, still in the dark, who harbors the Silver Blood, who has been instrumental in bringing about Lucifer's return."

"Who?"

"That, Schuyler, is what we have to find out."

Schuyler processed this information. The Martins had shown their hand, but there was still a puppet master offstage manipulating the strings. She thought of the files Priscilla Dupont had collected before she had died.

"Grandfather, whatever happened to Maggie Stanford? Does anyone know?"

Lawrence shook his head. "No."

The Forces—Charles, Jack, and Mimi—walked out of the courtroom together. Relief was evident in all of their faces.

Jack approached Schuyler. "Thank you," he said simply.

You kissed me, Schuyler thought. She remembered what else he had said that night . . . *How do you know he's not interested? You might be surprised.*

Did he know she knew?

She wanted to touch his cheek, to kiss his soft skin again, but she saw Mimi scowling. Even if Mimi Force owed her her life, it didn't mean she was going to be nice to Schuyler any time soon.

"You're welcome," she told Jack.

Charles joined them. "When we return to New York, I'll have my driver come by and pick up your belongings. We've already cleared the guest bedroom for you. I think you'll find it to your liking."

"What are you talking about?" Schuyler asked.

"Yeah, Dad, what the hell?" Mimi interrupted.

"Your grandfather has failed to mention it, I see." Charles smiled grimly. "Lawrence, you might have won the leadership of the Coven, but I have won the adoption battle. Schuyler, the Red Blood courts have decided, in their infinite wisdom, to put you in my custody."

"Grandfather . . ."

"It's true. The appeals have been rejected," Lawrence said, his head bowed low. "Charles, I did not realize you would insist on this. I'm sorry, Schuyler. I'll continue to fight it, but for now, you're going to have to live with the Forces. Charles, there is no need to send for Schuyler. I will drop her off myself."

Mimi glared at Schuyler, while Jack only looked shocked.

Live with them?

Were they crazy?

Schuyler looked from one twin to the other, and realized she had just survived the blood trial only to find herself facing a new and more complicated challenge.

FORTY-EIGHT

*C*oming back home to her stepmother's Penthouse des Rêves was a bit of a letdown after the pampering at Dr. Pat's clinic. Bliss had finally been discharged after several weeks, after being kept in observation to make sure she had stabilized and displayed no signs of corruption. She wondered what they were waiting for her to do—attack them? Slash her wrists? The nurses at the clinic acted as if they were afraid to come too near, lest something happen.

It was the first day of ski week, and usually the family would be on a plane to Gstaad by now, but Conclave matters had called her father to Venice. BobiAnne had gone with him, but only so she could hit the shops on Via Condotti in Rome. Jordan had accompanied their parents as well, since it was decided she was too young to be left behind. While Bliss was still recovering, she was left in the care of the household staff. Bliss had been at home during Mimi's trial and sentencing, but she was certain Mimi would come to no harm. It was just too easy to imagine a life without Mimi Force's dictatorial ways, and there was no way the universe would be so kind as to get rid of her.

Bliss was bored and alone in the apartment and decided to clean out her closet for want of something better to do. Maybe perform that spring-cleaning ritual women's magazines always advised: throw out clothes you hadn't worn in two years, or those that were too shabby or didn't fit any more—that sort of thing.

She was pulling out an old cable-knit sweater when a long velvet box tumbled to the floor and a necklace fell out of it.

It was the emerald. She had forgotten to return it to her father for safekeeping in the vault after the Four Hundred Ball. Bliss picked it up, still feeling wary at the story behind the jewel. Lucifer's Bane indeed. As she tucked it back into the box, a picture slipped out from underneath the velvet pillow.

Bliss reached down to pick it up, studying it. It was a picture of her father, looking young and slim in a hunting jacket and boots, with a woman at his side whom Bliss had always assumed was her mother. Her father kept a faded copy of the picture in his wallet. This one was more well preserved. Bliss noted her mother's long blond hair and large, doelike eyes. Bliss's eyes, her father always said. You have your mother's eyes. Her mother's eyes were green, like hers, as green as the emerald she held in her hand.

Bliss turned over the picture.

Forsyth Llewellyn and Allegra Van Alen, 1982.

Allegra Van Alen?

Wasn't that Schuyler's mother?

It must be a mistake. Her mother's name was Charlotte Potter.

What was that all about?

Bliss was still puzzling over the strange inscription when there was a crash at the window. Glass shattered at her feet and Bliss ran over to see what had happened.

The boy was shivering in the corner, his feet bleeding from the cut glass. He was wearing the same T-shirt and jeans she had last seen him in. His dark hair was wet and matted, but he looked at her with the same sad, hangdog eyes.

Dylan! It was truly him. He was alive.

He glanced up, his breathing shallow and ragged.

She ran toward him, still holding the emerald in her hand.

Dylan looked at Bliss, then flinched when he saw what she held aloft, almost as if it had hurt him.

"You're alive!" Bliss said joyfully. "But you're hurt—let me help you."

Dylan shook his head. "There's no time for that now. I know who the Silver Blood is."

NOVEMBER 23, 1872
MISSING HEIRESS FOUND DEAD IN THE RIVER

New York police discover the body of Maggie Stanford
two years after she was first reported missing.
A suspicion of foul play. Corpse found then missing again.

THE BODY OF A WELL-DRESSED and pretty woman was found this morning floating in the Hudson River. Policeman Charles Langford discovered the body at six o'clock this morning and reported the matter to the Tenth Precinct. The body was taken from the water and carried to the station house. There were marks on her head and body, which led the police to believe that the woman was foully dealt with. She had red hair, green eyes, and was dressed in a white silk ball gown trimmed with pink ribbons. In their efforts to establish the identity of the woman, the police found a white linen handkerchief which bore the initials "M.S." in the pocket of the dress.

The body was subsequently identified as that of Maggie Stanford, the daughter of deceased oil baron Tiberius Stanford and Dorothea Stanford, who passed away two months ago from dementia resulting from her daughter's disappearance. The clothes Maggie Stanford had reportedly worn to the Patrician Ball the night she went missing match the description of the ball gown worn by the dead woman. The body was inordinately well preserved, with almost no sign of decomposition. The body was sent to the hospital for further examination, but the next day it was reported missing from the morgue. The police continue to be baffled by this strange case.

The VAN ALEN Family Tree

Cordelia Van Alen —— (m) —— **Lawrence Van Alen**
Seraphiel   (b)   *Metraton*
The Angel of Song   *Heavenly Scribe*

z Catherine Carver   z John Carver

Steven Chase —— (m) —— **Allegra Van Alen** ————
(Red Blood)   *Gabrielle, the Uncorrupted*

z Rose Standish

Schuyler Van Alen
Dimidium Cognatus
(Half Blood)

Charles (Van Alen) Force —— (m) —— **Trinity Burden Force**
Michael, Pure of Heart

   z Myles Standish

Benjamin (Jack) Force —— (b) —— **Madeleine (Mimi) Force**
Abbadon   *Azrael*
The Angel of Destruction   *The Angel of Death*

   z Valerius   **z** Agrippina
   z Louis D'Orleans   **z** Elisabeth Lorraine-Lillebonne
   z William White   **z** Susannah Fuller

Acknowledgments

This book would not be possible without the constant encouragement and support from my readers. Thank you to everyone who e-mailed, blogged, reviewed, and posted on the *Blue Bloods* message boards. (Check it out at:[http://z13.invisionfree.com/Blue_Bloods). You guys rock!

Many heartfelt thanks to the wonderful team at Hyperion for their patience, support, and enthusiasm: Jennifer Besser, Helen Perelman, Brenda Bowen, Nellie Kurtzman, Jennifer Zatorski, Colin Hosten, Elizabeth Clark, Angus Killick, and Deborah Bass.

I am deeply grateful to Richard Abate and Josie Freedman at ICM.

Love and thanks to my family and friends, most of whom I have not seen in so long because I have been writing this book (and many others). I hope to have a social life at some point. Thanks especially to my favorite nephews and nieces, who are a joy and an inspiration: Nicholas and Joseph Green, Alexander, Valerie, and Lily Johnston.

As always, I would be nothing without my husband, Mike Johnston, who lives and dreams these books with me, but who hates sentimental speeches so I will spare him one. And finally, much love to our little vampire baby to come, who has been with me every step of the way.

The story continues in

Revelations

Turn the page for an exciting preview . . .

ONE

On an early and bitterly cold morning in late March, Schuyler Van Alen let herself inside the glass doors of the Duchesne School, feeling relieved as she walked into the soaring barrel-ceiling entryway dominated by an imposing John Singer Sargent portrait of the school's founders. She kept the hood of her fur-trimmed parka over her thick dark hair, preferring anonymity rather than the casual greetings exchanged by other students.

It was odd to think of the school as a haven, an escape, a place she looked forward to going. For so long, Duchesne, with its shiny marble floors and sweeping vistas of Central Park, was nothing less than a torture chamber. She had dreaded walking up the grand staircase, felt miserable in its inadequately heated classrooms, and even managed to despise the gorgeous terrazzo tiles in the refectory.

At school Schuyler often felt ugly and invisible, although

her deep-set blue eyes and delicate Dresden-doll features belied this. All her life, her well-heeled classmates had treated her like a freak, an outcast—unwanted and untouchable. Even if her family was one of the oldest and most illustrious names in the city's history, times had changed. The Van Alens, once a proud and prestigious clan, had shrunk and withered over the centuries, so that they were now practically extinct. Schuyler was one of the last.

For a while, Schuyler had hoped her grandfather's return from exile would change that—that Lawrence's presence in her life would mean she was no longer alone. But those hopes were dashed when Charles Force took her away from the shabby brownstone on Riverside Drive, the only home she had ever known.

"Are you going to move or do I have to do something about it?"

Schuyler started. She hadn't noticed that she'd been standing in a daze in front of her locker and the one above it. The bells signaling the start of the day were clanging wildly. Behind her stood Mimi Force, her new housemate.

No matter how out of place Schuyler felt at school, it was no comparison to the arctic freeze she weathered on a daily basis at the Forces' grand town house across from the Metropolitan Museum. At Duchesne, she didn't have to overhear Mimi grumbling about her every second of the day. Or at least it only happened every few hours. No wonder Duchesne felt so welcoming lately.

Even though Lawrence Van Alen was now Regis, head of the Blue Bloods, he had been powerless to stop the adoption process. The Code of the Vampires stipulated a strict adherence to human laws, to keep the Blue Bloods safe from unwanted scrutiny. In her last will and testament, Schuyler's grandmother had declared her an emancipated minor, but in a wily move, Charles Force's lawyers had contested its tenets in the Red Blood courts. The courts found in their favor, and Charles had been named the executor of the estate, winning Schuyler as part of the package.

"Well?" Mimi was still waiting.

"Oh. Uh. Sorry," Schuyler said, grabbing a textbook and moving aside.

"Sorry is right," Mimi narrowed her emerald green eyes and gave Schuyler a contemptuous look. The same look she'd given Schuyler across the dinner table last night, and the same look she'd given Schuyler when they'd bumped into each other in the hallway that morning. The look said: *What are you doing here? You have no right to exist.*

"What did I ever do to you?" Schuyler whispered, tucking a book into her worn canvas bag.

"You saved her life!"

Mimi glared at the striking redhead who had spoken.

Bliss Llewellyn, Texan transplant and former Mimi acolyte, glared back. Bliss's cheeks were as red as her hair. "She saved your skin in Venice, and you don't even have the decency to be grateful!" Once upon a time Bliss had been

Mimi's shadow, happy to follow her every directive, but a trust had broken between the two former friends since the last Silver Blood attack, when Mimi had been revealed as a willing, if ineffective, conspirator. Mimi had been condemned to burn, until Schuyler had come to her aid at the blood trial.

"She didn't save my life. She merely told the truth. My life was never in danger," Mimi replied as she ran a silver hairbrush through her fine hair.

"Ignore her," Bliss told Schuyler.

Schuyler smiled, feeling braver now that she had backup. "It's hard to do. It's like pretending global warming doesn't exist." She would pay for that comment later, she knew. There would be pebbles in her breakfast cereal. Black tar on her sheets. Or the newest inconvenience—the disappearance of yet another of her swiftly dwindling possessions. Already she was missing her mother's locket, her leather gloves, and a beloved dog-eared copy of Kafka's *The Trial*, inscribed on the first page with the initials "J. F."

Schuyler would be the first to admit that the second guest bedroom in the Forces' mansion (the first remained reserved for visiting dignitaries) was hardly the cupboard under the stairs. Her room was beautifully decorated and sumptuously appointed with everything a girl could want: a four-poster queen-size bed with a pillowy duvet, closets full of designer clothes, a high-end entertainment center, dozens of toys for Beauty, her bloodhound, and a new featherlight

MacBook Air. But if her new home was rich in material gifts, it lacked the charm of the old one.

She missed her old room, with its Mountain Dew–yellow walls and rickety desk. She missed the dusty shrouded living room. She missed Hattie and Julius, who had been with the family since she was an infant. She missed her grandfather, of course. But most of all, she missed her freedom.

"You okay?" Bliss asked, nudging her. Schuyler had returned from Venice with a new address and an unexpected ally. While she and Bliss had always been friendly, now they were almost inseparable.

"Yeah. I'm used to it. I could take her in a cage fight." Schuyler smiled. Seeing Bliss at school was one of the small reprieves of happiness that Duchesne afforded.

She took the winding back stairs, following the stream of people heading in the same direction, when out of the corner of her eye she saw the barest flicker and knew. It was him. She didn't have to look to know he was among the crowd of students walking the opposite way. She could always sense him, as if her nerves were fine-tuned antennae receptors that picked up whenever he was near. Maybe it was the vampire in her, giving her the ability to tell when another was close by, or maybe it had nothing to do with her otherworldly powers at all.

Jack.

His eyes were focused straight ahead, as if he never even saw her, never registered her presence. His sleek blond hair, the same translucent shade as his sister's, was slicked back from his proud forehead; and unlike the other boys around him, dressed in varying degrees of sloppiness, he looked regal in a blazer and tie. He was so handsome it was hard for Schuyler to breathe. But just as at the town house—Schuyler refused to call it *home*—Jack ignored her.

She snuck one more glance his way and then hurried up the stairs. Class had already started when she arrived. Schuyler tried to be as unobtrusive as possible as she walked, out of habit, toward the back seats by the window. Oliver Hazard-Perry was seated there, bent over his notebook.

But she caught herself just in time and moved across the room to sit next to the clanging radiator, without saying hello to her best friend.

Charles Force had made it clear: now that she was under his roof, she would have to follow his rules. The first rule was that Schuyler was forbidden to see her grandfather. The animosity between Charles and Lawrence ran deep, and not only because Lawrence had displaced Charles's position in the Conclave.

"I don't want him filling your head with lies," Charles had told her. "He may rule the Coven, but he has no power in my house. If you disobey me, I promise you will regret it."

The second rule of living at the Forces' was that she was forbidden to associate with Oliver. Charles had been apoplectic when he'd discovered that Schuyler had made Oliver (her designated Conduit) her human familiar. "First of all, you are much too young. Secondly, it is *anathema*. Distasteful. Conduits are servants. They are not—they do not fulfill the services of familiars. You must take a new human immediately and sever all relations with this boy."

If pressed, she would grudgingly admit that Charles was probably right. Oliver was her best friend, and she had marked him as her own, had taken his blood into hers, and there had been consequences to her actions. Sometimes she wished they could go back to the way they were before everything became so complicated.

Schuyler had no idea why Charles would care whom she made her familiar anyway, since the Forces had done away with the old-fashioned practice of keeping human Conduits. But she followed the rules to the letter. As far as anyone could see, she had absolutely no contact with Lawrence, and had refrained from performing the Sacred Kiss with Oliver.

There were so many things in her new life that she could and couldn't do.

But there were some places where the rules did not apply. Somewhere that Charles had no power. Somewhere Schuyler could be free.

That's what secret hiding places were for.

TWO

*M*imi Force liked the sound of stilettos on marble. Her patent-leather Jimmy Choos made a satisfying click, click, clack that echoed across the entire lobby of the Force Tower. The shiny new headquarters of her father's media empire comprised several buildings in the middle of midtown Manhattan. The gleaming elevator banks regularly disgorged a crew of "Forcies"—the beautiful employees of the Force media organization—design editors, fashion editors, lifestyle editors, heading off to lunch meetings at Michael's or into town cars that would escort them to various appointments around the city. They were a well-dressed group, with similarly pinched faces, as if their perpetually busy schedules didn't leave them time to smile. Mimi blended right in.

She was only sixteen, but as she walked through the crowd, past the lobby and into the dark alcove that concealed an elevator that could only be accessed through a secret and irreproducible key, she felt incredibly *old*. She remembered when the Force Tower had originally been christened the Van Alen Building. For years it had stood as a mere three-story foundation, since its planned tower had never been built after the Crash of 1929 and the Great Depression. Only last year did her father's company finally complete construction according to the old plans and christened the building with a new name.

Mimi looked around and discreetly sent a strong ignore-suggestion to anyone who might come near. She found the doorknob and pressed her finger against the lock, pricking it so that it drew blood. The blood analysis in the key lock was not the latest in security technology, but an antediluvian one. Her blood was being analyzed and compared to DNA files in the repository; a match would confirm that only a true Blue Blood stood at the gate. The blood could not be duplicated nor extracted. Vampire blood disappeared within minutes once exposed to the air.

The doors whooshed open silently, and Mimi took the lift down. What Red Bloods did not know was that in 1929, the building *had* been built to completion—except it extended downward instead of up.

The tower was actually a "corescraper"—a structure built underneath the ground, tunneling down to the planet's core, rather than up toward the sky. Mimi watched as the floors descended. She went fifty, then a hundred, then two hundred, then a thousand feet under the surface. In the past, the Blue Bloods had lived underground to hide from their Silver Blood attackers. Now Mimi understood what Charles Force had meant when he sneered that Lawrence and Cordelia would have the vampires "cringing in caves once again."

Finally the elevator stopped and the door opened. Mimi nodded to the Conduit at the desk. The Red Blood resembled a blind mole rat, looking as if he had not seen the sun in a long time. Rather like the false legends perpetuated about vampires, Mimi thought with amusement.

She could feel the wards, the heavy protections placed around the area. This was supposed to be the Blue Bloods' most secret and secure haven. Lawrence took great pleasure in the shiny, conspicuous new tower that had been built on top of it. "We're hiding in plain sight!" he'd chuckled. The Repository of History had recently been moved to several of the lower floors. Since the attack, the lair underneath the club had been abandoned. Mimi still felt guilty at what had happened there. But it wasn't her fault! She hadn't meant to bring any real harm. She'd just wanted Schuyler out of the way. Perhaps she had been naive. No need to linger on that thought now.

"Evening, Madeleine," an elegantly dressed woman in a chic Chanel suit greeted her politely.

"Dorothea." Mimi nodded, following the old crone to the conference room. She knew that several members of the

Conclave had not been keen on her admittance to the inner circle. They were worried she was still too young and not in command of her full memories, the entirety of the wisdom of all her past lives. The process toward a Blue Blood's complete self-actualization began during the transformation at fifteen, and continued until the end of one's Sunset Years (or approximately twenty-one years of age), when the human shell fully gave away, finally revealing the vampire underneath. Mimi didn't care what they thought. She was there to fulfill a duty, and if she didn't remember everything, she remembered *enough*.

She was there because Lawrence had come to the Force mansion late one night, soon after they'd returned from Venice, to speak to Charles. Mimi had overhead the entire conversation. When Lawrence had taken over as Regis, Charles had voluntarily resigned his seat on the Conclave, but Lawrence was urging him to reconsider.

"We need all our strength now. We need you, Charles. Don't turn your back on us." Lawrence's voice was low and gravelly. He coughed several times, and the smell of sweet tobacco from his pipe had filled the hallway outside her father's office.

Charles was adamant. He had been humiliated and rejected. If the Conclave would not have him, he would not have the Conclave. "Why do they need me when they have you, *Regis*," Charles spat, as if even saying it were distasteful.

"I will go."

Lawrence had merely raised an eyebrow upon discovering Mimi standing in front of them. Charles hadn't looked too surprised either. Finding a way through locked doors had always been one of Mimi's talents, even as a young child.

"Azrael," Lawrence murmured. "Do you remember?"

"Not everything. Not yet. But I do remember you . . . *Grandfather*," Mimi said with a smirk.

"That's enough for me." Lawrence smiled in a way that was not too unlike Charles's own. "Charles, it's decided. Mimi shall have your seat on the Conclave. She will report to you, as your representative. Azrael, you are dismissed."

Mimi had been about to protest, until she realized she had been glommed into leaving the den without her noticing. The old coot was clever. But nothing was stopping her from pressing an ear against the doors.

"She is dangerous," Lawrence was saying softly. "I was surprised to find that you had called up the twins to this cycle. Was it really necessary?"

"Like you said, she is strong." Charles sighed. "If there *is* battle ahead, as you want us all to believe, Lawrence, you will need her on your side."

Lawrence snorted. "If she stays true."

"She always has," Charles said sharply. "And she was not the only one among us who once loved the Morningstar."

"A grave mistake we all made." Lawrence nodded.

Charles said softly, "No, not all of us."

Mimi floated away from the door. She had heard all she needed to hear.

Azrael. He'd called her by her real name. A name that was etched deep into her consciousness, deep into her bones, her very blood. What was she except her name? When you were alive for thousands of years, taking a new moniker after another, names became like gift wrapping. Something decorative that you answered to. Take her name in this cycle, for example: Mimi. It was the name of a socialite, a flighty woman who spent her days maxing out credit cards and who cared only for spa treatments and dinner parties.

It hid her true identity.

For she was Azrael. Angel of Death. She brought darkness to the light. It was her gift and her curse.

She was a Blue Blood. As Charles had said, one of the strongest. Charles and Lawrence had been talking about the end of days. The Fall. During the war with Lucifer, it had been Azrael and her twin, Abbadon, who had turned the tide, who had changed the course of the last battle. They had betrayed their prince and joined Michael, kneeling to the golden sword. They had stayed true to the light, even though they were made of the dark.

Theirs had been a crucial desertion. If it were not for her and Jack, who could say who would have won? Would Lucifer be the king of all kings on a heavenly throne if they had not abandoned him? And what did they win anyway, but this endless life on earth. This endless cycle of reparation and absolution. For whom and for what did they make amends? Did God even know they existed anymore? Would they ever regain the paradise they had lost?

Had it been worth it? Mimi wondered as she took her seat at the Conclave, only now noticing the grumblings among her peers.

She looked to where Dorothea Rockefeller was staring. The shock almost sent her reeling. Inside the most protected, most secure haven of the Blue Bloods, and seated next to Lawrence in a place of honor, was none other than the disgraced former Venator, the Silver Blood traitor, Kingsley Martin.

He caught her eye and pointed two fingers in the shape of a gun in her direction. And Kingsley being Kingsley, he smiled as he pretended to pull the trigger.

THREE

nlike most designers' showrooms, which were decorated in minimal, almost clinical style with hardly a floral arrangement to break up the dazzlingly empty white rooms, the showcase interiors that housed the Rolf Morgan collection resembled the cozy quarters of an old-fashioned gentlemen's club: leather-bound books lined the shelves, while squat club chairs and comfortable shag rugs were arranged around a crackling fire. Rolf Morgan had come to fame by selling preppie, old-boy style to the masses, his most ubiquitous creation a plain-collared shirt discreetly embroidered with his logo: a pair of criss-crossed croquet wickets.

Bliss sat nervously on one of the leather armchairs, balancing her portfolio on her knees. She'd had to leave school a few minutes early in order to make her go-see appointment, yet had arrived to find the designer running half an hour late. Typical.

She looked around at the other models, all bearing the same classic American good looks commonly found in a "Croquet by Rolf Morgan" ad: sunburned cheeks, golden hair, upturned button noses. She had no idea why the designer would be interested in her. Bliss looked more like a girl from a pre-Raphaelite painting, with her waist-long russet hair, pale skin, and wide green eyes, than the kind of girl who looked like she'd just finished a rousing set of tennis. But then again, Schuyler had just booked the show the other day at the first casting, so perhaps they were looking for a different kind of girl this time.

"Can I get you girls anything? Water? Diet soda?" the smiling receptionist asked.

"Nothing for me, thanks," Bliss demurred, while the other girls shook their heads as well. It was nice to be asked, to be offered something. As a model, she was used to being ignored or condescended to by the staff. No one was ever very friendly. Bliss likened go-see appointments to the cattle inspections her grandfather used to perform on the ranch. He'd check the stock's teeth, hooves, and flanks. Models were treated just like cattle—pieces of meat whose assets were weighed and measured.